ALSO BY DIANA SAVASTANO

On the Breath of Angels

FOR CHILDREN

Winds of Pood - Book 1: Under the Puddle

Winds of Pood – Book 2: In the Blizzard

The Upside Down Inside Out Life of Maureen Kiernan

The Princess Who Loved to Swim

THE MARKER

A NOVEL

Diana Savastano

DRS PUBLISHING 2017

THE MARKER

ISBN-10: 0-9852089-5-3
ISBN-13: 978-0-9852089-5-0

DRS Publishing, Johns Creek, GA 30022

Printed in the U.S.A.
First Edition 2017

To Anthony Savastano

*Without you, this incredible story would have
ended on a hillside in Natchez, Mississippi,
and that would be the real crime.*

"And many of them that sleep in the dust of the earth shall awake, some to everlasting life, and some to shame and everlasting contempt."
—Daniel 12:2

Through swollen eyes, Taylor saw a blurry image of a magnificent
white stallion. This was the same horse he'd seen in a dream
before the war, standing beside a woman on a hill in a
cemetery lined with unusual headstones. The woman,
dressed in trousers and a tight-fitting sweater, held
a star-shaped object in her hand.

PROLOGUE

May 1863: Port Gibson, Mississippi

Early morning sun struggled to diffuse the heavy fog that blanketed a peaceful valley where battle-weary Confederate soldiers rested in makeshift tents.

As the first rays of sunlight penetrated the ghostly haze, a sea of blue advanced with lightning speed on horseback and on foot. A ragged Union flag flapped briskly as the blue-clad ranks moved swiftly and brutally, firing torrents of artillery into the enemy's camp. The earth trembled, and disoriented Confederate troops desperately scrambled for their weapons.

When the sound of gunfire awakened Dr. Bradley Taylor, he instinctively grabbed his medical gear and ran from his tent. With no concern for his own safety, he tended to both blue and gray troops, remaining faithful to the sacred oath he took when he became a physician.

Moving from one soldier to another, he doctored wounds until a single bullet found its intended mark. A searing pain ripped through his back as he slumped to the ground, writhing in agony.

In the midst of the chaos, Chaplin John Addison assumed the role of hero as he dragged Taylor, his childhood friend, away from the battle and into the safety of the forest.

After placing him down on the soft, damp earth, Addison backed away, clasped his bloody hands, and closed his eyes.

I must pray, he thought. *Bradley deserves at least that.* But as hard as he tried, he couldn't. He sulked away and whispered mournfully. "Many of them that sleep in the dust of the earth shall awaken, some to everlasting life, and some to shame and everlasting contempt."

Taylor stirred. "John, where are you?"

Drifting back in time, Taylor's thoughts turned to the day before they left for Port Gibson and the words Addison spoke from the pulpit:

"This war has many faces. To those who started this battle, the pledge and commitment to victory are all that matter. To the men who fight, honor is the battle cry that will mask deep scars of pain, loneliness, and fear. War is ugly!" he shouted, slamming his fist on the wooden pulpit. "The battlefield has many voices: the roar of countless rifles, the thunder of cannon fire, the stampede of charging cavalry, and the screams of dying men. The cries of victory and the moans of defeat will echo in our ears forever. This is a war that will tear the very fiber of our nation, pitting brother against brother. May God forgive us for what we are about to do."

Hours passed as Taylor drifted in and out of consciousness. In the darkness of night, he felt someone tugging on his uniform, but weakness rendered him powerless to resist. It was only after hearing the sound of something moving through the forest that the looter ran off.

Through swollen eyes, Taylor saw a blurry image of a magnificent white stallion. This was the same horse he'd seen in a dream before the war, standing beside a woman on a hill in a cemetery lined with unusual headstones. The woman, dressed in trousers and a tight-fitting sweater, held a star-shaped object in her hand.

"That belongs to me," he'd said to her, reaching for it. But before he could take it, she vanished.

His thoughts turned to his family and to Benjamin, Tilly, and Little Ben. *We never called them slaves; nevertheless, to all appearances, we owned them. How can one man own another man?*

A sharp pain in his stomach caused him to press his hands against his belt buckle. His swollen fingers followed the outline of two raised metal initials. Panic swept over him when he realized this was a Union buckle. He pulled at it, but it wouldn't break free from its belt.

As life ebbed from his body, he slid his hand across the ground and found a small rock. He believed that if he scratched his name on the brass surface, he would be identified. But all he could do was scrape a small T above the US engraving before his hand froze over the buckle.

In the tranquil confines of the hereafter, Taylor felt a peace that passed all human understanding. His wounds were gone; he felt no pain, hunger, or thirst. There was no sense of time in this place: no war to fight, no battle to win, no life to live.

Seasons passed, and life returned to the land once so brutally violated. It wasn't until the summer of 1867 that a group of men trudged up a muddy hill beside horse-drawn wagons stacked with simple pine caskets. Their somber demeanor revealed an unspoken reverence for the job they were about to perform.

Taylor watched as they exhumed the remains of those buried in hastily dug graves. Some were identified, others were not. For him, there was nothing but the Union buckle in his skeletal hand.

One of the workers offered a silent prayer and then whispered, "This one's Union; may he rest in peace."

Taylor cried out his name. He bowed his head, wishing it were judgment day so he could stand face to face with the man who left him to die as an Unknown Soldier.

"And this," he whispered as they carried away his remains, "is how hate can turn human beings into devils."

CHAPTER 1

Present Day-New York City

"I'm tired, Sam. I desperately need a vacation, and this assignment, even if it's in Florida, isn't going to help me."

Sam Baldwin, a heavyset man in his early fifties, averted his eyes from the glaring stare of his senior writer, Jennifer Beasley. This was definitely not the norm for Sam. His usual behavior was that of a giddy schoolboy with a bad case of puppy love whenever she was near.

At this moment in time, however, he needed to be levelheaded, to keep his mind on the mission at hand. He could not—would not—be distracted by her strikingly gorgeous features, the soft curves that embraced her killer body, and the air of self-confidence that turned him on in so many ways. First things first: he had to get her to agree.

His chair creaked loudly as he brusquely swiveled it to face the broad sweep of office windows overlooking Third Avenue. Dark, billowy clouds hid the morning sun, which dampened his mood and heightened his concerns. He certainly didn't care about the view, but he didn't dare turn to face her.

With an air of superiority, which he thought befitted his position as publisher of News in Review, he leaned slightly forward and abruptly pushed on his chair, causing it to tip back awkwardly. To hide his embarrassment, he lifted his sneakered foot and defiantly banged it on the windowsill. With an arrogant smirk, he sucked a long drag on his cigarette.

By no means was Sam aggressive, but he so enjoyed playing the role. His attitude amused Jennifer. She knew first hand how hard he had to work at being a tough guy. To those who knew him, the tacky, fake persona he portrayed was laughable.

After holding a mouthful of smoke—for what he deemed an appropriate amount of time—he exhaled a series of smoke rings that drifted slowly toward the ceiling.

He stared out the window in quiet contemplation, trying to give the impression that what he was viewing was far more important than the conversation with her.

"You should be happy to get away from the unseasonably cold weather we're having," he muttered after a long pause.

Jennifer's back stiffened against the chair. *If it's a fight he wants,* she thought, *it's a fight he'll get.* She coughed to get his attention; he ignored her. She coughed again—only this time it was from the second-hand smoke that filled the room. "Turn around and face me like a man," she insisted.

Her tone caught him off guard, and he jerked forward in his chair, swearing under his breath as his hands reached out to the windowsill to break his fall. A pained expression filled his face. Slowly, like an old man looking for pity, he turned his chair around and calmly lit another cigarette. He deliberately blew the first puff of smoke in her direction, as if she were the root cause of his suffering.

"Bury that cigarette in the ashtray or swallow it," she demanded. "You know there's a no smoking ordinance in this building. Why do you always have to push the envelope? For goodness sake, Sam, tell me why you want *me* to do this story. We have freelancers in Florida. Why not tap into one of them? Anyway, I have vacation time; I need to get away, or I'll have a breakdown."

Sam narrowed his eyes, hoping that she wasn't telling the truth. This was not something he wanted or needed to hear right now. He took one last drag on his cigarette and waved his hand to dismiss her remark. A long cigarette ash fell to the floor. He glanced down and stomped on the residue as if it were a vile cockroach. Then, ignoring the dark spot on the carpet, he stared into her piercing hazel eyes. *Oh, how I love those warm, sultry eyes*, he thought. He shook his head to get rid of the distraction.

"You're not having a breakdown!" he said emphatically. "You're the strongest woman I know. I'll admit you look a little tired...those dark circles under your eyes are certainly not a pretty sight. That's why I'm giving *you* this story. You'll rest, take in the sun, and tell our readers about life after retirement. This is a gift to my favorite writer."

Jennifer's icy calm revealed that this approach wasn't going to work. She clenched her jaw, holding back a tirade of nasty words. She reasoned that this was Sam's standard way of going into battle. Nothing personal. It was a cunning game used to intimidate and manipulate his staff.

Determined not to allow him to bamboozle her with phony smiles and empty words, she eased back with a slight sympathetic expression on her face.

But Sam Baldwin knew how to play in this arena. All he had to do was remain passive and non-threatening. If he didn't overreact, he could drop the net over her head in one fell swoop, catching her off guard.

He offered an apologetic shrug. "You know I wouldn't ask you to do this if Ellie didn't up and quit on me at the last minute—not at all professional."

Jennifer stared at him. She was sure he was lying but didn't want to outright accuse him of that. So, instead, she quietly looked him in the eyes, and, with a slight smile, said: "You see, Sam, here's where I'm confused. This whole quitting thing doesn't add up. Why was she given this mediocre assignment? Is that why she left?"

"Who knows? But the good news is that she did all the legwork and scheduled the interviews. Anyway, this is your kind of story—human interest and all that stuff. Think of it as a fun assignment. You'll get to meet some interesting senior citizens, go for early-bird dinners, and find out if there really is life after retirement. After all, someday we'll all be old, and, maybe, we'll want to retire to Florida."

Jennifer laughed. "Are you kidding? I'm thirty-five! I have another thirty years before I can even think about retirement. And besides, how much fun and sun can I get in two days?"

Sam ignored the question because she took the bait. He steadied the net over his prize catch, but his common sense sent up a warning flare: *She's not like the rest of them. Give her a few more soft-spoken words, and she'll be yours.*

He appeared to be sincerely apologetic. "I would never ask *you* to do this if I weren't in such a terrible bind. I know you're overworked, but you're the only one who can save this issue."

Jennifer had to admit he was right. Without the cover story, the next issue wouldn't meet production deadline, and the entire staff would have to work overtime. The image of Sam standing over everyone with whip in hand made her reconsider the assignment. She crossed her legs, fingered the soft cashmere scarf draped loosely around her neck, and exhaled a soft sigh of defeat.

He won. With a quick wiggle of his bushy eyebrows, he returned to his usual self: ogling her shapely figure. He wanted to tell her that she had the greatest legs of any female he'd ever known. *One touch and I'd die a happy man*, he thought.

"Stop staring at my legs!" Her voice had a cold, sharp edge to it, but she didn't care. "You act like you've never seen a pair of legs before. Your wife has great legs. Why don't you slobber over them?"

"What man wants to slobber over his own wife? What do you think I am a…a pervert? Go to Florida, have a good time, write me a great story. I promise, on my mother's grave, you can have vacation time—no questions asked."

And so, the deed was done. Jennifer got up to leave but not before aiming a scolding finger at him. "I want a business class seat, non-stop reservation…not like the last time when you had Missy book a connecting flight to save a couple of bucks. I ended up in the back of the plane near the toilets. And I want two weeks off with pay in writing, on my desk, by the time I leave today. If it's not there, I'm no longer here."

Sam grinned and blew a kiss that bounced off the door as it slammed shut. "That's my beauty," he whispered. "It works every time.

CHAPTER 2

Jennifer's angry footsteps went unnoticed as she passed the editorial offices leading to her own inner sanctum. Not one writer, editor, or assistant observed anything out of the ordinary. It was a daily, normal occurrence for someone to stomp out of Sam Baldwin's office, grumbling that he was insufferable and condescending.

The newsroom buzzed with its own electrifying activity and drama. Conversations ran the gamut from the fluctuating stock market to the latest international crisis. The incessant ringing of phones and rattling of printers could turn a sane person into a madman.

By the time Jennifer reached her office, the hostility of having to go to Florida to do someone else's work had reached its boiling point. She slammed her hand against the door, and it swung open, banging the wall. "Damn!" she said, looking around for something to break or tear into shreds.

The only thing that caught her eye was the latest edition of the magazine on her desk. The cover headline screamed at her: *The Act of Adultery* by Jennifer Beasley. She regarded it thoughtfully, remembering how every writer on staff wanted that assignment.

It was a story she'd hoped would ease the humiliation of her ex-husband's infidelity. But after interviewing others who went through the same demeaning experience, it only deepened her hatred for him. *Two years of marriage to Michael Milner—not one day of faithfulness,* she thought.

The adultery article had her name on it from the time Sam suggested it at an editorial meeting.

"That's my story!" she'd demanded.

Sam tried to talk her out of it, making the argument that she wasn't ready. "Give this whole mess some healing time," he'd said in a fatherly tone. "After a while, you'll just want to kill the bastard and get on with your life."

She threatened to quit; it worked. However, if one were keeping score, Jennifer may have won that battle, but she definitely lost the war. She got the story and paid a heavy emotional price that ended in expensive therapy. *Nevertheless,* as she reasoned more than once, *it only took a few months to rid myself of that parasite and admit failure on my part because I never loved him.*

When Sam first read the article, he bragged that he'd made the right decision. "She wrote an award-winning piece," he'd said, adding in confidence that nowhere in its text did the article reveal the writer's own anger or frustration. According to Sam, Jennifer Beasley was a consummate journalist who wrote a fair and comprehensive account without prejudice.

Now, she could only stare at the cover, knowing she wouldn't read the story. She didn't have to; every word was etched in her mind. There were times when she found humor in some of the accounts reported, but an avalanche of anger always followed, which quickly buried any attempt to lighten the mood. It was as if even the slightest expression of jollity condoned infidelity.

A tap at the door brought her back to reality. Before she could respond, Missy Sanders—the latest in a long line of receptionists—fluttered into the office like a carefree butterfly. Her long, thick eyelashes batted gracefully over expressive sky-blue eyes. Dressed in a shocking green retro dress that puffed out from the waist down to her knees and dotted with (what else?) butterflies—certainly not appropriate for an office environment or a cold, rainy day in April—she stood, hands on hips, waiting for a compliment. When there was none, she questioningly tilted her head from side to side. A bundle of corkscrew blonde curls bounced like bungee cords against her child-like face. In a wispy Southern drawl, she whined that New Yorkers are just plain rude.

After a long pause, Jennifer said, trying to sound sincere, "Your dress is really...bright. And your perfume is like a blast of springtime."

"I'm making a statement that we should all work together to enhance our environment. And while we're doing that, we should celebrate the season—even if this is the worst April ever in Manhattan. I've decided to bring a touch of spring into our rather dull, drab office with flowers and scented candles. Of course, Sam offered one of his predictable, negative comments, but I certainly don't care. Between his chain-smoking…by the way, has anyone told him that smoking is not allowed in this building?"

"Yes, many times."

"And what about those smelly onion sandwiches he keeps in the conference room? The entire office smells like a gym locker. I want this place to be as inviting and pleasant as possible. Unfortunately, some people simply don't get it. Sam said my perfume reached his office before I did and that I look like an overstuffed pea pod. Well, pardon me for saying this, but cigarette smoke is offensive to me, and he looks and smells like an overstuffed ashtray."

Jennifer remained quiet, knowing that if she uttered a single word she'd burst into fits of non-stop laughter.

Missy took no offense to the silence. She made a quick assumption that it would be impolite for a senior staff member to agree or speak ill of the boss. She shrugged and said, careful to enunciate every word as if Jennifer didn't understand the King's English, "I have your reservations: two business class seats, two suites at the Hilton, dinner at The Towers, and a mid-size car—since Jake has camera equipment."

Now, she got Jennifer's attention.

"Jake is coming with me? Who said?"

"Well, it was Sam. I surely don't know what goes on here. I do my job, and everyone yells at me. Isn't anyone in this office polite enough to speak softly and calmly? It's as if no one here has good manners. Sometimes I feel unappreciated. I do declare!" She dug her knee-high stiletto boots into the carpet, waiting for Jennifer to tell her that *everyone* at the magazine thinks she's darling and cute and delightful. Instead, without apology, Jennifer explained that writers and editors are sometimes loud. "We can be rude, at times…well, most of the time. No excuses, but it's the nature of our business. Anyway, I'm not yelling at you; I'm annoyed with Sam. You're doing a great job, and everyone here thinks so too."

Missy smiled and reassured herself that Sam probably liked her, but something in his twisted personality prevented him from acknowledging it. "Thank you," she said. "I appreciate your kindness. Anyway, you have two messages. A man by the name of Milner called and said to call him ASAP. Billy Beasley from the market called and said he left you two text messages, and why aren't you answering your cell. He also said you lost more money than you could afford, so call him before you become penniless. I hope that's not true."

"For future reference, Billy is my cousin, and the market is his organic food store on the corner of East 84th and Third Avenue. I can see he's already forgotten that we spoke this morning at the crack of dawn."

"Don't you live on 84th Street?"

"Yes."

"Well, I'm sorry to hear about your financial loss."

"There's no loss; it's a family joke."

Missy didn't get it.

"Next time anyone with the last name of Milner calls, tell him or her I've moved to Alaska," Jennifer said. "As for Billy, always put his calls through; he's my absolutely favorite everything."

For a moment, Missy's eyes clouded with bewilderment. "This place makes me crazy. Sam won't take calls from his mother, whom I thought was dead because he's always swearing on that poor woman's grave, and Jake won't take any calls from someone named Gloria, who calls here three times a day. Who is she? His wife or something?" She lowered her voice. "I hear Jake has a child."

"Jake's not married. And yes, he has a daughter. As for Sam's mother, she's very much alive. Sam's a big teaser. By the way, his mother is Ann Baldwin, and she owns this magazine. Better get used to this place; we're a crazy group. And try to ignore Sam because he's really a softy underneath that arrogant, brash, rude behavior he so likes to portray."

Missy stood in the doorway long enough to show her disapproval by shaking her head. With a swish of her dress, she bolted down the hall, mumbling all the way about the absence of good manners. She was convinced that the only person at the magazine who showed any politeness and dignity was its creative director, Jake Cohen.

In an attempt to disperse the sickening smell of jasmine, Jennifer fluttered her hand across her nose. She checked her cell messages and sent a text to Billy. *Call later, busy now.*

The thought of him made her smile. He was always caring and loving. He never showed any unhappiness over the fact that his mother died when he was born or that his father abandoned him shortly thereafter. Jennifer's parents adopted him, and the two of them grew up more like brother and sister than cousins.

Shoving two extra copies of the magazine into her laptop case, she looked up at the clock on the wall. It was 3 p.m., and her day was over. She had to pack, clean out the refrigerator, take Morton—her lovable tabby—to her neighbor, Carolyn Saber, and try to do some preliminary research on people who migrated south for the rest of their lives. "A little sleep in between wouldn't hurt," she mumbled, walking out into the corridor.

"Where are you going?" Sam yelled from the other end of the hall. In one hand he held a coffee mug, in the other a doughnut and cigarette.

Jennifer grimaced at the sight of smoke billowing around the doughnut. "How very disgusting you are," she said, ignoring his question.

A squeaky laugh came from within Candy Jenson's office. The petite blonde managing editor stretched her head and caught Sam's eye. "Listen to Jen, or we'll ban together and report you to the fire marshal."

From across the hall, Jim Weiss, the magazine's senior editor, slapped his hands together and said, "Now that's what I call a splendidly good idea."

"Very funny!" Sam bellowed. "How 'bout I fire all three of you? Didn't anyone ever tell you prima donnas that glazed doughnuts rolled in cigarette smoke are *splendidly* delicious? Once again, Beasley, where are you going?"

"Ah, let me spell it out for you: F.L.O.R.I.D.A! Remember? And why, may I ask, is Jake the Cohen tagging along? I don't need a bodyguard now that Bilinski is in prison."

A hearty laugh spilled out of Sam's mouth, and it lightened Jennifer's mood. Eddie Bilinski was an infamous fictional character created by Sam to divert any would-be suitors while Jennifer was going through her divorce.

"Jake will take your shots and go on to Charleston," said Sam. "I'm doing you a favor. At least you won't have to take your own photos. Come on, Jen, you and Jake get along great." Sam took a deep drag of his cigarette and then a quick bite of the doughnut before exhaling. "Hmmm. Delicious."

Jennifer scowled. "You're nauseating! By the way, where's my two-weeks-with-pay letter?"

Sam swallowed hard, paying no heed to the question. He stuck his head into Candy's office. "Want a bite, beauty?"

"Close my door!" Candy yelled.

"Okay, calm down. As for you, Beasley, if you check your inbox, you'll find my sworn word that you can have two weeks off. Now, go and have a ball. Don't forget to send postcards, and use your sunscreen."

"Sunscreen? She's lucky if she sees the light of day," Jim said, closing his office door against a barrage of cigarette smoke, deliberately aimed his way.

Jennifer walked out to the reception area, trying to shake the nasty image of Sam chewing on a smoky doughnut.

Missy wasn't at her desk. She peeked across to Jake's office. He, too, was nowhere in sight. A red light over his darkroom signaled that no one should enter. She knocked twice. "You in there, Cohen?"

The door flung open, and Jennifer jumped back. "Well, well," she said, staring into the flushed faces of Missy and Jake. "What have we here?"

At forty-eight, the boyish expression on Jake's face could make a woman's heart melt.

But Missy's face was quite the opposite. She grinned like a Cheshire cat that just swallowed a mouse. With a light touch of her finger, she stroked away traces of pink lipstick off his lips. She meant it to be a sensual message, but it was lost on Jake.

"Wait till Sam hears about this," Jennifer said, holding back a laugh. "Missy, I think I hear your phone ringing."

Eco-friendly green flitted by, followed by the familiar fruity scent. Missy disappeared, not realizing that the phone was quiet.

Jake licked his lips. "Such a sweet girl. She wanted to see my darkroom. Want to know what she said in that ever-so-delicate voice? 'I do declare, Mr. Cohen, but it sure is quiet in here.'"

"You could be arrested for child molestation. Isn't she eighteen or something?"

"Believe it or not, the woman is twenty-eight. Came in to give me a telephone message. Before I knew it, she had me pinned against the wall. Then, she kissed me. And not like you kissed me last Christmas. What's a man to do?"

"Don't ask *me* for advice. You're single. She's single; do whatever you like."

Jake wiggled his nose and inhaled the air around him. "I'm not going to do anything with that sweet, smelling child. As for you—"

"And you're telling me this because I'm…what? Interested? I don't think so! I'll see you at the airport tomorrow. Don't call me after ten this evening because I'm going to bed early. In fact, don't call me at all."

"May I tweet, text, and stalk your Facebook page?"

"No tweeting, no postings, no nothing!"

Jake laughed and retreated back into his darkroom. The attraction he felt for Jennifer was, at times, overwhelming. He couldn't be in the same room with her for more than two minutes without wanting to take her in his arms and kiss her. He knew, however, that any advancements in a romantic way and she'd dice him up for cat food. *Someday I'm going to kiss her and not stop*, he thought.

Jennifer hurried from his office. He frustrated her, but she would not allow herself to analyze why. On her way to the elevator, she thought of going back to apologize for being abrupt but changed her mind when the door slid open.

CHAPTER 3

A strong clap of thunder shook the glass façade of the Western Publishing Building just as the elevator reached the lobby. Along Third Avenue, a sea of people huddled under building overhangs and umbrellas, trying to avoid the heavy downpour and gusty winds that whipped around the corner of 51st Street.

Deciding it would be impossible to hail a cab without getting drenched, Jennifer walked into the small café off the lobby. She stood patiently in a long line, waiting to order coffee and a blueberry muffin. Inside her jacket pocket, her cell pinged repeatedly. She ignored it. By the time she placed her order, the rain had stopped, but the continual sound of messages coming into her cell didn't.

Minutes later, Candy walked in and spotted her. "Thought you might be in here. When I saw the rain, I knew you'd never get a cab. Thanks for taking the assignment in Florida. I told Sam I'd work it out with one of our freelancers, but he said this assignment was too important and, anyway, you needed some time away."

"What? This is weird. He's playing one of his silly games, and I'm afraid this one might backfire on him."

"I hope you're going to get something good out of this."

"Two weeks off."

"Oh, sure," Candy laughed and rolled her eyes. "Like he's ever going to live up to that promise. Trust me; he'll come up with something to keep you tied to your desk."

"Not this time. I'm tired and need time off even if it means I have to hide away at home. No computer, no phone, no nothing."

Candy moved closer. "Still dealing with the past?" she asked in a low voice. "Is there anything I can do to help?"

"Thanks for asking, but it's not the past. It's me. I'm indecisive and not sure where my life is going. It's as if I'm waiting for something to break through so I can break free. Does that make sense?" Jennifer asked with a puzzled expression.

"It certainly does. I waited years for the right person, the right job, the right everything. And then, out of the blue, I met Ann Baldwin. She told me how her first husband blew through her family fortune and left her penniless with a son to raise. She determined never again to allow anyone to use her. Her words still resonate in my mind that I should stop being the victim. I took hold of my life, applied for the job of editorial assistant at the magazine, and, much to my surprise, Sam hired me. Four years later, I'm the managing editor. I joke about him, but he and Ann were a huge support system when I needed it the most."

"They're definitely the good guys in our lives. But I'm serious about getting two weeks off; I desperately need time away."

"Count on me to back you up. Give me a call if you need anything, and keep your ears and eyes open because something is going on, and it has Sam's name written all over it. Ellie left because of something far more important than this assignment. By the way, calls and e-mails are already pouring in regarding the adultery article, all extremely positive. The entire staff got a copy of Ann's message to you. It's hard to believe that such a polite, elegant lady could spawn a man like Sam."

They giggled like two schoolgirls, checking around to see if anyone was listening.

"One thing is for sure," Candy said, "picking on Sam is fun, and I honestly believe he loves the attention. Well, I'd better get back before the smoking furnace discovers I'm gone."

"Thanks for coming down to find me."

With a wave, Candy pushed her way through a crowd of people, managing to slip into a packed elevator just before the doors closed.

Outside, bright rays of sunshine broke through clouds that moved swiftly across the sky, revealing patches of blue for the first time in weeks. The rain washed away the last residue of snow, bringing hope that the worst winter in decades had finally ended.

Later that evening, as Jennifer was cleaning her refrigerator of half-eaten, long forgotten containers of food, she remembered to check the rest of her messages on her cell.

The first message from her cousin made her smile. The second from Michael Milner brought a frown. She tapped the return call icon, and, within seconds, Billy's answering machine picked up. He screened all calls, even though he talked to everyone, including telemarketers.

"It's me!" she yelled.

"It's about time!" Billy yelled back and then rambled for three minutes with nothing more than unnecessary verbiage about how the economy was killing the gourmet food industry. "That's how my life's going; what's new with you?"

"Nothing since we last spoke this morning when you woke me up with one of your delightfully silly songs."

"We've been talking every single day—three times a day—since we were kids. You don't think that's going to stop now that we're big kids, do you? I need to connect with you cause you da CUZ!"

"Well, da cuz is going to Florida tomorrow morning, so we can't talk long."

"Oh…my…gosh! You're not going to believe what I'm about to tell you. But first, is there anything you need me to take care of while you're gone?"

"Thanks, but no. I have to finish cleaning the refrigerator and bring Morton across the hall to Carolyn. By the way, I'm sorry about the economy, but if I had your money, I'd burn mine."

"Hey, what's mine is yours. Forget about money and refrigerators. Anyway, listen to this. Elaine the Polish lady—the one who's filled with that ESP stuff—told me that you're on your way to an exciting journey. Once again, she's right."

"If Florida's an exciting journey, I'd rather stay home."

"I think she meant that it's an adventure. You know, something that leads to the discovery of new places, people, and things. Please remember to take me with you."

"Isn't this the same Elaine who reads tea leaves and palms? Didn't she tell you that you had the winning lottery ticket last week?"

"I didn't win the lottery, but I won on a scratch off—five hundred big ones. Elaine might be off a little here and there, but I'd bet my money on her any day. Your life is taking a turn, and I'm turning with you."

"I'll call you when I get back. Take care, and don't believe everything you hear from Elaine. I'll check in with Dad later tonight. As soon as I get back, we'll make plans for his birthday."

"Already on that, Il Capitano. Have a safe trip."

Jennifer went back to her cleaning, feeding the garbage pail a half-eaten brown apple, a tasteless chunk of meatloaf, and two pieces of stale pepperoni pizza.

Morton sat quietly, eyeing every morsel of food as it went flying into the trash. He walked over to the pail and gave it a disapproving hiss.

"Everybody in my family is a food critic. Come on boy; time to go visit Aunt Carolyn. Do you want to walk across the hall or get the royal treatment?"

Morton decided to play dead, so she carried him.

Carolyn greeted them with a happy giggle. "Welcome to the Hotel de Feline, Morton," she said, patting him on the head.

"Thanks for watching the big baby," Jennifer said, placing him on the windowsill. "I'm not looking forward to Florida."

"Are you going to retirement land alone?"

"Jake will be with me…to do the photos."

"I think he's crazy about you."

"Don't care. And I'm not encouraging anything."

"Silly girl. No offense, but you need to come out from under the I'm-so-sorry-for-myself cloak. Get over it, and get it on with Jake."

"Don't see that happening. I like him, but…let's concentrate on *your* love life. What's going on with that crossing guard?"

Carolyn laughed. "He's not a crossing guard; he's a retired cop, working as a security guard at the school…and much needed security, I might add. You wouldn't believe what some of these kids are doing today."

"Okay. Sorry."

Carolyn opened a bottle of Pinot Noir and filled two wine glasses to the top.

"Whoa!" Jennifer said. "Are we celebrating something? That's a lot of wine, even for you."

"I have a date this weekend."

"So, are you starting to drink from now?"

"I'm excited and happy, and I need to loosen up. So do you. Anyway, you'll never guess who it is…go on, take a guess."

Jennifer sighed. "Somebody from school?"

"No! You know I don't like to date other teachers or, heaven forbid, students."

"Please don't ever do that. I don't want to read in the tabloids that you've been arrested for seducing a student."

Carolyn laughed, flashing a perfect set of teeth. Jennifer studied her soft features and remarked, to herself, how much alike she and Billy were. *They're both adorable, have gorgeous features, and playful natures. What a great couple they'd make.* She quickly dismissed the idea because neither of them showed any interest other than friendship.

"Who's this mystery man?" Jennifer asked. "Is it the guy from the bookstore?"

Carolyn squealed. "Yes! Dinner and dancing and…whatever. I think I could fall for this guy. He actually reads, and, this is incredible, the man speaks another language—French. After all the airheads I've been dating, I think I may have hit the jackpot. If this date goes well, I'll see if he has a friend. You really need to get out and start dating."

"Not now, maybe never. I can't believe anything I hear from men, and I simply don't trust any of them—except for my father and Billy."

"That would be a ditto for me. But you can't have a touchy, feely relationship with them. Your dad is adorable, and Billy, well, he's wonderful. But as for you, now is the time. If you want to play it safe, start with Jake; he's one of the good guys."

This was a conversation Jennifer didn't want to continue. She patted Morton on the head, gulped down the remaining wine in her glass, and went back to her apartment. By ten o'clock, she turned off the phone, went to bed, and didn't wake until the alarm clock rang the next morning. Within one hour, she was heading to the airport.

CHAPTER 4

When the aircraft broke through the clouds and sunlight flooded the cabin, Jennifer thought that maybe Sam was right. She inhaled deeply and relaxed. She sneaked a peek at Jake's scrunched face and his tight grip on the armrests as if he were guiding the plane upward. His fear of takeoffs was over the top.

A gentle tap of encouragement on his arm went unnoticed.

"It's okay," Jennifer said convincingly. "We made it through the clouds. You can open your eyes."

He didn't reply.

She studied him. *Good looking*, she thought. He wore a pale blue shirt, jeans, and a navy blazer. She lowered her eyes and gazed at his Armani brown leather loafers. There was no doubt that he had expensive taste.

"Jake," she said, tugging at his arm. "Open your eyes."

He flashed a goofy grin and gave her a wink. "Did we make it off the ground?"

"I certainly hope so. Here comes the drink cart."

Without missing a beat, he flashed a flirtatious smile at the flight attendant. "I'll take coffee. Black, no sugar," he said in his sweetest voice. "However, my traveling companion will have a glass of milk with a splash of coffee. She's still not able to handle the dreaded caffeine."

The flight attendant ignored Jennifer, staring down at Jake as if he were a scrumptious dessert. "Do you think she'd like decaf?"

Jennifer looked up and made it known that she could answer for herself. "I'll have regular, thanks." She turned away, reached into her laptop case, and retrieved a folder marked *Retirement*.

Jake shifted his attention to the folder. "Ellie may have been a proficient journalist, but she fell short in people skills. Leaving the magazine without a word to any of us was strange. If the rumor mill is correct, she and Sam had more than a falling out over editorial issues."

"Do you think they were romantically involved?" asked Jennifer.

"Whatever happened, it doesn't matter now. Thank goodness the interviews were scheduled. What's the itinerary?"

"Retirement communities in Miami, Boca Raton, and Fort Lauderdale. There's a diverse list of retirees—the owner of a New Jersey garbage company, a celebrity chef from Michigan, and a lawyer from Boston⊠that gives this otherwise bland assignment a much-needed boost."

While jotting notes, sipping coffee, and occasionally looking out the window, Jennifer's mind wandered through the months of what her life had become before and after her divorce. She was thirty-three when she met Michael. More than once she commented that he wasn't her type, but she continued to date him. He had just passed the bar and entered his father's law firm. He seemed charming, a person who literally loved women. According to those who knew him, he was everything a woman could ask for in a man. If that was true, then Jennifer felt cheated.

After their first year of marriage, everything changed. Sex was infrequent and soon stopped completely. Michael said there was nothing wrong with their relationship and, certainly, nothing wrong with him. "If anything," he'd said, "it's probably because we're busy people with active careers."

But Jennifer knew that wasn't true. They'd made a mistake, and neither was willing to admit it.

Jake cast his eyes in her direction and immediately sensed that trouble was brewing. He always hated to see her in what he called the *M Factor*. Anyone close to her knew the difference between work thoughts and Michael thoughts. He continued to stare at her until she tilted her head in his direction.

"At last, you noticed I'm still here and hungry as ever," he said, eyeing her breakfast. "I'll take whatever you don't want. Sharing is caring, and caring is love."

She suggested he take it all, and he did.

With Jake occupied, she tried to remember which thoughts disturbed her the most. Of course, there was always the same nagging question: why did it bother her so much? She reasoned that carrying old baggage was a lot easier than moving ahead with her life.

By the time the aircraft landed, she didn't remember fastening her seat belt or yawning at least a dozen times to release the pressure building in her ears.

Once in the rental car, Jake mumbled and fumbled with all the dials, trying to set the GPS and the air-conditioner at the same time. He brushed the sweat from his brow. "I forgot how stinking hot it is here. Look at me; I'm a mass of sweat. We left New York shivering, and a couple of hours later we're sweltering in this humid heat. Did I use deodorant this morning?"

Jennifer turned up the AC. By the time they exited the airport, the car had cooled down, and the navigational system dutifully commanded the way.

"Where are we staying?" he asked. "Miami? Fort Lauderdale? Where?"

"Have a little patience, Jake. We're staying at the Hilton in Fort Lauderdale. There's no way we can get lost."

Just then, he made a left instead of a right turn. By the time the system recalculated the route and gave a new command, he was thoroughly frustrated, red-faced, and still complaining about the heat.

"Let's try to remain calm," Jennifer said, leaning her head back and closing her eyes.

"Will do, chief," Jake replied, tapping his fingers on the steering wheel. He stared ahead and began humming. His confidence grew as the monotone voice directed the way. He looked over at Jennifer; she still had her eyes closed. Lowering the AC, he drove in silence, until the final command announced they'd reached their destination.

"You can open your eyes, Jen. We're at the hotel," he said proudly, sounding like a kid who just solved a complicated math equation.

Check-in went quickly. Once in her room, she unpacked, changed into her swimsuit, and wrapped a beach skirt around her waist. She stuffed her small beach tote with sunscreen, lip-gloss, cell phone, and an e-book reader.

A disturbing thought popped into her head. In a flash, she pulled out an imaginary tennis racket and—swat!—the thought went sailing across her balcony and out into the vast ocean. To her surprise, she laughed.

Gentle waves rolled up the beach and around the few remaining umbrellas planted too close to the shoreline. Neat rows of blue and white lounge chairs circled an inviting pool where waiters outnumbered hotel guests. Off on the horizon, storm clouds formed, and Jennifer knew it was a matter of time before a late afternoon storm would make its way inland.

A young boy skipped along the path just below her balcony. He looked up at her and stuck out his tongue. Suppressing a giggle, she returned the gesture and quickly stepped back into the room before he had a chance to retaliate. "Got you last," she said with a laugh.

She dialed Jake's room and asked if he wanted to meet for drinks and a walk along the beach.

"Yes and yes. We deserve it," he replied.

"We deserve more than that, but I'll settle for a drink right now."

"I need sunscreen."

"What makes you think I brought it?"

"You? I'd venture to guess that you forgot nothing and brought everything."

"Are you trying to say I'm predictable?"

"I'm saying you're dependable and organized; someone who thinks and plans every move. You're a what-if person. That's good, especially for someone like me who forgets a toothbrush and underwear."

"I have extra panties if you need—"

Jake laughed hard and loud, causing Jennifer to hold the phone away from her ear.

"Thanks for the offer," he said. "I'll let you know when or if that becomes necessary."

"I'll be at the pool. Hurry down, or we'll be sitting under dark clouds and rain," she said.

A group of squealing kids gleefully splashed in the shallow end as Jennifer followed a garden path to a table away from doting mothers and screaming children.

After ordering a glass of white wine, she stretched her neck to see if Jake was in sight. Knowing he probably got lost somewhere between his room and the pool, she sighed and shook her head.

After circling the pool, he finally saw her waving at him.

"What took you so long?" she asked.

"Well, you see, it's like this…I have no sense of direction."

"Ya think?"

Without checking the menu, he ordered a club sandwich and a scotch on the rocks. "Why don't we step out of the box with this article," he suggested.

"What do you mean? This is a straight, no-nonsense piece about retirement. Not much room for creativity, and I still don't understand why Sam made this our cover story."

"Don't you know? This wasn't his idea. Ann suggested it as a way to introduce her brother, Henry Marshall, a big-shot attorney from Boston who's looking to start a political career. He's the interviewee at The Polo Club in Boca. You didn't figure that out?"

"No. How would I know that? It's not the same last name, and Sam never mentioned it. Anyway, I didn't give this much thought and, truthfully, I didn't read all the bios from Ellie's notes. I accepted the assignment because I knew we'd all have to work double time if I didn't. What does it matter? We'll get the story, the photos, and we're out of here."

"Not so simple. Marshall wants to be the mayor of Boca. This story idea is the first in a long line of public relations to launch his political career, which he hopes will take him to the Senate. And you, my dear, are the only one who can turn this caterpillar into a butterfly."

Jennifer shook her head in disbelief. "Wow! Sam played me like a fiddle. Okay, he'll get his story, but I'll write it as I see it."

"Let's enjoy ourselves and forget about Sam. How about a swim in the ocean?" he asked, downing his Scotch and consuming only half of his sandwich.

"I'll walk, you swim. The waves have picked up, and I don't like being in the water when a storm is approaching."

Jake darted ahead, yelling back that she was a wimp. She laughed when he nosedived into a wave. When he didn't surface, she picked up her pace and moved toward the shoreline. Just as she was about to rush into the choppy water, his head popped up.

"Come in you big sissy!" he hollered.

"No, and don't get lost in another wave!"

He laughed and disappeared under the water.

She wanted to tell him to come out but thought better about it. *He's a big boy,* she reasoned. *I'm not his mother.*

She walked along the beach and picked up shells, examining each one as if they were rare treasures, only to cast them into oncoming waves.

The sun dipped behind fast approaching storm clouds. A flash of lightning and a loud rumble of thunder caused Jake to rush out of the water. They barely made it into the hotel when the rainstorm slammed into the coast.

"Want to come to my room and watch the storm?" Jake asked.

"No, I'll pass. I need to shower, put some notes together for the story, and take a nap."

"Good idea. Our dinner reservation is for eight, so you have plenty of time to relax."

"How about we leave at seven?"

"Still don't trust my navigational skills?" Jake asked.

"I don't think we'll have a problem finding the restaurant. I'd like to see if there are any shops along the way. My dad's birthday is coming up, and I haven't found a gift yet."

CHAPTER 5

Jennifer Beasley had always been a stickler for detail; especially when it came to her job. As a journalist, it was essential to report facts accurately, without interjecting her own opinion. So when she scrutinized Ellie's organized notes, she became curious when she saw a red circle around Henry Marshall's name, followed by a red line out to the margin. One word with exclamation points caught her attention: *BASTARD!!!*

She snapped a photo of the page and sent it to Jake. He responded with a question mark and an angry emoji.

Within seconds, her cell beeped. "Why do you think she wrote that word?" Jake asked.

"It's obvious that she either knew Marshall personally or knows something about him. Perhaps that's why she didn't take the assignment. The burning question is…did she quit or was she fired?"

"I don't know. I heard something happened between Sam and Ellie. The office chatter alluded to an affair, but that never made sense to me. Give Candy a call and see what she knows about Marshall."

Candy Jensen eagerly reached for her cell when she saw Jennifer's number. "How are things in Florida?" she asked.

"Everything here is good; we're settled in. I'm going over Ellie's notes, and I noticed something odd. Do you know Henry Marshall?"

"Sure, he's Ann's brother. I don't know him personally. Is there a problem?"

"Well, for one thing, Sam never mentioned that Marshall was a relative or that Ellie may have known him personally."

"I wasn't aware that he didn't tell you. When the article idea was presented, he only told me not to worry about it and that he'd take over. I welcomed the help and didn't think two shakes about it."

"What's strange is that Ellie circled Marshall's name and wrote the word *bastard* in the margin."

"Whoa! Oh, gosh, let me think. I met Marshall years ago at an office party. The one thing that sticks out in my memory was his loud, obnoxious behavior. And he flirted with every woman. Do you think he's going to be a problem?"

"I doubt it. It's clear Ellie didn't want to do this interview. And now, the question is, was she fired or did she quit?"

"I'm under the impression she quit, but that could be a lie."

"I'll tread lightly and keep you posted. In the meantime, let's keep this away from Sam. It's business as usual."

"Got it. Call me anytime."

After jotting a few meaningless paragraphs about Florida and retirement, Jennifer set her cell's clock alarm for one hour, plumped the pillows, and got into bed. Within minutes, she dropped off into a deep sleep, but not for long. Loud music and boisterous laughter, coming from a group of happy-hour drinkers, destroyed her peaceful rest.

She dressed quickly in a floral off-the-shoulder dress with matching heels. Her long, silky auburn hair hung loosely around her shoulders.

By the time she reached the lounge, Jake was sitting at the bar, checking his e-mails. When he saw her, his eyes lit up. "You look fantastic!" he said, flashing a wide grin.

"Thank you. I have to say, in New York, you're one of the best-dressed men. As for here, well, you'll have some mighty stiff competition with all these polyester retirees showing off their vintage clothing," Jennifer teased.

"Don't laugh, but I do have a poly jacket that my uncle left me when he passed away. I cherish the ugly thing."

"That's sweet. You should have brought it along for evening wear."

"Did you speak to Candy?"

"Yes, but she doesn't know anything more than we do."

They drove in silence along coastal A1A, passing lofty condominiums that showed little evidence of being fully occupied. On the opposite side of the road, empty shops and neglected motels revealed that the failing economy had hit this area hard.

Jake slowed the car into an abandoned strip mall where dilapidated stores were being demolished. In the middle of the rubble, only one shop remained intact.

"Talk about depressing," he said, pointing to the scribbled words on a large poster attached to the grimy front window: *The End is Near! Going Out of Business! Everything MUST GO!*

"Aww, this is sad," Jennifer said. "I'd like to return in the morning. I might find a birthday gift for my dad. Maybe this trip won't be a waste after all."

"Your wish is my command," Jake said. "By the way, what scent are you wearing? It smells like a vanilla candle."

"You have one good nose there, Cohen. It's vanilla scented body wash."

"Simple. Understated. Gives me a warm feeling inside. I'm having a Christmas flashback. My mom loves vanilla candles…has them all over the house."

Jennifer laughed. "You don't celebrate Christmas."

"That's how much you don't know. My mother's Irish Catholic. We celebrate Christmas and Hanukkah. I've had a very diverse upbringing. I also speak Gaelic and Yiddish."

"I'm impressed. You're multilingual and have a good nose. Wow, you're quite a catch!"

"You're laughing at me."

"No, I'm not. I'm just boring in comparison. Grew up with one religion, one culture, and one language."

He pulled into The Towers valet lane. "We made it. No directions and no fuss."

"How did you manage this?"

"Can't tell a lie. The concierge at the hotel gave me detailed directions. Oh, and another thing, I have a photographic memory."

"Now, I know you're lying."

Before he could respond, his cell rang. "Want to take bets as to who it is?" he asked.

"Gloria? Sam?"

"Not Gloria. It's Sam the man, and I'm not going to answer it."

Jennifer nodded in agreement. "I ignored two text messages and one call earlier from him. I wonder if he has something important to share with us?"

"Probably not. He's nosey and intrusive." Jake's voice revealed his annoyance.

"He just wants to know our every move. How about we keep him guessing until tomorrow. Agree?"

"Absolutely!"

A panoramic view of the Intracoastal Waterway and downtown Fort Lauderdale greeted them as they walked through the atrium of the restaurant. A dazzling three-tier crystal chandelier loomed over an imposing mahogany table topped with a centerpiece of fresh tropical flowers. Placed around the centerpiece were trays of fruits, cheeses, and desserts. Music from the piano lounge drifted through the tastefully decorated dining room, illuminated by soft lighting and candles.

"Sam said the atmosphere would be to our liking. For once, he's right on target," Jake said.

A rather snarky maître d' led the way to a corner table. Right on his heels, a waiter appeared with a wine list.

Jake selected a pricey bottle of Cabernet, knowing that when he turned in his expenses for this trip, Sam would disapprove.

A sommelier with a silver tastevin around his neck presented the bottle for Jake's approval. He nodded, and a small amount was poured into a glass.

Right on cue, Jake held the glass firmly by the base and took a deep sniff before swirling the bold, full-bodied red, making sure it had legs. One sip was all that was needed.

"Perfect," Jake said with the authority of a true wine connoisseur, and the wine—that cost more than his shoes—was slowly decanted before being poured into two crystal glasses.

Jake raised his glass. "To new beginnings."

And the soft melodious ping of crystal hitting crystal sealed the toast.

"You sure know your wine, Cohen."

"Watch the waiter," Jake whispered. "He'll eye the bottle, and as soon as we take a few sips, he'll swoop in and fill our glasses. This is the way they get a second bottle ordered even before we eat."

"And why not?" Jennifer said with a hearty laugh.

"Why is it that the sound of your laughter is like music

to my ears?"

She smiled thoughtfully. "Sounds like a pick-up line. You do know that wine has a way of enhancing the moment. None of it really matters; tomorrow, it will be business as usual."

"Ouch! That hurt."

They perused the menu as if it were a prized manuscript. Food was their common denominator, and tonight was no different. Jake painted the picture, while Jennifer added just the right text.

During dinner, the evening sky came alive with bolts of lightning and sounds of rolling thunder.

"I love storms," Jake said. "As a child, whenever there was a storm, I would take photos through my bedroom window until the skies cleared."

"The night my father got sick, there was a big snowstorm. They said it was a heart attack. Not bad enough to take his life but bad enough to change it. I'm still amazed by how quickly he adapted. He went from a busy doctor to a collector of everything from Civil War memorabilia to porcelain figurines."

"Everything about Alex is spot-on," Jake said, filling her glass.

"I think I've had enough. I don't want to be up late nursing a sick stomach. I need to be fresh and alert for the interviews."

"I think you'll be pleasantly surprised. We're going to retirement villages, not nursing homes."

"That's true," Jennifer said. "Some of the people I'll be

interviewing are my dad's age."

It was after eleven by the time they left the restaurant. Jake drove slowly out of the parking lot and then stopped the car. He looked at Jennifer, wanting to pull her into his arms and kiss her—like Missy kissed him. But he stopped himself when she tapped the steering wheel.

"What are you waiting for?" she asked. "Are you unable to drive?"

"You must be kidding. Takes more than a couple of glasses of wine to stop Jake Cohen from functioning. What time is our first interview?" he asked, wanting to change the subject.

"Ten thirty, here in Fort Lauderdale. Three o'clock in Miami, and seven o'clock in Boca, right after a homeowners meeting. That should prove to be interesting."

Jake agreed. "Let's see what else we can make interesting over the next few hours."

Jennifer didn't respond, and the evening ended.

CHAPTER 6

At breakfast the next morning, they reviewed the day's agenda.

"If we stick to this schedule, we'll be able to keep our flights tomorrow morning," Jennifer said, munching on a bagel. "I want to get this assignment into Sam's greedy hands ASAP."

"I'm heading for Charleston before I return to New York," Jake said casually. "Want to tag along?"

"Ah...tempting, but I can't. There's a pile of work on my desk, and this assignment has brought me to the edge."

"I understand. Hurry and finish your coffee; we'll stop at that antique shop before going to the interview."

"You remembered...thanks. How come you're so kind to me?"

"I like you. Well, it's beyond like, it's—"

"It's a great friendship," Jennifer said, finishing his sentence.

After a brief moment of uncomfortable silence, Jake laughed. "Friendship it is."

By the time they were in the car, the uneasiness had passed. But Jennifer remained quiet, focusing on the shoreline where rough waves pounded the deserted beach along the highway.

Jake made a wide sweeping turn into the strip mall and parked next to a wrecked van with a faded *GOING OUT OF BUSINESS* sign taped to the back window. He turned off the ignition and shook his head. "This place looks haunted! I'm not letting you go in there alone."

"You're sweet, but I don't think you have to worry."

"I'm going to ignore you because I *do* worry," he said, leading the way into the store.

The jingle of a rusty bell, dangling precariously above the door, announced the arrival of potential customers. Only a single lamp on a back table dimly lit the cluttered shop. But even in the dimness, it was apparent that years of neglect had taken its toll. The walls were stained, and the ceiling was cracked beyond repair, giving the appearance that it might collapse at any moment.

A strong, musty odor, combined with the unpleasant stench of cigarette smoke, permeated the air. A slow, squeaky ceiling fan offered no relief from the heat or the smell.

Jennifer covered her nose, hoping that the scent of her body spray would mask the unpleasantness.

Jake shook his head and crinkled his nose. "I'm not sure which is worse, the stench or the deplorable state of this place."

At the rear, two six-foot totem poles with matching carved eagles flanked a closed door. The tips of their wings touched over the doorframe. A handwritten sign, affixed to the door, foretold the shop's future: *Over 55 Years in Business. The End is Here!*

"I feel sorry for whoever owns this place," Jennifer whispered. "You need to buy something."

Jake rolled his eyes. "Great! Just what I need…garage sale junk in my newly furnished apartment."

"Shh," Jennifer hissed in his ear. "Someone's coming."

From the rear of the shop, the door swung open and banged the side of the totem pole, giving it a wobble. A short, stout woman looked at it with a scowl on her face. She swore under her breath. "One of these days, that stupid thing is going to fall and kill me." She stretched her worn, faded sweater tightly across her chest and fumbled toward the front counter.

To say she looked old would be a masterpiece of understatement. Wrinkles crisscrossed her face and neck like deep fissures in a dried out stream. She leaned on the counter and let out a rattling, choking cough. Extreme sun damage and chain smoking evidently took its toll on what was once an attractive woman.

"Everything is seventy-five percent off," she said gruffly. "The more you buy, the more you save," she said in a raspy voice.

"Do you have anything from the Civil War era?" Jennifer asked.

"Oh, let me see. We had a friend who bought everything we had, which wasn't a lot. Don't get many calls for Civil War stuff."

Jennifer nodded and looked into a display case filled with costume jewelry. She chuckled to herself when she saw a brooch that looked exactly like the one her dad threw away when Grandmother

Beasley passed.

"Wait!" screeched the woman, startling both Jennifer and Jake. She turned and bellowed to someone in the back room. "Where's that cemetery thing Junior found back in 1952? You know—the one from Mississippi!"

A deep, shaky voice responded, "Edna! I don't know where that dang thing is! Maybe it's in my desk drawer."

A gruff burst of laughter spilled from Edna's mouth and almost made her dentures pop out. "My husband has a problem with his memory," she said, clamping down on her false teeth. "He's ninety-one and barely able to get around now."

"What thing is he referring to?" Jake asked.

Edna shrugged. "We've had it forever."

"Can you describe what it is?" Jennifer asked.

"Our son…well, let me start at the beginning. We were visiting my sister, Edith, in Natchez, you know, Mississippi. Junior, I think he was four at the time, and very inquisitive, found this thing sticking up out of the ground at the cemetery. He took it, stuffed it into his jacket, and then hid it in Carl's suitcase. Didn't see it till we got home to Florida. Did you ever? Kids! They do the craziest things."

"Who's crazy?" asked Carl in a gruff voice. He sat in a transport chair, using his feet to inch forward. He moved slower than a slug.

Edna ignored her husband. "There was nothing we could do about it," she continued. "The boy took it, and we put it away. If you want, I'll look for it."

"We're here on business," Jake said. "We can stop back later today. What time do you close?"

"We make it a practice to never stay open beyond five o'clock. Been closing at that time since we reached our eighties…still following the same habits."

Carl pointed at an old Mickey Mouse alarm clock, which was off by one hour.

"Are you going by *that* clock?" asked Jennifer.

Carl nodded. "Sure am, tells perfect time."

"Sorry, but it's wrong," Jennifer said. "We're on daylight saving time."

Edna frowned and reached for the clock, setting it ahead by one hour. "I'll look for that cemetery thing...be sure and come back," she said, following them to the door. She gave a wave and waited for them to get into their car before locking the door.

Jake looked back at the store. "Do you believe the story that their kid took something from the cemetery?"

"Not a word! I think Carl and Edna saw something they thought had value and took it."

"It's possible. But I think the whole thing is morbidly amusing."

"What could they possibly have taken?"

"Maybe some of dem bones, dem bones, dem dry bones. Who knows?"

Jennifer laughed. "I'm intrigued. Let's come back later before we go to Miami."

Sea Rest Retirement Village in Fort Lauderdale—a private, gated community situated along the Intracoastal Waterway—enjoyed a sophisticated lifestyle with all the amenities, including an eighteen-hole golf course, two swimming pools, seven tennis courts, fitness and wellness centers, nature and biking trails, and an elegant clubhouse.

From the moment they entered the clubhouse, it was apparent that this community was anything but restful. In fact, the only one resting was Jake. Once he found a comfortable chair, he began chatting with the ladies and nibbling on whatever food they handed him. Every once in a while, he'd aim the camera lens at something he deemed interesting, and a succession of rapid clicks followed.

Whenever Jennifer motioned for him to take a photo, he'd rush over, take a few shots, and then return to be pampered by the group of well-dressed, overly made-up women that found him charming and witty. Jake relished the attention and accepted it all with a shyness that made him endearing.

Jennifer's interview with the owner of a waste collection company was nothing short of boring. He spoke without emotion about starting out as a garbage man and ending up owning the company. More than once he interjected the fact that he was not connected to the Mafia. "Organized crime in the hauling industry is a myth," he said, and then joked that it wasn't only garbage he hauled away.

And with that, Jennifer ended the interview.

With tins of cookies and enough hugs to last a lifetime, they left and headed back to the antique shop.

Carl and Edna sat behind the counter, surrounded by a haze of thick cigarette smoke. A marble ashtray with a bronze art deco figurine overflowed with cigarette butts and gum wrappers.

"I found it!" squealed Edna with a welcoming smile. "It was at the bottom of our trunk."

"What is it?" asked Jennifer.

"I'm not sure what to call it," she answered, handing a cast iron, star-shaped object to Jake. She gave him a flirtatious wink.

Jake studied it carefully. "It's kind of heavy...at least three pounds. The embossed words are barely legible, but I think it says... Our Comrade Soldier 1861-1865." He turned it over. "The back has an aperture for a mounting pole. The date indicates that it's postwar."

Carl stared knowingly. "It's a grave marker!" he bellowed as if addressing a bunch of halfwits.

"You can have it for two hundred dollars," Edna said.

"What cemetery did you say your boy took this from?" Jennifer asked.

"The national cemetery in Natchez," Edna replied impatiently.

Jennifer looked at Jake. "What do you think?"

"Two hundred is a bit steep," he said, looking at Edna. "We'll give you seventy-five dollars…no more than that."

Edna no longer portrayed a friendly demeanor. "Cash only!" she snapped.

"I'll take it," Jennifer said. But when she and Jake were in the car, she expressed doubts about its authenticity. "It could be a repro."

"Whether it's authentic is anybody's guess. Carl and Edna just might be the biggest cons we've ever met."

"Or, it's possible they don't know anything more than we do."

Two hours later at Marina Cove in Miami, Jennifer was well into her interview with a popular chef who once had a lucrative TV career and best-selling cookbooks to his credit. It wasn't until the dialogue took a sharp turn into revelations about other well-known chefs and their escapades—nothing of which she could use in the article—that she signaled Jake it was time to leave.

They headed to The Polo Club where a buffet and full bar were a welcoming sight. Many of the residents were already slightly tipsy.

By now, Jennifer knew that although the cast of characters in this retirement article had different careers and enjoyed much success in the past, only one looked to the future with a career in politics. And that man was Henry Marshall.

Unlike his sister, Marshall was opinionated and brash. He repeatedly rattled that his knowledge of law and business management gave him a superior edge when it came time to pull his retirement community out of bankruptcy. "I also thwarted a major lawsuit from a local developer. Imagine what I could do for Boca and the state of Florida," he said, flashing a pretentious smile.

Jennifer ignored most of his vague and long-winded ramblings but managed to steer him into rephrasing some of his foolish remarks to make him sound less obnoxious.

It didn't take long for him to figure out what she was doing. And while he didn't appreciate a woman having the upper hand, he did realize that even though his sister owned the publication, she would never agree to an article slanted to fit her or his personal goals. And so, he took the suggestions and then made it seem that he was the one with the brilliant responses.

As the interview continued, he grew tired of the mundane questions and kept interrupting and contradicting. When his cell phone rang, he was thankful to break away. "Sorry, have to take this call…very important."

Jennifer took this time as an opportunity to go online and search for information about the so-called lawsuit, which turned out to be a simple case of a disgruntled retiree over the color of his condo. As for the bankruptcy claim, nothing popped up.

Marshall sauntered back to the table. He sat down with a hard thud and exhaled slowly. "Sorry for the interruption. Where were we?"

Immediately, she sensed a change in his disposition. His face was flushed, and his smile was definitely forced.

She opened a folder and flipped casually through some papers. Every now and then, she'd circle a word and make a note in the margin. "I'm reviewing Ellie's notes," she said without looking up.

Marshall remained silent.

"I stepped into this assignment at the last hour," she said, lifting her eyes. "It appears that Ellie knew you well."

The icy glare in his eyes, and the flare of red that spread across his face and down his neck, were a convincing sign that he had something to hide. He pushed back in his chair and folded his arms defensively across his chest. "I hardly knew her. Isn't it her job to get detailed information?"

And then, he rattled off a list of everything he thought was wrong with the city. Thankfully, the din swirling about them became so distracting that Marshall had to stop talking. "Let's join in the fun," he said abruptly. "I think you have enough for your article."

"More than enough," Jennifer said with a discerning tone.

Marshall sensed that she knew about him and Ellie. But he also believed she would keep his private life confidential—if she valued her job.

For the rest of the evening, Jennifer kept her distance.

"All in all this was fun," Jake said, as they were getting ready to leave. "Where else can I have free food, women fussing over me, and the friendship of a beautiful, charming colleague?"

"There's a lot to be said for all three. Remember, though, they all come with a price."

"Ah, always the voice of reason. So, how did the interview go with old Harry? Seems like quite a character. He's nothing like Ann."

"You got that straight. When Ellie's name came up, he got defensive, and there's no doubt in my mind that those two were more than mere acquaintances. Nevertheless, only time will tell if he's going to be successful with his political aspirations. As for his private life, it will stay that way—for Ellie's sake."

"Maybe she was in love with him, or maybe he promised her the world."

Jennifer shrugged. "Perhaps it was a love story that took an unfortunate turn at the corner of Infidelity Street and My Wife Found Out Boulevard."

"Now that's funny," Jake said with a laugh. "But really, I think love is an elusive emotion that we have no control over. Reminds me of when I was a kid. I loved to hunt for seashells and bury them close to the shoreline. I'd no sooner fill the hole, and a big wave would roll in and wash away the shells."

"Let me get this straight. You equate love with digging holes in the sand, burying shells, and losing them to waves?"

"Think of it as a metaphor. The hole is my heart, and the shells are the loved ones I place there for safekeeping. And, of course, the waves are life. Don't you get it?"

"Well…okay. How about we wave our way out of here?"

CHAPTER 7

When they returned to the hotel, Jake suggested a nightcap at the tiki bar. Jennifer could see the change in his mood. A strong ocean breeze temporarily doused his obsession with the heat, but not his obsession with her.

"You're really quite beautiful. But of course, you know that," he said.

Jennifer gave him a blank stare. "First a compliment and then you imply that I'm a narcissist. Well, thanks for nothing. I think your statement might suggest that the heat melted your brain."

"I think it would be nice if the heat melted your heart," he shot back.

"Hey, that's not nice. My heart doesn't need melting; it's in a protective mode."

"If I were a betting man, I'd say you enjoy using Michael as a shield against getting close to anyone. Tell me if I'm wrong, but you were never in love with him or vice versa."

"I won't argue that point because it's true. But I don't believe I'm using him to keep my distance from anyone. And truthfully, I got caught up in the moment and should have known better. From the beginning, we had an agreement that if either of us wanted out, we'd exit without causing embarrassment. He broke that contract on all levels."

"You've changed. I liked you before, but now you're different. Less dependent, more your own person. One thing I can't stand is a woman who's weepy and clingy."

"I was never that type," she said, taking his remark personally. "I simply did my job and didn't make waves. Now, I like to make waves while I'm doing my job."

"I didn't mean *you*; I'm talking about Gloria. She was always weepy and clung to me like a wet tee shirt. I hated it, and the more she knew I hated that type of behavior, the more she did it. I can't get that woman off my back."

"Excuse me, but she's the mother of your child. If you didn't care for her why did you let the relationship go on for so long?"

"I thought she'd change. Instead, she became pregnant."

Jennifer rolled her eyes and laughed sarcastically. "Change? That's the magic word that can destroy a relationship. No one should have to change to suit another person's blueprint. And—I don't mean to sound tactless—but I suppose she became pregnant by herself? You men are all the same; you want it all, and to hell with the consequences."

Jake looked grieved. "I'm not like that, Jennifer. Stop trying to put me in the same box with other men, or should I say bed. While I was with Gloria, I didn't cheat on her. Furthermore, I never told her I loved her. She knew from the beginning that there was no love on my part."

Jennifer bit her bottom lip. "Sounds a lot like my story. I'm sorry, let's not talk about this anymore. I'm tired, and this is not a good subject for me. I'm resigned to the fact that there is no happy-ever-after in my future."

"That's ridiculous! You make your own happiness when you determine to change. It's time to move on. How about a date—a real date—with me? When I get back to New York, we'll go for dinner and a movie. What do you say?"

She didn't reply. Instead, she stood up, gently touched his shoulder, and walked to her room. Once the door clicked shut behind her, she cried. She blubbered in the shower and sniffled while downloading her notes. She dabbed at eyes and finally stopped just before calling his room.

"Want to have breakfast with me before I fly home tomorrow?" she asked, trying to tone down her sniffling.

"I'll have breakfast with you if you have dinner with me Friday night."

"It's a deal. By the way, I need a ride to the airport."

Jake laughed. "Now I know why you invited me for breakfast."

She felt better, and he did too. She packed her work and looked at the marker. A cold shiver swept over her. *A grave marker should never have been removed from a cemetery,* she thought, placing it at the opposite end of the room.

Sleep didn't come quickly. After tossing and turning, punching down pillows, and fluffing the covers, she finally felt a quiet release, and her body relaxed. She drifted off into a peaceful sleep, but it didn't last. A dream sequence began, and she became agitated. Sam was arguing with someone, while Jake kept tugging her hand. There was another man—a stranger—dressed in a military uniform. She heard the sound of gunfire in the distance. Then, there was dead silence.

She felt her body levitate through a door that led to a moonlit field surrounded by oak trees. A soft breeze stirred the branches, and she shivered. Her soul filled with despair, and she began to sob when she saw someone standing in a haze on a hill. It was the stranger in her dream. She felt his pain and sorrow.

"What a terrible loneliness!" she cried. "Where am I? Who are you?"

A voice she could barely hear answered: *Please help me. I don't belong here.*

Before she could respond, the door closed and the vision grew dim. She found herself sitting at the edge of the bed, eyes filled with tears. Her nightgown was saturated with perspiration, and her hand trembled as she reached to turn on the light. She collected her thoughts and moaned. "It was just a dream; a silly dream."

It was four o'clock in the morning. She retrieved a bottle of water from the fridge and her parched throat welcomed the cold liquid, gulping it as if she'd just come from the desert. Water dribbled down her chin and splashed on her chest. She stared, at nothing in particular.

The six o'clock wake-up call wasn't needed. After a long shower, hoping to wash away the sadness, she dressed and met Jake for breakfast.

"You look tired, Jen. Didn't you sleep well?"

"No. I had one hell of a nightmare."

Jake reached for her hand and held it tightly. He shook his head, feeling guilty that his words may have played a part in her restless night. "I'm sorry for being insensitive last night. I'm probably to blame."

She looked down at his hand and was reminded that in the dream, he held her hand. She pulled away. "Please, Jake, no more talk. I just want to go home, finish this article, and plan for a quiet vacation."

"Vacation?" he laughed. "You honestly believe that Sam is going to give you some time off? Dream on, my girl."

"We'll see," she said smugly.

Over the next several hours, Jennifer fought hard not to think of anything disturbing. She stopped at the airport newsstand, bought a candy bar, a bag of peanuts, and a magazine. While waiting for her flight, she read the magazine from cover to cover, ate the candy, and devoured the peanuts.

Her flight took off on time, and it wasn't until she finished two cups of coffee that she allowed time to recall her crazy dream. The voice she'd heard touched her soul. It amazed her that it could be so real.

I don't belong here.

"Belong where?" she answered, turning sharply to see who spoke. Except for her laptop case with the marker in it, the seat next to her was empty. "Oh…my…gosh!" she said under her breath. In her mind's eye she saw tall trees swaying in a breeze she could almost feel.

Please help me!

She looked at the empty seat. *I'm having a breakdown,* she said to herself. *I knew this would happen. Too much work, too much stress. I thought I was okay, but I'm not.*

A quick peek out the window made her feel better when she saw the Hudson River and the New York City skyline.

She forced her thoughts back to childhood. Whenever she was in a sad mood, her mother would sing silly songs to make her laugh. One of them was about a little girl and her pet pig. The melody and words rolled over and over in her head. She laughed out loud before realizing that the flight attendant was standing over her.

"Are you okay?" she asked, somewhat concerned.

"I'm fine. Just thought of something funny."

"I could use a good laugh too. Please fasten your seat belt. We're getting ready to land at LaGuardia."

As soon as Jennifer exited the airport, she realized that winter was over. It wasn't as warm as Florida, but it was a pleasant day bathed in sunshine. She hailed a cab and settled in for the ride home, hoping that the traffic and noise of the city would drown out the pleading from the unnerving, strange voice she'd heard on the plane. As soon as she saw familiar landmarks, she perked up.

It wasn't until she entered her apartment that she allowed herself to listen. Nothing. Quiet. She inhaled and smiled. *It's gone*, she thought happily. *Whatever it was is gone.*

The familiar fragrance of peach potpourri reassured her that this was a safe place to be. She locked the door behind her and, for a moment, thought that *safe* was a strange way to feel. "Safe from what?" she whispered into the quietness.

She opened the blinds to let in the brightness of the day. A few clouds dotted the early afternoon sky. Her window boxes were empty. She began making mental notes that she would plant pink geraniums in one box and herbs in the other. "In fact," she said, opening the windows, "I'll buy them today."

A feeling of renewed strength overtook her. She unpacked and dressed in jeans and a sweatshirt. The message machine indicated three calls. The one from her father was calm. The one from Tom Milner sounded desperate. And the one from Billy was a rambling mess of words ending with an urgent plea to call him as soon as possible.

Without hesitation, she called her cousin.

"Boy, am I glad to hear from you. How was your trip?" he asked.

"Okay. What's so urgent?"

"Can you come to the market? I have a lot to tell you, and I'll give you all the food you need."

"I'll be over soon."

She called her father. Four rings and his answering machine picked up: *Out in the garden. Leave a message.*

"I'm home. Going to the market. Will call later."

When she left the apartment, she heard meowing and scratching from behind Carolyn's door, which meant Morton knew she was home. She crossed the hall and tapped the door. "You have to wait until Aunt Carolyn comes home from work."

Less than five minutes later, she was at the market.

"Come on," Billy said excitedly. "Fill up the cart with everything you need, and I'll have Sonny deliver it." But he didn't wait for Jennifer to start shopping. Instead, he began selecting items, placing them gently into the cart.

"This," he said, holding up a bottle of extra virgin olive oil, "is imported from Italy. Just got a shipment, and the customers are clamoring for more."

Jennifer knew better than to stop him.

"Look at these tomatoes!" he exclaimed, holding one up as if it were a prized possession. "Nowhere in the city will you find fruits and veggies like these. You look like you haven't had a decent tomato in days. What else?"

"Bread, milk, butter…things like that."

Billy ignored the mundane list of staples and pointed to a row of imported anchovies. He took a jar off the shelf. "This is delicious for

Caesar salad, on pizza, or a pasta dish."

"Be real—as if I have time to cook."

Billy pretended not to hear. "What else do you need?"

"Wine, and I also want four pink geranium plants and some herbs."

Billy motioned to Sonny, who came over like a loyal pup and gave him a list of everything Jennifer wanted. "Get a couple of bunches of tulips too. Tell Angelo it's for my cousin. Put it all on my account," he added, and Sonny offered a perfunctory salute as he dashed away.

Jennifer stretched her head to look into the quaint bistro Billy opened a few months ago. It was packed with hungry diners. She sighed. "I was hoping to have a salad and—"

Billy grabbed her arm. "Come on, let's have lunch. I have a table for us in the corner where it's quiet. No salad today. Our specialty is grilled mahi-mahi, coleslaw, and jasmine rice."

The table was set for three people.

"Who's the third plate for?" Jennifer asked.

"Elaine will be joining us. She has something important to tell you," he said, stuffing a breadstick into his mouth. "She called me late last night, and told me she was thinking about you."

Jennifer looked at her watch. "She'd better get here soon. I have a ton of work to do at home."

"Relax. You need some time to unwind after your flight. And anyway, Sonny's not ready. Now, tell me, how was the trip? Good stuff for your article?"

"Yeah, but I managed to find time to buy a present for Dad. Now that I think of it, I'm not going to give it to him. I'm going to get him something else. Maybe a new set of paints or a fishing rod."

"A fishing rod sounds good. I'll call my friend at Herman's. He'll drop something off tomorrow. What did you buy that you're not going to give him?"

"This is going to sound weird, but it's a grave marker."

Billy's eyes widened. "You bought Dad a grave marker? Are you insane?"

"Listen…it's a Civil War piece…small…I can hold it in the palm of my hand. It's a long story. Anyway, I'm not going to give it to him. If it's the real thing, I'll give it back to the cemetery."

"This is sounding bizarre. I'm getting the heebie-jeebies thinking of you owning a grave marker. Get rid of that thing."

At that moment, Elaine swept around the corner and fell into the chair next to Jennifer. Her arms waved frantically, and the jingle-jangle of two clunky charm bracelets made heads turn throughout the café. She was out of breath and begged Billy to pour her some wine.

"Look at me," Elaine moaned. "I'm a wreck. I threw on this old dress. You like it? It belonged to my grandmother. I ran all the way here; I didn't want to miss you. My dear girl, you're in the stars. You're going to write a best seller that will become a movie. Yes! It's true!"

Billy gaped at Elaine as if she had two heads. He was mesmerized by what she'd said. He poured a small amount of wine in her glass and drank it. "What did you say?" he asked, wiping his lips. "My cousin is going to be famous? This is incredible! How do you know these things?"

"I just know," Elaine answered coyly. She twisted her head to see who might be listening. "Things come to me. Jennifer, say something."

"I'm speechless. Imagine me, a writer, writing a book," she answered, holding back a sarcastic giggle.

Elaine laughed and took no offense to the remark. She knew that skepticism was very much a part of how people reacted to her predictions. "Of course you're a writer," she said politely. "But this is different. Your life will change. I see exciting things in your future."

Jennifer stared at her, more impressed with how great she looked for her age than by her ability to predict the future. When Billy first told her that Elaine was in her late sixties, she didn't believe him. She looked incredible, not a wrinkle on her face.

Elaine continued. "You're planning on writing a book, aren't you?"

Jennifer didn't know how to respond. Writing a book was not part of her immediate plans. "I guess, someday, I might write a book."

Elaine frowned and shook her head as if trying to reason with a child. "Not someday! I feel you *must* start now! You have an idea, don't you? Someone has given you an idea. I can't make out who or what. Well, it doesn't matter. You're to start now, this much I know."

Jennifer remained silent, stunned by her words.

"Tell her about the grave marker," Billy insisted.

Elaine clasped her hands and raised them to her lips. "O mój Boze!" she wailed in Polish. She reached for Jennifer's hands, holding them tightly. "What is this about a grave marker?"

"I bought a Civil War…actually a post-war piece. It's small, in the shape of a star with a different symbol on each of the five points. I haven't researched it yet, so I'm not sure if it's authentic or whether it's Union or Confederate," explained Jennifer.

Elaine closed her eyes and tightened the grip on Jennifer's hands. "What happens when you hold it? Do you feel or sense anything? Anything at all?"

"I had a dream…." Jennifer hesitated.

"A dream? Are you sure it was a dream?" asked Elaine.

"It felt like a dream, but I was awake. I'm not really sure. All I know is that I moved through a door and found myself in a field."

Elaine bowed her head and remained silent for a moment. "You weren't sleeping, my dear," she said, lifting her head. "You had an out of body experience. Go on."

"Someone was there, but I didn't see him clearly. It was…strange and truthfully, Elaine, I don't believe that it was anything more than—"

"What else happened? Quickly! Tell me everything!"

"He spoke to me. He said…oh, this is crazy, he told me to help him and that he didn't belong somewhere."

Elaine jumped from her seat and her chair fell backward, hitting the floor with a loud bang. She covered her mouth with both hands, closed her eyes, and swayed like a pendulum.

Billy rushed to pick up her chair and eased her into it.

After composing herself, she sighed heavily. With bulging eyes, she stared at Jennifer. "Anything else?"

"While I was on the plane, I heard the same voice, and he asked again for my help. Look, I'm getting nervous about this whole thing. You know I have an overactive imagination. Or, worse yet, I'm having a breakdown from too much work and stress."

"I don't believe that," Billy said. "You know there's something here, Jen. Don't be afraid to find out what it is. You found an object connected to someone in the past that needs to connect to someone in the present. That person must be caught between two worlds. He's trapped, and you have to help him. Does that sound right, Elaine?"

"Exactly correct, my precious friend," Elaine answered. "Jennifer, you owe it to yourself and this stranger. You need to explore this phenomenon. There's a story here, and you will not only find the mystery behind this person and the grave marker, but I truly believe you'll finally find some peace in your own life. Don't dismiss what you don't understand. I'm here to help you. May I see the marker?" Elaine asked.

"Of course. Anytime."

Elaine looked at her with pleading eyes. "How about this evening at eight?"

"That's fine, but I have to go now. Sonny is waiting for me."

CHAPTER 8

★————~~~~————★

Sonny drove the delivery van slowly up 84th Street and found a space in front of Jennifer's brownstone.

"Luck is with us today," he said, flashing a happy smile. "The stars are aligned. Elaine said so."

"Oh no, not you too?"

"Oh, yeah! She's always telling me things. Half I doubt, half I believe. It's fun stuff. She told me I was going to open a Chinese restaurant."

"Sonny, you're Chinese…your father owns a restaurant. Ah, get the picture?"

"Yeah!" he said with a laugh.

After making two trips into her apartment—carrying boxes with everything from imported pasta to pâté—Sonny helped unload and even placed things into her small pantry. He put the plants on the floor under the kitchen window.

When he was finished, she walked him out to the van and handed him twenty dollars.

"No," he said, shaking his head. "Can't take this. Your cousin will skin me alive."

"You take this and don't say a word to him. I've learned that what he doesn't know won't hurt him." With a warm smile and a quick wink, she stuffed the money into his shirt pocket.

Late in the afternoon, she unpacked her suitcase but left the marker in her tote by her desk. A knock at the door startled her. It was Carolyn.

"Hi, Jen. You're not going to believe this, but as soon as I walked into my apartment, Morton began purring and scratching at my front door. I let him out, and he trotted right over to your door and scratched at it. This cat acts more like a dog every day."

Jennifer bent down and rubbed Morton's head. "Such a good boy. Did you miss me?"

Morton purred and rubbed his tail against her leg. He immediately took off to check his food bowl.

"He didn't miss me, he missed his crunchy treats," Jennifer said.

"When did you get home?"

"Around noon. I went to Billy's, did food shopping, and I got some plants. This summer we'll have herbs. No more of that dried stuff."

Carolyn sniffed the plants and critiqued the wine.

"Is it too early for a glass of wine?" Jennifer asked.

"Never too early for that, but I can't stay right now. Got papers to correct. Maybe I'll see you later."

Morton sniffed the plants. Something across the room caught his attention. The fur on his tail puffed.

"What do you see? A bug?"

Morton sauntered off, and she laughed. She opened a bottle of white wine, poured a glass, and settled on the couch with a plate of cheese and crackers. The phone rang. She took a sip and waited for the machine to answer. In a few seconds, she heard Michael's pleading voice for her to pick up.

"I know you're there, Jen," he said.

She pointed her finger at the phone. "Bang!" she yelled. She laughed and nibbled on a piece of Brie. "I don't take orders from you, Michael!"

It took thirty seconds for him to call back. He left the same message before slamming the receiver down.

Another laugh. Only this time, Jennifer wasn't angry. "I've finally got him going," she said to Morton.

She went to her desk and pushed her flash drive into the USB port. The retirement article filled the screen. She liked the lede and was pleased with the way the text flowed. It always amazed her how well she wrote while under pressure. If there was such a thing as writer's block, she'd never experienced it. Quite the contrary; she had dozens of articles and story ideas hidden in folders and in the deep crevasses of her mind.

The phone rang, and this time she picked it up. She was ready to yell at Michael, but it was Jake calling from Charleston.

"Just wanted to say that I'll be in the office day after tomorrow. You do remember what we have planned for Friday evening, don't you?"

She thought for a moment. "What's Friday? Oh, sure I remember. We have a real date. I look forward to this, Mr. Cohen. I hope you'll spring for an expensive dinner and, instead of a movie, how about a play?"

Jake laughed. "The more expensive the date, the more I'll expect from you. No. I think we'll stick to dinner, a movie, and perhaps a bag of popcorn. I don't want you to feel that you have to be in my debt."

Now it was her turn to laugh. "See you on Friday. By the way, let's keep this our little secret. No need to tell the world that we have a date, right?"

"You're not ashamed of me, are you?"

"Certainly not. I just like to keep certain things private, especially from Sam. You know how annoying he can be when it comes to *his* staff."

"My lips are sealed. See you Friday."

She returned to work and lost track of time until the doorbell rang. She looked at her watch. It was eight o'clock. She placed the marker on the coffee table and walked to her intercom. "Who is it?" she asked.

"It's me…and Elaine!" Billy yelled, and Morton hightailed it out of the room.

Half an hour later, with wine glasses filled and gourmet snacks laid out on the coffee table, Elaine and Billy stared blankly at the object they came to see.

"May I hold it?" Elaine asked softly.

Jennifer handed it to her and waited for a reaction. But there was none.

Elaine examined the front and the back, turning it over and over. "This is going to sound strange, even for me," she said, squinting her eyes as if trying to get a clearer picture of something or someone. "The only thing I see is a white horse. How incredibly odd is that? Oh, gosh! This is intense. The presence of this magnificent animal awakens an excitement within. Jennifer, if you ever see a white horse speak to it."

Jennifer suppressed a laugh. *A horse? I'm supposed to talk to a horse? How silly is this?*

Holding the marker securely, Elaine covered it with her other hand and closed her eyes. A heavy sigh escaped her lips. "Oh, my!" she blurted. "I feel warmth flowing from the palm of my hand to my elbow. It's warm and soothing. That's better, much better. Pain is gone. What a relief."

Jennifer turned and shot a questioning stare at Billy.

"She has a severe case of tennis elbow," he whispered. "Doctors tried everything; told her surgery was the only answer."

Elaine opened her eyes. "It has power," she said with authority. "I will be bold and say that it has curative power. Right now, I am free of pain in my arm. It's just that simple." She handed the marker to Billy. "What do you feel?" she asked, beaming.

"It's cold," he said slowly, scrunching his face and squeezing his hands as if trying to will the marker to do something. "There's no warmth, only cold metal against my hand."

"Close your eyes," demanded Elaine. "Stop trying to control its power."

Billy began to fidget. Afraid of what might happen next, he tried to give it back to her.

She refused it. "Relax," she said. "Let it guide you."

He listened, and a sensation of warmth slowly flowed through his hands. A startled look crossed his face.

"Don't let go," Elaine said.

"I feel weird. I can see inside my body. This is scary."

"No!" screeched Elaine. "Don't allow fear to take over. Where are you?"

"I'm moving through a sea of red."

Elaine got the chills. "Go inward. Don't stop."

Billy took a deep breath. "I can feel warmth in my chest. Why is that?"

"Because it's where your heart is…because it's where your condition must be." She turned to Jennifer. "What's wrong with him? Tell me the truth."

Billy nodded, giving Jennifer permission.

"Billy had rheumatic fever when he was a child. His heart valves are damaged."

"Where are you, Billy?" Elaine asked harshly. The intensity of her voice frightened Jennifer.

"I don't know," Billy answered. "It's dark, and there's a steady, soft thumping in my ears. Gosh! For the first time in my life, I feel a quiet settling inside my body."

Jennifer began to cry.

Elaine bowed her head, traced the sign of the cross from her forehead to her chest and shoulders, and murmured a Polish prayer.

Billy opened his eyes. He gently placed the marker on the coffee table and pushed back. "I'm not sure of what just happened, but I feel different," he said calmly.

They sat quietly, afraid to speak, fearful that if they said something negative, it would change the outcome of what had happened.

Everything in the room seemed surreal. Morton sat in the corner, looking curiously at the coffee table where the marker rested.

"A soldier died before his time," Elaine explained. "His life was stolen. I don't like these types of feelings…too much pain. But oh, what a lovely young man. Jennifer, you must pursue this. This unusual piece of history will rectify many wrongs. I have never felt a phenomenon such as this. You must find out why *you're* the conduit. Look at me…I can move my arm without pain. It's the most exciting thing that has ever happened to me."

"What about me?" Billy asked, pressing his hands against his chest. "My heart condition could have been the death of me. I never heard of anyone dying of tennis elbow."

"Okay, so your heart is more dramatic. But," Elaine said thoughtfully, "I don't think that everyone will feel the same thing when they hold this piece. Jennifer, keep this marker close to you and in a safe place. What has happened tonight is nothing short of a miracle. But there's a danger I can't explain. I don't know if it's from the past or the present. You must be very careful, please."

"I will," Jennifer murmured. "But tell me, Elaine, do you know if the soldier was Confederate or Union?"

"I'm sorry, but I don't know anything about that."

"According to the man who sold it to me, it was taken from a Natchez cemetery," Jennifer explained.

Billy took his tablet and searched for cemeteries in Natchez. "Here's one...the Natchez National Cemetery." He jotted down the number and clicked on the website link. "If this marker is from there, then it has to be from a Union soldier's gravesite because it's a Federal cemetery. Maybe it's a commemorative piece."

"Sometimes you're so smart," Elaine said.

"Not really," Billy replied. "I think I remember seeing Union medals in one of my dad's books, and they looked very similar to this. Look here," he said, touching the points of the five stars. "Each point has the insignia of the armed forces. Dad would know for sure, though. Call him, Jen."

Alex Beasley answered the telephone with his usual greeting. "Dr. Beasley, on call."

"Hi, Dad. How are you doing?"

"Great. Where are you?"

"Home. Billy and I were talking about a Civil War piece I found in an antique shop in Florida. She went on to describe it in detail and noted what Billy found online.

"Hold on while I check one of my books."

After a few minutes, Alex returned to the phone. "Medals of Honor for Union soldiers were sometimes in the shape of a star with insignias imprinted on each point. It's probably Union, but whether it's a grave marker, I'm not sure. I think it would have been expensive to put on all the graves. If you like, I could try to dig up—excuse the pun—some information about it."

"Thanks, Dad. Whatever you can find out will be great. Billy and I will see you Sunday for lunch. I'll email you a photo and website info about the cemetery. Take care, and call me if you need anything," she said affectionately.

Within the hour, Billy and Elaine were gone. Jennifer crawled into bed, hoping that sleep would come quickly.

A diffused glow of light from the street lamp directly in front of the brownstone filtered into the room, casting just enough light so she could see her cat sleeping at the foot of the bed.

In the distance, the sound of a car alarm awakened Morton. He jumped off the bed and sauntered to the window. Leaping up, he gracefully balanced on the edge of the windowsill and looked outside.

Jennifer turned over, closed her eyes, and drifted off into a deep sleep.

CHAPTER 9

Jennifer awoke at dawn, surprised that she'd slept soundly without waking. She felt refreshed, eager to get to her office. She dressed, scoffed down a bowl of cereal, and was out the door in less than 30 minutes and in her office before most of the staff.

From the hall, the aroma of freshly brewed coffee reached her with an insistence that whatever smelled that good had to taste even better. She went into the kitchenette, poured a cup, and reached for a cinnamon twist.

"Who's there?" Sam called from his office.

"It's me, the bogeyman. Good morning, Sam. Great coffee."

"Well, if it isn't the lost lady writer," Sam said, shuffling into the room. "Where have you been? Yesterday I called you all over Florida."

She ignored his remark, knowing that he was exaggerating.

"If you check your file," she said sweetly, "you'll find the retirement article. I slugged it *Old.*"

"You're finished? I knew you were the right person for this assignment. And now that you're back, I want you to know that I will not forget this favor."

"Of course you won't," she said playfully. "Right after I send my own assignment to Candy, I'm out of here for two long, glorious, lazy weeks of nothing but rest and fun and anything else that life throws my way."

"Two weeks? Now? Impossible! I can't do without you at this time. I said you could go, but not now. You have the cover story for June," he said, lowering his eyes.

Jennifer glared at him. "I'm leaving this Tuesday. As for the cover story, it's not mine. Have a great morning, Sam. If you need me, I'll be glued to my desk until lunch."

He frowned, knowing that he wasn't going to win. He'd have to think of something brilliant before next week. His cell rang, and he covered his face with his sticky hands. "And that," he said with a heavy sigh, "has to be my mother."

By eight o'clock, the staff started dribbling in with idle chatter about everything from weekend plans to the latest crisis somewhere in the world. Unless office doors were closed, it was open season for general gossip.

Jennifer peeked in Candy's office, and she waved her in.

"Something definitely happened between Ellie and Marshall," Jennifer said. "But it has nothing to do with the article. I don't believe we'll ever know the truth. As for Sam, I didn't mention anything about my suspicions."

"It's good to have a grown-up on staff," Candy said with a laugh.

For the rest of the morning, Jennifer kept her door open. Heads popped in and out, and she welcomed the boring chatter that had a way of finding her ears.

When her phone rang, she picked up the receiver. It was Michael's father. He begged her not to hang up.

"Jennifer, please speak to Michael," he said in a concerned voice.

"What does he want?" she asked impatiently, putting him on speaker. She got up and closed her door.

"He needs to tell you something. Something private. I wouldn't bother you if it weren't important," he whispered.

"I'll call him—"

"No need, I'll transfer you. Hold on, don't hang up, please."

She looked at her watch. "Five, four, three, two—"

"Jen," Michael said sweetly. "I need to talk to you. It's a matter of life and death."

"Stop being dramatic."

"I can't discuss this over the phone. Please have lunch with me and—"

"Absolutely not! No lunch, no dinner, no nothing. If you don't tell me what's going on, I *will* hang up."

"I have a sexual disease." Michael waited for a response.

Jennifer held back a laugh. "A disease that you might or might not have doesn't concern me."

"It's not AIDS!" Michael said emphatically.

"I hope for your sake it's not. But this is your problem—you and whomever you're with right now. If I were you, I'd post this information on your social media pages. It's one sure way of reaching the masses in record-breaking time," she said calmly.

Then, instead of slamming down the phone receiver, she laid it in its cradle, as if it were a newborn babe. "Jennifer Beasley has left the drama," she said, opening her office door.

Missy was standing there with an apologetic expression on her face. "Sorry...I forgot," she whined. "He was so sweet. But you can count on me to never again to put that man through to you. While you were on the phone, you had another call from Dr. Beasley. Same name as yours...said you had the number. I hope you're not sick." Missy sounded genuinely concerned.

"Dr. Beasley is my dad. Thanks for the message. I'll call him now."

Alex Beasley immediately picked up, and the cheerful tone in his voice lifted his daughter's spirits. She told him about Michael's call.

"I think he's lying to gain sympathy from you. Forget that jerk. I found something interesting about your marker. It's true that it came from the Natchez National Cemetery. I called Alfred Copeland, the cemetery director, and he confirmed that it's a post-war memorial star. One was reported missing in the early 1950s. He also said it's not uncommon that something connected to the Civil War would mysteriously disappear. I don't understand why the people in Florida sold it after keeping it for so long."

"That's what I thought, too. In the meantime, I feel much better talking to you."

"Good. Forget about Michael."

"Okay. It's a done deal."

At five o'clock, she left the office under gloomy, dark clouds. She hailed a cab and got in just as a rainstorm drenched the city.

I'm waiting for you.

"Where are you?" she asked.

The driver adjusted his rearview mirror. "You talking to me? We're stuck in traffic."

"Sorry," she murmured and lowered her head. *It's time for me to document every single event that's happened since I bought the marker.*

As soon as she walked into her apartment, Morton meowed. He jumped off the windowsill to greet her. She opened a can of cat food and plopped it into his bowl. After pouring a glass of wine, she checked the refrigerator to see if there was anything good to eat. She shut the door without making a choice.

She closed the blinds in the living room, turned on the desk lamp, and began transcribing precise details since the marker came into her possession.

The house phone rang. It was Billy.

"Elaine had a dream," he said breathlessly. "Listen to this, Jen. She saw you with, and these are her words, 'a good-looking, kind, and gentle man.' Isn't she something? She wasn't clear as to *who* it is, but she's sure that love is headed your way."

"It sounds like she's talking about Jake. I don't know if we should believe every single thing Elaine says. This love stuff is not what I want to hear."

"How about if we believe the things that have come to pass so far. She told me the market would be very successful. This was when I first opened. She was right about that. Oh, she also told me about meeting a woman in a bookstore. I met Marianne at the library. She said that I would like her, but not fall in love. True, again. I'm excited to think that my soul mate is still out there."

"Does Marianne know this?"

"No. You know that Marianne and I have an understanding. I'm not in love with her, and she knows that. Why are you having such a hard time believing that someone has the ability to see into the future? Furthermore, Elaine has never asked me for a dime or takes money from anyone else. Doesn't this prove she has a real gift?"

"You have a point. Too bad it's your head!" she said, laughing.

"Remember when Dad first said that to you? I laughed so hard I fell off the porch."

"Dad does say funny things. But, to answer your first question, I don't have a hard time believing that someone could see into the future. Aunt Louise was always saying things that came true, especially about her second husband, Edgar."

"I forgot that story. Do you remember when we were hiding

in the closet and heard Aunt Louise telling Mom about her dream? I'll never forget that day. When I heard her say that she saw Uncle Edgar naked in his office with his secretary, I thought I'd bust. I had to cover your head with a jacket to keep you from screaming out loud."

"Poor Aunt Louise. I also remember Mom telling her that if she knew anything at all about Dad, she was to keep it to herself."

"She never said anything about him, did she?" Billy asked.

"Never. They seemed very much in love, didn't they?"

Billy had a faraway look in his eyes. "If we could have what they had, life would be perfect. But now, there's love in both our futures. Elaine said so."

"Well, if Elaine said so, then it must be true."

CHAPTER 10

The next morning, Jennifer opened the windows in the kitchen. From her second floor apartment, she had a bird's eye view of the block and the swelling buds on trees that lined the street.

Her cat sat on the window ledge where a decorative iron grill protected two potting boxes from falling to the ground. "The season of spring brings hope to new beginnings," she said to him. But Morton was only interested in a passing dog.

Jennifer called out to her neighbor, and he waved. His dog offered a bark, and Morton hissed.

"That's not nice," she said, and her cat purred an apology.

Her thoughts turned to the house where she and Billy grew up and how glad they both were when her father decided not to sell it after her mom passed away. She and Billy loved their weekly visits, especially during spring and summer. Billy planted vegetables and herbs and liked to claim that it was the Beasley special brand of TLC that made everything grow abundantly.

Despite her love of gardening, the plants were still on the floor under the window. "Tomorrow morning, without fail, I'll plant you guys," she said.

An hour later, she was in her office reading the draft of her article. She worked through lunch, stopping only to eat a piece of fruit and a cup of yogurt.

The office was unusually quiet, as most of the staff scrambled to meet their respective deadlines. Assured that her article was ready, she uploaded it to Candy's file and headed to the kitchen. To her disappointment, the coffee pot was empty, and the doughnuts were gone.

"I'm going down to the café," she said to no one in particular.

"So am I," said Jim from his office.

Jennifer smiled at him. "Did you nibble on all the doughnuts? What if I wanted one?"

"No one should be eating doughnuts at this time of day. It will ruin their appetite. Speaking of appetite, do you want to have dinner with Trudy and me?"

Jennifer held back a laugh. Jim, fifty-five, overweight, and married forever, never ate in a decent restaurant in all his life. Dinner to him and Trudy meant a fast-food tray containing dried-out hamburgers and greasy fries.

Jennifer wrinkled her nose. "No, but thanks for the invite. I would have liked just a small bite of something, but you ruined that for me."

Jim waved as Jennifer rushed to answer her phone. Missy yelled from the front that it was Jake.

"Hey, Cohen! Where are you?"

"I just got home. The traffic from the airport was unbelievable. I'm not going to complain because it's going to be a perfect evening for eating al fresco. Can you meet me at Cognac at 7:30? I'm famished. Hope you are too."

"Can't…having dinner with Jim and Trudy."

"Don't make me laugh. Since when do you eat crap on a bun?"

"You know me so well. Seven-thirty it is. It's a good thing Jim sampled all the doughnuts or I'd be nursing a sour stomach right now."

"Tell Jim he's a slob. Gotta run. See you later."

Jennifer started to say that she already called Jim a bunch of names, but the line went dead. No sooner had she hung up, the phone rang again.

"Jennifer, I need to see you right away," Sam said with a note of urgency in his voice.

"On my way," she said. She walked at a snail's pace, stopping at Candy's office door. "Here it comes," she whispered.

"Give him hell," Candy said. "By the way, thanks for having your article in before deadline. I'm already hearing every excuse imaginable from some of our writers."

Jennifer laughed all the way to Sam's office where he sat slumped behind his desk, shuffling nervously through stacks of papers.

She stood in the doorway, held her hands out in front, and wiggled her fingers. "I need a manicure," she said. She was in control, watching as Sam's face changed from a pathetic smile to a hopeless frown. "And a pedicure," she added, tapping her shoe on the floor.

"I just spoke to the printer," Sam said in a shaky voice. "Seems we're having trouble with this issue, and I'm at my wit's end. I'm going to fly to Michigan early Monday. I need you here—just for a couple of days. I'm sure I can straighten out this mess by the end of next week."

Jennifer remained silent. She shifted her position and leaned against the doorframe, crossing her arms over her chest. She felt like a warrior, bracing for a fight.

Sam widened his eyes. He had no idea what was coming.

"Sam," Jennifer began. The sound of her voice, sweet and non-threatening, threw him off guard. And then it came, swift and precise. "Look at me and hear what I'm saying. I'm leaving for vacation Tuesday morning. Nothing in this world is going to stop me. No problem, no mishap, nothing! Now, I hope you and your lovely family have a wonderful weekend. I'll be here all day Monday, just in case there's a problem with my copy. I'll see you then." She blew a kiss in his direction.

As she passed Candy's office, she gave a triumphant thumbs-up and left.

As usual, Friday's traffic was heavy, but she didn't care. She was ready to begin the weekend. Weaving her way through the masses, she suddenly felt his presence. At the bus stop, she held her breath and listened. Only the wail of distant sirens echoed through the streets. She boarded the bus and stood quietly. When she reached her stop, she walked home confident that he was gone.

After a hot shower, she rummaged through her closet and found a lavender linen dress with a matching knitted jacket. Her hair curled loosely around her face and over her shoulders. She seldom wore makeup but took special care to do her eyes. A little blush, a dab of lipstick, and she was out the door.

When she turned the corner at Broadway and 55th Street, she saw Jake sitting at a table reading a newspaper. At first, he didn't see her. By the time she came into view, he was on his feet, moving a chair so she could sit facing the sidewalk.

"You look fantastic," he said. He beckoned for the waiter and ordered her a vodka martini, straight up, lots of olives.

"Am I that predictable?" she asked.

"Not usually. The specials tonight are excellent. But I'll let you choose your own dinner."

"Mighty big of you."

They scrutinized and discussed the menu as if it were a best-selling novel. After skipping over the appetizers, Jennifer ordered the grilled branzino, and the waiter nodded approvingly.

"Is that all?" Jake asked. "Are you on a diet?"

Jennifer shook her head and looked up at the waiter. He waited for Jake to say something.

"Let's try it this way," Jake said. "We'll share the goat cheese and tomato tart, and we'll each have the arugula and fennel salad."

"Well then, okay," Jennifer said. "I'd still like the branzino."

Possibly the most surprising thing about the evening was the simple realization that they got along so well. They talked, they ate, they laughed—taking no notice of the time.

"I think we missed the movie," Jake said, looking at his watch.

"Let's have coffee and dessert at my place," Jennifer suggested.

Jake's eyes brightened.

Morton was sitting by the door when they arrived. He gave Jake a curious glance and sauntered away.

Jennifer opened the kitchen windows and observed a skinny teenager being dragged along by five dogs on long leashes. He was wearing disposable gloves and holding a bunch of plastic bags. She paused for a moment. *Boy does this kid have his work cut out for him.* She giggled; unaware that Jake was watching her.

He wanted to touch her, to kiss her, and to feel her body against his. He thought about how her lips would taste, they were full and sensual, and he often found himself staring at them. One time he had to ask her to leave his office for fear he would kiss her in front of his assistant. She had a look that drove him crazy. He was still staring at her when she tilted her head and squinted at him.

"What's wrong? Do I have something on my face?" she asked

laughingly.

"I'm admiring you. I want to kiss you. The question is, will you let me?"

Jennifer walked toward him. *I need to know*, she said to herself, *if there's something here.*

He intended to hold her hands, but the feeling that bubbled inside his stomach reached the boiling point. His hands went around her waist, and he pressed her close to his body. His lips traced her face until they rested gently on her mouth. Barely touching, they felt soft—like the delicate petals of a rose. "Don't say a word," he said breathlessly. "Just let me kiss you."

And he did, over and over. His hands moved along the outline of her body, the feel of her made him moan. He wanted her. When he whispered her name, she pushed him away.

"No...I'm sorry, Jake. This is not what we...I should be doing."

"Jennifer, I want to make love to you."

"Not going to happen," she said. "I won't...it will complicate our friendship. I'm not going to lie to you, Jake. I'm not ready to fall in love. And yes, I do equate sex with love; one without the other is worthless."

Jake wasn't going to tell her that he's been in love with her from the first moment they'd met. She touched something in him that no other woman had. *No*, he thought, *now is definitely not the time to tell her.*

"Jake, say something."

"I want this to be right. I want you to feel good about the decision to share one of the greatest things two people can have."

"I like that line, but I think the greatest thing is a love that will last a lifetime."

He reached for her hand. "I understand. Just so you know, I'm looking for that too."

Long after Jake left, she felt satisfied with her reaction and words. She went to her computer and began typing when a sound caught her attention. It was Morton. He jumped down from the windowsill and stalked his way to the middle of the room, twitching his tail. He lifted his eyes and hissed.

Jennifer also felt a presence. She looked around the room not knowing in which direction to speak. Morton's eyes fixed on an empty space between the hall and the living room. She was sure her cat sensed something, so she spoke in that direction.

"Speak to me, please. My name is Jennifer Beasley."

"I'm Dr. Bradley Taylor. I have been waiting for you."

A shiver of fear ran through her when she realized that this encounter was real. This was not her imagination.

Morton continued to stare into the empty space. She wondered if her cat was able to hear him.

She waited. For what, she didn't know. *A question; I need to ask him a question.* "Where are you from, Dr. Taylor?" She turned on her recorder.

"My home is in Brandon, Mississippi. I need you, Miss Beasley. You are the only one who can help me."

"I don't understand." She stood up. "Can you see me?"

"No, but I sense your presence. We are connected because of the marker. It was placed at my resting site…a place where they put me…a grave for an Unknown Soldier. I am not an unknown; I do not belong in this place."

"Where do you belong?"

"With my family."

Jennifer stood up. "Is that what this is all about? You're in the wrong cemetery, and you want me to…to do what?"

"Please come to Natchez. You will understand everything once you are here."

"Dr. Taylor, please understand—" Jennifer stopped talking. It was too late; he was gone.

Morton ran into the kitchen, took a drink from his water bowl, and then licked his paws, unconcerned by the event that just took place.

She poured a shot of scotch and drank it in one gulp. It burned her throat all the way down to her stomach. She sat on the couch, holding the empty glass. Morton jumped onto her lap, and the glass went flying. It hit the carpeted floor with a thud and rolled under the coffee table. She made no attempt to pick it up. "I just had a conversation with a dead man."

After composing herself, she rewound the recorder and played it back. All she heard was her own voice. "Silly," she said aloud. "You can't record a non-physical entity."

She picked up her cell to call Billy, but when she saw that it was after midnight, she changed her mind. She went to her bedroom with Morton close behind.

Surprisingly, sleep came quickly, and Jennifer didn't stir once in the night.

And, somewhere far off, within the vast chasm that separates life and eternity, Bradley Taylor rested in the dust of the earth.

CHAPTER 11

"Morton, what do you think?" Jennifer stepped back to admire the window boxes, now bursting with flowers and herb plants. "It isn't much, but it's better than nothing."

Her cat wasn't interested. Instead, he slinked over to his empty food bowl and gave it a swat with his paw.

She reached for her cell, took a photo of the window boxes, and sent it to her dad and Billy with a simple title: *My little garden!* Both responded immediately with clapping hands and red flower emojis.

Jennifer turned her thoughts to last night's conversation with Bradley Taylor. *He can't see me. Thank heavens for that,* she thought, and her heart rate increased when she recalled the distinct plea for her to come to Natchez.

As a journalist, she felt compelled to follow the path—wherever it might lead. She called the airline and booked a flight, searched the Internet for a hotel in Natchez, reserved a rental car, and made an appointment to see Alfred Copeland at the cemetery.

She thought about calling Billy but wasn't sure if she was ready to discuss last night's encounter. Everything was moving quickly now and most of it was beyond her comprehension. She reasoned that unless someone else heard this soldier's voice, they couldn't possible understand the magnitude of this event. *A stolen grave marker started this. Perhaps a visit to the library and a microfilm search will reveal something.*

As soon as she left her apartment, her cell rang.

"How about lunch?" Jake asked in an upbeat voice. When she didn't answer right away, he decided to tempt her with Chinese food.

"I'm on my way to the library," she answered.

"Which library?"

"Where Patience and Fortitude live."

"Great, I'll meet you there, and then we'll go to lunch."

She didn't have a chance to agree or disagree because the call ended.

Jake sat on the steps in front of the historic New York Public Library in Midtown Manhattan. He observed everyone who passed. The quirky expression on his face made Jennifer laugh as she crossed Fifth Avenue.

"If only you could see your face," she said. "What are you thinking?"

"We live in the best city in the world and the craziest. I just love it all!"

Jennifer walked over to one of the majestic stone lions that flanked the wide front steps. "Hi, Patience," she said, giving the sculpture a tap.

"Didn't your great-grandfather help in the construction of this library?" Jake asked.

"Yes, he was a stonecutter in the early 1900s and did a lot of marble work here."

"No wonder this place is special to you," he said. "You're like the lions: brave and strong."

She smiled, and they walked through the portico and into the massive white marble entrance of Astor Hall. Two magnificent staircases led to the Milstein Microform Reading Room where it was unusually quiet for a Saturday.

Jennifer sat at a reader, and her search began with newspaper articles about thievery at cemeteries in Natchez in the early 1950s.

Jake took a seat beside her. His foot touched her leg, and he moved it up and down to get a reaction.

"I know what you're doing, Jake Cohen, and it's not going... wait, look at this! I found something."

He tapped his finger on the table, pointed to his watch, and then his stomach. "I'm starving," he whispered.

Jennifer was excited. "Not now!" she said, leaning closer to the reader. Her finger touched the screen, tracing an article from *The Natchez Times*, dated May 5, 1952. "Listen to this, Natchez Trace Park Rangers reported that vandals removed memorial markers from the Natchez Trace gravesites of unknown Confederate soldiers. In an unrelated incident, the Natchez National Cemetery also reported one memorial marker missing from its mounting pole at gravesite 1186,

Unknown Soldier."

"Well, at least this does confirm part of Edna's story," Jake said. "Can we go now?"

"Not until I make a copy."

"Food…I need food. How about I get take-out and we eat at my apartment?"

"Good idea." She picked up her copy, and they left.

During lunch, Jennifer told Jake about her encounter with Dr. Taylor the night before. She left nothing out, even though most of it sounded crazy.

Although Jake wasn't sure what to make of it, he knew that she was not one to exaggerate. Her common sense and logic sometimes baffled him. But if Jennifer Beasley said that a Civil War soldier was talking to her, without a doubt, it was so.

"I'm going to Natchez next week to sort things out," she said. "Whatever's going on begins there."

"Did your soldier ask for anything specific?"

"I'm confused as to what he wants. I heard the urgency in his voice, but the whole thing sounds ridiculous."

"Obviously, there's more to this. Why not let go and see where it takes you," he said, sounding like the voice of reason. "You haven't said anything about my decorating. Since you were last here, I've had the whole apartment done over. I'll take you on a tour."

His office was especially interesting to Jennifer because of all the memorabilia and family photographs.

Jake ran his hand lovingly along the rich mahogany finish of his desk. "This belonged to my grandfather," he said. "Did you know he was the editor of the old Herald Tribune back in the 1940s?"

"Yes, of course. Everything in this room is fascinating. I really like the phone and typewriter."

"They're original...from the early 1940s. There are so many memories connected to practically everything in this room."

"This reminds me of my father's office. He, too, kept so many of my grandfather's possessions. It's wonderful to be connected to the past in this way."

A large photo of a cute, pigtailed little girl, with eyes as bright as her dad's, took center stage on his desk.

"Elizabeth looks so much like you, Jake."

"She's a sweetheart and so much fun now that she can read and write. She's eight, going on twenty."

"How often do you see her?"

"Every Sunday we go to my mom's for family dinner. Sometimes she sleeps over, and we go to the movies or the theater. We're planning a trip to Europe this summer...her first time away from Gloria. She's the best thing that ever happened in my life. I just wish...."

"I know," Jennifer said. "We don't know what tomorrow will bring. Maybe you and Gloria—"

"Ah, not going to happen. I'm concerned about her, though.

Elizabeth said she coughs a lot and has been missing work because of her allergies."

"Life changes, Cohen. Look at me, just a few days ago I was walking along, minding my own business, and then WHAM! Never say never."

"Let me show you the bedroom," Jake said, changing the subject. He made his way slowly down the hall and stepped aside. "What do you think?"

"Absolutely gorgeous! There isn't a thing I don't like."

"I just got the four-poster bed and highboy. Actually, I can't take credit for it, my daughter picked it out."

"Tell Elizabeth I like it very much."

"Everything in here is new. In fact," he added coyly, "no other person has ever been in here, or in my bed."

"Why, Jake Cohen, you mean to tell me this bed is chaste? I'm impressed."

"I'm saving this for—"

"Don't say another word." Jennifer walked to the doorway. "Whoever it is, I'm sure it's none of my business."

"What if it's you?"

She left the room ignoring the comment.

"I guess we're leaving," Jake said. "Are you afraid of what might happen if we stay?"

"I'm not afraid of anything."

"I think you are," he replied.

Dark, gloomy clouds swirled high over the city by the time they reached her apartment. They just made it inside, when a bolt of lightning lit up the sky. A loud bang of thunder rattled the windowpane and sent Morton running under the desk.

"Something smells good in here. Is it lemons?" Jake asked, walking into the kitchen.

"It's a lemon pound cake. Would you like a piece?"

"Maybe later," he replied.

She went to her desk and transcribed the information found in the library into her computer. She got so absorbed in her work that she didn't see Jake sitting on the couch, holding the marker.

Morton jumped up and sat next to him. They both stared at the object as if waiting for it to send a message.

Jennifer continued writing, unaware that it was seven o'clock and still raining heavily.

Jake stood up. "What is it about this piece?" he asked. He paused, and then continued: "Is it my imagination or does it get warmer the longer you hold it?"

"Elaine and Billy believe it has curative powers. What do you feel?"

"Warmth, all the way from my hand down to my knee...the one I injured playing football in college."

"Does your knee still hurt?"

"It did before I got here. Could be the storm; it troubles me just before it rains." He marched around the room, lifting his knees up and down. "But now, I don't feel any discomfort."

He placed the marker on her desk and looked out the window. "What a storm. I think I'll be here for a while. I like a rainstorm at the end of a lazy Saturday. Don't you?"

Jennifer nodded and joined him at the window.

"I'll miss you next week," he said. "Will you let me know where I can reach you?"

"Of course—"

Jake didn't allow her to finish. He kissed her, and she pulled away just as the doorbell rang.

She rushed over to the intercom. "Who is it?" she asked in a raspy voice.

A loud shout told her it was Billy. "I forgot my key!"

Her cousin bolted up the steps, carrying shopping bags. "Hey, Jake, great to see you. You can help eat all this food—leftovers from the bistro," he said, looking slightly bewildered. "What's going on? Did I interrupt something?"

Jake shook his head. "I just took some shots of the marker. Interesting piece."

"Boy, you can say that again," Billy said, removing three flat serving dishes from the kitchen cabinet.

"Whatever you brought sure smells good," Jake said, licking his lips. "Good thing I passed on the pound cake."

"I brought enough food to feed all of New York," he said, giggling like a schoolboy. "Ask Carolyn if she's hungry."

"I think she's out, but I'll try," said Jennifer. She walked across the hall.

"Hey! What's up?" Carolyn asked.

"Billy brought dinner. I thought you had a date."

"Long story," she replied, following Jennifer to her apartment.

"Who's going to open the wine?" Billy asked, reaching for another plate.

Jake raised his hand and brushed passed Jennifer, giving her arm a squeeze.

The touch went unnoticed.

After coffee and double helpings of pie and lemon pound cake, Billy and Carolyn settled in the living room, discussing the city's educational system.

Jake helped Jennifer clear the table and moved closer to her as she washed the dishes. "Why do you always smell so good?" he whispered.

"Maybe I just smell good to you," she answered, squirting water at him. "That should cool you off."

"Want to play rough?" he said, as he tied her hands behind her back with the kitchen towel. "Now let me see you wash the dishes."

"Hey, you two!" yelled Billy. "No fighting while the grownups are here."

"Just having some fun, Gramps," Jennifer said with a laugh.

Jake moved closer to her. "What are you doing tomorrow?" he asked, hoping that she wouldn't brush him off.

"Billy and I are going to my dad's, but I'll be back in the city by five o'clock."

"Call me when you get home. I won't sleep a wink tonight. In fact, I don't think I'll be getting much sleep anymore. You've gone and messed up my life," he whispered.

"Want to talk about a messed-up life? I have to meet a dead man at a cemetery in Mississippi next week. If that isn't messed up, what is?"

"Jennifer!" Carolyn called. "I'm going. Thanks for feeding me."

"Gosh, Carolyn, I almost forgot. I'm going to Natchez Tuesday. I'll probably be gone for a couple of days and—"

"Yes, I'll take care of Morton. He's great company for me," Carolyn said.

Billy jumped up from the couch, offered to give Jake a ride home, and within minutes the apartment was quiet.

CHAPTER 12

Alex Beasley's home was impeccably maintained. The stately brick Tudor, with cross-gables and slate tile roof, stood on the corner of a tree-lined street in the quiet village of Rye Brook, New York.

Alex eagerly waited at the front door for his children. When he saw them pulling into the driveway, he gave a wave and rushed to meet them at the side kitchen entrance.

Within minutes, the sweet harmony of their voices filled the house with cheerful chatter and childish laughter. It never ceased to amaze Alex how much joy these two individuals brought into his life.

Billy placed a case of wine on the counter, while Jennifer held up two cake boxes for inspection. And even though they always brought the same dessert, it didn't diminish the excitement.

"Your favorites, Dad!" she explained, opening the boxes to show him the strawberry shortcake and chocolate éclairs as if he didn't know what they looked like.

After popping open a bottle of sparkling wine, Billy poured a little into three stemmed glasses. "We need to toast the season…even though it had a slow start. Are we ready for planting, Dad?"

"The flowerbeds and garden boxes are ready," Alex answered. "I got flats of herbs from the nursery. Our vegetable seeds have already sprouted and are ready for planting. Everything is under the breezeway."

"This year we should try watermelon. What do you say, Dad?" Billy asked.

Alex thought for a moment. "Sounds good to me. What else?"

And so, the garden dialogue began between her two favorite men.

Jennifer tiptoed out of the kitchen and dashed upstairs to her bedroom. Nothing in the room changed since her sixteenth birthday when she and her mother redecorated to give it a grown-up look.

She wandered around the room, touching everything as if seeing it for the first time. Her bookshelves still held books she'd collected and read during her school years. Her old computer, where she wrote her first story, was still on the desk. Propped up in the middle of her window seat was an antique doll that once belonged to her great-grandmother. She smoothed the doll's vintage frilly dress and wiped a smudge from her rosy cheek. "You're still beautiful, Lucia," she said, gently touching the doll's porcelain red lips. "Remember all the wonderful late night conversations we had about boys?"

Lucia's blue-glass eyes stared blankly.

"There's no new boy in my life right now, but I'll keep you posted if that changes."

Jennifer took one last look at her room and left with a smile on her face.

Billy and Alex were still in the kitchen, working together, cutting potatoes and slicing onions.

"Did you have a pleasant talk with Lucia?" Alex asked.

Jennifer shook her head. "Dad, forget about talking to a doll, now I'm talking to a dead soldier."

Alex paused. "Does this have something to do with that grave marker?"

Jennifer nodded.

"Talking to your doll is one thing—a dead person is quite another. You have a very vivid imagination, but this goes beyond that."

"I heard him. We had a conversation."

"Is he in the room with us?"

"No, he's not here."

"Dad, this whole thing is incredible," Billy said. "I didn't see him, but I did hold the marker and…well, I feel great! Whatever I had is gone."

Alex tilted his head and moved his questioning eyes from Jennifer to Billy. "Let me see if I have this right. You held the marker and a condition you've had since you were a child just disappeared?"

"Well…yes!" exclaimed Billy.

"You mean to tell me that this marker has, or so you believe, healing powers?"

Billy raised his voice an octave. "Isn't it amazing?"

"What's amazing is that, once again, the two of you are up to your ears in trouble——just like when you were kids. Where one goes, the other follows. When one lies, the other swears to it. I want to believe what you've told me, but this healing thing is a little too much. Do me a favor, don't invite the soldier to lunch."

Jennifer laughed and patted her father on the back. "Daddy, you told me that all my friends are welcome to stay for dinner."

"Set the table," Alex said, rolling his eyes. "Oh, and set an extra plate. Let's use all the good stuff. I feel festive."

Billy and Jennifer exchanged puzzling looks.

"An extra plate? For the soldier?" Billy asked.

Alex shook his head. "For a special guest," he said with a sly wink. He went to the kitchen sink and washed a head of lettuce. "I ran into an old friend at a garage sale last week, and I've invited her for lunch. We dated long before I met your mother."

The look on Billy's face was comical. He reached for Jennifer's hand and squeezed it so hard she flinched.

"You can both close your mouths now," Alex said. "You know I have eyes behind my head."

"Who is she?" Jennifer asked, taking the good china from the cabinet.

"Kathryn Olmstead."

"Is that the same woman Mom mentioned whenever she was angry with you?" Jennifer asked.

"Your mother was seldom angry with me. And if she did mention Kathryn, it was all in fun. Your mother wasn't a jealous woman...never had a reason to be."

Billy raised his eyebrows and shot Jennifer a *don't go there* look. "We think it's great that you ran into each other. Is she married?" he asked.

"Of course not," Alex said.

Billy pulled Jennifer into the dining room. "This should prove to be an interesting afternoon," he whispered. "Your soldier now takes a backseat to this new turn of events."

"I think it's great that Daddy is interested in someone," Jennifer whispered back. "In fact, maybe we should be looking for someone special too."

"Boy am I stupid, or what? I noticed vibes between you and Jake last night, but I wasn't sure what to make of it."

"There's nothing to make of it. We have a great friendship, but one thing is certain: it ends there."

"Elaine said that love is in your future."

"Well, then, let's wait and see what happens. As for now, I'm not in love with anyone."

As soon as Kathryn arrived, Jennifer noticed the change in Alex's demeanor. He seemed to move with new vigor. Much to her surprise, Kathryn was a lot like her mother. Her manner was sweet, and the calm quality of her voice made everyone pay attention when she spoke. She seemed comfortable in the house as if she were there before. A cloth napkin was missing from the table, and she went to the china closet drawer to get it.

Jennifer noticed everything.

Billy noticed nothing, except that Kathryn looked ten years younger than her age.

The afternoon flew by pleasantly. They enjoyed a delicious lunch and great conversations that brought laughter and some heated debates, which Kathryn eagerly participated in.

When it came time to leave, Billy and Jennifer affectionately embraced her and said they hoped to see her again.

"When you come back from your vacation, Jennifer, we'll have lunch at my house," Kathryn said.

Once Billy pulled out of the driveway, he and Jennifer screamed with laughter.

"Daddy has a girlfriend!" Jennifer yelled in a singsong voice.

"Yeah! I'm so happy, I could spit. What are you doing tonight? Gonna see Jake?"

"Nope. In fact, I'm sending him a message right now that I'll see him in the morning at work. And…there it goes."

Jake's return message was a sad emoji.

At the office the next day, Sam deliberately avoided Jennifer. He couldn't come up with anything creative to keep her from leaving the following day, so he decided the best thing was to let her go. Just before lunch, he called a meeting.

The conference room filled quickly. Sam wasted no time telling everyone they were behind schedule with the upcoming issue.

Jennifer sat back in her chair and stared out the window, knowing that he was exaggerating.

"Miss Beasley!" Sam called in a hostile tone. "Focus, please. Your vacation didn't start yet."

"Sam, don't be such a bully," Candy said.

"What's wrong with all of you?" Sam said. "Where is your article, Jennifer?" He lit a cigarette.

Everyone in the room moaned.

"Put that foul thing out!" Jim yelled.

Surprisingly, Sam did exactly that.

"Candy has my article," Jennifer said. "Seems to me there's a bit of dementia here."

"I'm as sharp as the rest of you clowns," Sam said. "You're the one confused. I never received your article."

"I sent you a copy," Candy said seriously. "Not to worry."

Sam gave Candy a glaring stare.

Jennifer laughed. "Sam, I'm leaving tomorrow."

"Okay, just kidding. Have a good time. I'll even take you to lunch today." He lit a cigarette before anyone had a chance to yell at him.

"What part of no smoking in this building don't you understand?" Candy asked.

Sam dropped the smoldering butt into his coffee mug. It sizzled, and he shrugged. "Happy now? Anyone else for lunch?" he asked, hoping that no one would take him up on the offer.

All hands went up, and Sam grumbled.

At lunch, Jake made sure that he sat next to Jennifer, and Missy made sure that she sat next to Jake.

"Jennifer. Be sure to give Missy your itinerary," Sam said with a scowl. "I don't want to track you down like a bloodhound if I need you."

"Missy and I will be in constant communication. NOT!" Jennifer said.

Jim laughed. "Where are you going?" he asked.

"Natchez."

Except for Jake, everyone at the table gawked at her.

"Why are you taking a vacation in Natchez?" Jim asked.

"Going to visit a friend," Jennifer answered.

"Is it male or female?" Sam asked.

"Neither," she replied, and everyone laughed.

"I guess she told you it's none of your business," Jim said.

Sam shot Jim a dirty look.

"Okay, Sam," Jennifer said seriously. "To pacify your inquiring mind, it's a man."

"I'm jealous," Sam said.

"What about you, Jake?" Missy asked. "Are you also jealous?"

Jake shook his head. "I'm only jealous of the living."

"What in the hell does that mean?" Sam asked.

"It's an inside joke," Jake replied.

"I don't like inside jokes," Sam said in an annoyed tone. "Jennifer, you need to cancel this trip. I don't have a good feeling about Natchez."

"Why don't you go along, Sam?" Jim asked.

Jennifer sighed. "Please! I want to have a good time."

"You can have a nice time with me; I'm fun to be with," Sam said seriously.

"Of course you're fun to be with." Jennifer rolled her eyes. "I just...I don't want your mother to find out that you and I have this special relationship that passes all the boundaries of anything that even resembles normal."

"Don't mention my mother," Sam whispered. His eyes scanned the restaurant.

"Is she here?" Jennifer asked.

"She's everywhere!" Sam replied with half a smile.

"I'd like to meet her," Missy said.

Sam suggested that Missy bite her tongue.

"Ann Baldwin," Jennifer said, "happens to be a lovely woman. If you must know, most men don't like strong women."

Sam nodded. "I'd like to divorce my mother."

Everyone ignored his remark.

"Ann doesn't give any attention to those who are rude or indifferent," said Candy. "I get along with her so well, you'd think we were sisters."

Sam frowned. "I will admit that she likes you, but sisters? That's a stretch."

Missy was fascinated with the conversation, but the witty sarcasm eluded her.

For the rest of the day, the office was unusually quiet. Everyone on staff took the time to stop by Jennifer's office to say good-bye.

She was clearing her desk when Jake knocked on the door. "Are you hungry?" he asked with a boyish grin.

"Yes, and I'm about to leave."

"I'm going home to make a special dinner, and you're invited to share in the magic of great food, candlelight, and music."

The expression on Jennifer's face was that of disbelief.

"Yes, I can cook! You can take that surprised look off your face," he said, pretending to be insulted.

"I'm not surprised by anything you do," she replied. "But I'll take a rain check. I have an early flight and need to finish packing."

The hurt expression on Jake's face didn't deter her.

"Are you bored with me already?" he asked.

She looked away, wishing he would stop pressuring her. "You're moving too fast. I need space, and I have a lot on my mind right now."

"Okay. No more pressure from me."

She gathered her things and walked over to him. "We'll do dinner when I get back from Natchez," she said, touching his arm to reassure him.

He kissed her on the forehead and left.

Chapter 13

Eighteen hours later, a female robotic voice from the rental car navigation system guided her to the Dunleith Historic Inn in the heart of Natchez, Mississippi.

Over the last few hours, her mind restlessly roamed from Bradley Taylor to Jake Cohen. At times, her brain felt as if it was engaged in a game of table tennis, and she always came up the loser. Up to now, everything in her life had been topsy-turvy, but things seemed to be getting better. She knew how Jake felt and what he wanted from her, although she wasn't quite sure if the *L* word was for love or lust. But it didn't matter because she wasn't ready for either. She did, however, feel satisfaction knowing that she didn't succumb to temptation.

By the time she turned into the driveway leading to the inn, a quiet calm had settled over her. Ahead, the stately 1856 Greek Revival-style mansion came into view. Lofty white columns and a wide, inviting porch with rocking chairs offered a friendly, welcoming sight.

After checking in, she headed to the Natchez National Cemetery.

The quiet beauty of Natchez was in stark contrast to the bustle of Manhattan. Writing assignments and vacations took her around the world, but this was the first time she'd been to Mississippi. And although interviews ran the gamut from celebrities to politicians, the thought alone of interviewing a Civil War soldier should have made her turn around and head back to New York.

The wind picked up as she drove through the wrought-iron gate that led to a one-story clapboard house used as an administrative office. In the distance, rows of white marble headstones stood at reverent attention where thousands of soldiers lay at rest. Far beyond, live oak trees led to a bluff that overlooked the Mississippi River.

She pulled into a visitor's parking space and got out of the car. *What if this turns out to be a dead end?* she thought and then laughed inwardly.

An attractive man in his mid-fifties greeted her at the front door. "How do you do, Miss Beasley. I'm Alfred Copeland." A firm handshake and a warm smile put her at ease.

"Nice to meet you, Mr. Copeland."

"Please have a seat," he said, pointing to a leather chair at the front of his desk. "I'm delighted that you've decided to visit."

Jennifer clicked the top of her pen and placed it down on her notebook. "Do you mind if I record our conversation?"

Copeland smiled. "I've seen those pens. Do they work?"

"Yes. Saves me a lot of time, but I still take notes. It has a video application as well."

Copeland swiveled around in his chair and reached for a folder on top of a credenza. "This is it," he said casually, pulling out a photo.

"It's the only one we have in our archives of this memorial star, which was once located at gravesite 1186."

Jennifer confirmed it as the one she'd purchased.

"I believe it's rare," Copeland said. "There's a handwritten notation in the file from a worker who notified his supervisor that it was last seen in 1952." He handed her the note.

"That coincides with the story I heard from the shopkeepers in Florida and the newspaper article I found in my research."

"Allow me to tell you a little bit about those who are buried here. After the war, many bodies were found along the levees near the Mississippi River. Once they were exhumed, they were brought to cemeteries for burial, but unfortunately, many of the remains were difficult to identify. Union troops had wooden tags with names and units inscribed on them. And even that wasn't one hundred percent because there were times when they were lost in the heat of battle. Articles of clothing were another important way to identify which side they were on. A fragment of uniform, a buckle, or even a button could distinguish between Union and Confederate."

He went on to explain that by 1871, the cemetery held the remains of 3,086 Union soldiers, with only 253 identified.

"Are there any Confederate soldiers buried here?" Jennifer asked.

"I don't think so. Even in death there was a separation between the North and the South. In the case of an unidentified soldier, well, that's another story. As for the soldier at 1186, this is a good example of how identification was established. When the digging crew disinterred his remains from Port Gibson, they found a US buckle tightly clasped in his hand. Would you like to see his burial site?"

"Yes, thank you."

"It's not a long walk, just over the hill. By the way, Miss Beasley, the Veterans Administration and I want to thank you for offering to return the marker once your project is completed. It's not often that someone returns an object of value. We certainly do appreciate your kindness and would like to have a special dedication when the piece is returned."

"That'll be wonderful. It's my pleasure."

A soft breeze carried a sweet scent of honeysuckle as Jennifer and Copeland walked along a gravel path. As far as the eye could see, rows of tombstones stood at attention as caretakers busily went about the task of keeping the grounds neat and trim.

Jennifer felt heaviness in her chest. It was as if she were mourning all the souls of those who found their way to this final resting place. "Rest in peace," she whispered softly.

Copeland nodded. "I've often muttered those same words while walking along here." His cell vibrated. "I have to go back to my office. Just ahead is 1186. You can't miss it. Take your time."

Like all the other headstones, 1186 was simply marked Unknown U.S. Soldier. Her heart thumped in anticipation as she gently placed her hand on the cold stone to steady herself. She listened, hoping to hear his soft, familiar voice, but all she heard was the chirping of sparrows and the gentle rustling of leaves in the trees.

"I'm here," she said, and her words hung in the warm spring air. She inhaled deeply when she saw a figure standing in a mist between the trees. Their eyes locked, and all doubts and concerns quickly dissipated.

Bradley Taylor wore a faded blue uniform. A belt hung loosely around his waist. He was strikingly handsome. Brown, wavy hair and a beard framed his soft, even features. She drowned in the intensity of his blue eyes. She studied him, wanting to reach out to move a lock of hair that curled over his forehead.

She removed the marker from her tote. Her first thought was to place it near his gravestone, believing that if she gave it back, all of this would go away.

He stood expressionless. "Please do not be afraid."

"Right now, I'm not sure what I feel. Until last week, this marker was in the possession of other people. Why didn't you speak to them?"

"This is beyond understanding. I can only thank you for coming. Please contact my family. Tell them where I am."

"The war ended over one hundred and fifty years ago."

"Years? There are no years here. This place is timeless."

"Tell me what happened to you."

"Union forces attacked our camp. I was tending to the wounded when I was shot in the back."

"Dr. Taylor, are you telling me that you're a Confederate soldier?"

"Yes. I had identification," he replied softly. "My Bible was in my medical bag. I had it up until the time I was shot. I also had personal belongings—a photograph of Rebecca, my wife, and Bradley, my son. Everything that could have identified me was stolen."

"What about the buckle in your hand? Where did it come from?"

"Someone replaced my CSA buckle." He extended his open hand, and Jennifer saw the US buckle with a small *T* on the upper part of the plate. "I tried to scratch my name on it, but I could not. That is when the eyes of my soul opened, and I caught a glimpse of heaven's light, and its brightness embraced me. I heard my name as it floated through endless space."

She placed the marker in her tote and removed a notebook, pen, and cell phone. She held up her cell and tried to capture a photo of him; but no image appeared.

"What is that?" he asked.

"It's a cell phone—a wireless electronic wonder that takes photographs and makes phone calls from anywhere in the world. I just tried to take a photo of you. Unfortunately, as advanced as we are today, we can't capture non-physical entities."

"Will you help me, Miss Beasley?"

"Who do you think did this to you?"

"I do not know. My best friend, John, carried me across a field into the confines of the forest. Then, he said something rather strange.

Back home, he was my church pastor, so I dismissed it as nothing more than regret over the war."

"Do you recall what he said?"

"Yes, I can still hear his somber voice and agonizing words. He said, '…those who sleep in the dust of the earth shall awaken, some to everlasting life, and some to shame and everlasting contempt.' "

Jennifer's hands trembled, and he saw her emotion. She tried to compose herself as the last remaining rays of sunlight streamed through the trees. Until that moment, she never thought about the men who fought in a war some called *Brother against Brother*. Now, this story was weaving itself into the fibers of her mind so tightly she couldn't think of anything else.

"What happened to your friend?"

"John Addison is more than a friend. We are like brothers."

"Please tell me about your family."

"I was born in Brandon, Mississippi. I live there with my wife and son. My father is a doctor. We have a home called Tall Oaks."

He spoke in present tense as if everything in his life still existed.

"Did you own slaves?"

"No. Benjamin, Tilly, and Little Ben Jackson lived with my aunt and even had her last name. She took care of them. Just before she passed, she instructed my father to sell her estate and give the money to Benjamin and Tilly once the war ended. She wanted them to have their own property. They were never slaves in her home, and when they came to live with us, I told Benjamin they were free to go, but he chose to stay. He said we needed each other, and he was right.

"I grew up in a family dedicated to preserving life. This is why I chose medicine as my profession. I wanted to do whatever I could to help those on the battlefield, regardless of the uniform they wore." He lowered his eyes. "Will you find my family?"

"You must understand that if I find them, they'll think I'm a lunatic. I have no evidence to present that you're the person at this gravesite. The only way to prove who you are is to compare your DNA to a relative."

"What is DNA?"

"Oh, gosh, let's see if I can explain. Within the cells of one's body is genetic information—a code that links us to family members over generations. But your family and government officials will want more than my word before they even consider a body exhumation. I have no evidence to present that the person here is you," she said, touching the top of his headstone. "There's so much involved, but it all comes down to proof. And right now, I have none."

"What is it like in your world today?"

"People are very much the same as they were back in the 1800s. Technology has increased, but human nature hasn't changed. There's still hatred in the world, and I believe that will eventually destroy civilization."

"I saw you in my dream," he said softly. "There is no doubt that we are connected."

"Now that I've been here, will you be able to see me…my every move?" she asked, hoping that he couldn't. Just the thought of that made a flush of pink rise on her cheeks.

"No," he answered, unaware of what she was thinking.

"I'll try my best to find your relatives. But first, I'll need names, dates, and places."

He presented his family history in detail. When he was finished, their eyes locked, and a silent understanding passed between them that could not be explained in words.

"Thank you, Miss Beasley," he whispered, and his physical form slowly faded into the mist.

"Good-bye for now," she said softly, fighting back tears.

Alfred Copeland closed the blinds in his office and looked at his watch. He was about to leave when Jennifer came through the front door.

"You were gone a long time," he said. "I was beginning to worry."

"Is there anything else you can tell me about the soldier buried at 1186?"

Copeland unlocked a file drawer and thumbed through a number of folders. He removed an official document dated 1912 and read aloud.

"A memorial star was placed at gravesite 1186 by Civil War veterans to honor an Unknown Soldier. This dedicated soldier was found holding a US buckle. As it was impossible to free it, without breaking bones, he was buried with it in his skeletal hand. The belt plate has the letter *T* scratched on it." He went on to explain that three veterans signed the letter.

Jennifer sighed heavily and closed her eyes. Her body swayed, and he gently led her to a chair.

"Are you all right?" he asked.

"Yes, I am. It's all true, Mr. Copeland; every word he said is true."

"Whom are you talking about?"

She wanted to tell him about her conversation with Dr. Taylor but knew that her story was unbelievable. "I was referring to the man in Florida…the one who sold me the marker. I'm going to Brandon. Can you tell me how far it is from here?"

"Yes, I know exactly where it is. It's in Rankin County. Let's look and see," he said, unfolding a small map of the state. He traced his finger from Natchez to Brandon.

"You'll want to take 84 East to 55 North," he said. "I'll make a copy of this map that shows many of the historical landmarks and plantations." He went on to explain that although many of the plantations were destroyed, Metcalf Manor is one that remained untouched. It was used as a hospital during the war. "The Metcalf's were one of the biggest and wealthiest families in the state. They had two sons. One fought for the North, the other for the South. There's quite a story about that family. The plantation is now a bed and breakfast…one of the most famous in all of Mississippi for its own Civil War library and museum. Here's a brochure if you'd like to visit."

Jennifer stared off, lost in her thoughts. She knew that her training as a writer and researcher would be an enormous help in the days ahead. This was a puzzle with so many old and odd pieces that it would be an almost impossible fit. But she also knew that giving up was not an option.

She left the cemetery and called the Metcalf Plantation to reserve a room. The rate was outrageous, but she took it.

She tapped #5 on her speed dial and waited for Ralph Mancuso to answer. Ralph, a good friend and a retired New York City detective, was now a private investigator and a consultant for the magazine. He was also someone who could be trusted.

"Where've you been, sweetheart?" he said in a reassuring voice. "Sammy told me that you were out of the office, shopping or something."

"As usual, Sam's in denial," she answered with a laugh. "I'm in Natchez, Mississippi."

In the background, Ralph's wife screamed out, asking who was on the phone.

"Stop yelling, Alice! It's Jen, and it's none of your business," he said laughingly.

"I need a favor, and Sam can't know about this," Jennifer said.

"Hold on while I take this in my office."

She pulled into a parking space at the Dunleith.

"Okay, Jen, give me the details," he said in a serious voice.

"I need to find anything and everything about two families living in Mississippi during the Civil War. Dr. Bradley Taylor, Sr. and Chaplin John Addison both from Brandon. I'll e-mail all the details when I get to my room."

Ralph coughed and cleared his throat. "What are we dealing with here?"

"At this point, I'm not sure. Dr. Taylor's death took place during a skirmish. I'm particularly interested in what happened to Addison. He was Dr. Taylor's pastor. Did he die in the war? Was he married? Children? The works. I'll be leaving Natchez early tomorrow morning, but you can reach me on my cell or by e-mail anytime. I'll be staying at the Metcalf Plantation in Brandon."

"Is Brandon in this country?" he asked jokingly.

"I know that anything outside of New York City is foreign to you, but Mississippi is quite progressive. They have highways, restaurants, and hotels. And, yes, they do speak English—albeit with a drawl."

They both laughed.

"Alice's brother, Carl, is a Civil War buff and a Professor of History at NYU. He'll be a good source for us. I'll get right on this. Is this something you're working on for the magazine?"

"Not sure yet. If it goes the way I think it will, this could be my first novel."

"Say no more. When the time comes, we'll see who gets the bill. If Sam makes a fuss, we'll work something out. By the way, Jen, you sound terrific. Whatever's going on, keep it going."

"Thanks. I knew I could count on you. One way or another, you'll get paid. Tell Alice I send my best."

"Ok. Stay out of trouble, but if you need help, my nephew is with the FBI in Atlanta. And if you think I'm charming—"

"I don't think I'm going to need FBI help, but thanks for the offer."

As soon as she disconnected, another call came through. It was Billy, and he was worried and curious about Dr. Taylor.

"What does he look like? Could you see him clearly?"

Jennifer gave him all the particulars.

"I can't wait to tell Elaine that you saw him," he said. "Is there anything I can do to help?"

She thought for a moment, knowing if she didn't come up with something, his feelings would be hurt, and he'd call every hour for an update.

"Check eBay for Civil War grave markers. See if you can find one that's similar to mine. Search the Internet. Any info you get will be helpful."

"I'm right on it. I'll call you when I have something. I'm having dinner with Carolyn tonight…we'll work together on it. By the way, I really like her. How come I never noticed how beautiful and intelligent she is?"

"You were always too busy looking for the wrong types. Of course, I should talk. I made a real mess of my life. You and Carolyn! I'm happy to hear this news. She's wonderful, and I think the two of you are a good match. Give her my best, and get to work."

"First of all, just for the record, you weren't the one who made a mess of things. Anyway, we've both made mistakes along the way. Most people do."

"We'll talk more about this later. In the meantime, you have your assignment, so get going. By the way, please water my garden boxes and tell Morton to be a good boy while I'm gone."

Early in her career, Jennifer learned the importance of backing up her files. Later that evening, she inserted her pen's USB cable into the laptop and saved all her notes.

After reading the description of Bradley Taylor, she got into bed, closed her eyes, and thought about the way he looked. *Strikingly handsome.* She wondered how it was possible to see the blue of his eyes and the color of his uniform through the ethereal mist that surrounded him. *I should have asked him more questions. But he's unreachable. There's no direct phone line, social media access, Skype, or e-mail.* She knew that unless he contacted her, there couldn't be any communication between them.

CHAPTER 14

It wasn't until seven o'clock the next morning that a loud ringtone from her cell woke her up. It was Billy, and before she could say hello, he spilled every detail how he and Carolyn stayed up all night searching for information.

"We had the best time and never realized it was four in the morning. We didn't get a wink of sleep. By the time I left for the market, Carolyn was still working the Civil War websites. So far, we found similar markers, but none that look exactly like the one you have. We'll keep searching," he said excitedly.

"I have no doubt of that. Talk later."

By nine o'clock, she was heading to Brandon. She drove in silence—radio off and pen recorder at the ready. All she could think of was yesterday's visit to the cemetery. *This is an impossible undertaking,* she thought and then quickly dismissed the negativity of that statement. The challenge to find the proverbial needle in the haystack is what she enjoyed most. She smiled, assured that her analytical mind and journalistic training qualified her to follow the leads that would bring this story to fruition.

With that in mind, she acknowledged that Elaine was right:

there's a book here. But first, she had to locate the Taylor family and share a bizarre story that they'd probably never believe.

The drive gave her plenty of time to think. The two-lane road had little traffic, and there wasn't much to see. For miles, on either side, there was nothing but untamed woodland. There wasn't a gas station or fast-food restaurant in sight. *How is one to survive?* She laughed and reached for a candy bar on her dashboard.

After what seemed an eternity of monotony, a warning sign blinked for traffic to slow down. Ahead, a truck blocked the road as workers cleared debris from a fallen tree. She pulled over and waited for them to finish.

Annoyed that they were working slowly, she got out to stretch her legs. She checked her cell for messages. Nothing interesting, so she clicked off and looked up. And that's when she saw him: a magnificent white stallion. He stood motionless, staring at her from behind a fence. She approached him cautiously, fearing that he might get spooked and run away. But he didn't. And that's when she remembered the words: *If you see a horse, speak to him.* When Elaine said it, it was laughable. Now, it was chilling.

Without a moment's hesitation, she aimed her cell and snapped a photo. "Are you real?" she asked.

A bobbing head and a gentle swish of his tail gave her the answer. She checked the camera to be sure it captured the beautiful image. It wasn't an apparition.

"I'm a reporter and seldom at a loss for words, but I simply don't know what to ask you." She held out her hand, and the stallion whinnied softly and tapped her palm gently with his nose.

He lifted his head and held her gaze.

"Oh, I understand," she whispered, nodding. "*You're* the confirmation." A smile softened her face and her heart.

She watched as he turned and disappeared into the woods.

From the road, a worker waved the all clear, and she returned to her car.

After driving quietly for some time, she initiated a conversation with her pen. "So here it is: the great American novel is about to unfold. And for some strange reason, this entire thing fell into *my* lap. If all of this leads to a dead end, I'll pave a new road. If this turns out to be nothing, I'll make it something. But, oh, if it's all true then I have a treasure to share."

While still fresh in her mind, she rattled off descriptions of the cemetery, Copeland, and Bradley. The intensity of her commentary almost caused her to miss the turn into Metcalf Manor. She pulled up to iron gates and the lens of a surveillance camera focused on her from atop a speaker box.

"Welcome to Metcalf Manor." The voice was as fresh as a spring breeze.

"Hi, I'm Jennifer Beasley. I have a reservation."

"Follow the road to the main house, Miss Beasley. Valet will unload and park your car."

The gates opened, and she steered along a private road that weaved its way through pristine landscape. The winding road, bordered by towering trees, formed a dense canopy of drooping silvery moss, resembling giant spider webs. Crepe myrtles, rose hedges, hydrangea, and magnolias, provided a botanical feast for the eyes. Pebbled walking paths meandered around a lake with fountains, statuaries, and gardens. Swans and egrets completed the picture-perfect scene.

She imagined that Bradley grew up nearby and must have walked through these woods as a youngster.

When the historical Metcalf Manor came into view, she slowed to a crawl, stretching her head to capture the broad sweep of the grand Colonial mansion. Her reaction took her by surprise. *Magnificent!* She scanned the full porch that wrapped around the entire three-story structure. At one side, a breezeway led to two other smaller buildings: Magnolia Cottage and The Lake House. A large wooden sign pointed to the Library and Museum.

She drove to the front of the manor where a young man with a welcoming smile greeted her. He opened the car door and escorted her into the main hall. The interior was beautiful, warm, and inviting.

"Hello. Welcome to Metcalf Manor. I'm Marci," said the manager. "We're so delighted to have you as our guest."

Check in went quickly, and she and Marci strolled along a path where the sun's warmth embraced flowerbeds brimming with azaleas, tulips, and lilies. Baskets and planters of red, pink, and white begonias provided a colorful setting to scenery that needed no accompaniment. After a long, cold winter in New York, Jennifer delighted in seeing full blooms of bright flowers.

"You'll be staying in Magnolia Cottage," Marci said. She stopped at a picket fence in front of a whitewashed brick cottage complete with its own English garden and slate terrace. Two rocking chairs faced a lake with fishing docks.

"The bass fishing is excellent," Marci said with a smile.

"I don't think I'll have time for that this trip. But it certainly would be nice."

When Marci opened the cottage door, Jennifer felt as if she'd stepped into another world. It was charming, reminiscent of a cottage in Cornwall where she spent the last year of college studying English literature. A large brick fireplace, surrounded by comfortable sitting chairs, led to a bay window bench complete with puffy pillows that captured her heart. *I should write my book here. A perfect place to relax, read, and sort out life.* And another fleeting thought popped into her mind: *honeymoon.* She shook her head, dismissing it as a silly idea.

A carved mahogany tea table, laden with a silver tea set, a plate of scones and teacakes, and small jars of lavender jelly, honey, clotted cream, and lemon curd immediately caught her eye, and she sighed happily.

Marci filled a cup with orange jasmine tea and gestured

for Jennifer to sit. "Please let me know if there's anything else you'll need. Dinner is served in the Oak Room from six o'clock on. There's information in the desk drawer on all our amenities. We have a spa, but you'll need an appointment."

She left, and Jennifer settled in. She drank tea and nibbled on cakes and biscuits. *So this is life below the Mason-Dixon line. I could take to this quite nicely.*

She looked at her watch and called the front desk. A pleasant voice said, "Miss Beasley, how may I help you?"

"Would it be possible to speak to Tom Metcalf?"

"Tom is out of town. This is Susie, his sister."

"Hello, Susie. I was wondering if I could visit your library this afternoon? I'm a journalist and—"

"Of course," Susie said quickly. "Please come up to the main house, and I'll take you on a tour."

"I'm on my way." She grabbed her tote, took one last bite of a teacake, and scooted out the door.

When she reached the main house, a smartly dressed woman in her early forties greeted her at the front door. "I'm Susie Metcalf. We're so happy to have you staying with us. We hope your accommodations are to your liking."

"Thank you. Everyone has been so gracious."

"Are you a freelance writer?"

"No, I work for News in Review."

"How exciting! We've had many writers stay with us but none from such a prestigious magazine as yours. This is a paradise of inspiration for so many talented authors. I love to write, but I haven't had anything published. Rejections are all I get."

"What do you write?" Jennifer asked, knowing that she'd just opened a can of squiggly worms and would have to endure a litany of stories and ideas.

Much to her surprise, though, Susie smiled and explained that she wrote a children's story, rejected over thirty times. "I won't bore you with the details," she said sweetly.

"Rejection is a big part of a writer's life. I hope you'll keep trying. For now, I'm looking for information about two families who lived in Brandon during the Civil War, specifically the Taylor and Addison families. Will you be able to help me?"

"Our archives are complete with information about families who lived here before, during, and after the war. My 3rd great-grandfather saved this house from destruction by turning it into a hospital during the war. Many local families brought their belongings here for safekeeping. After the war, my family restored one of the houses on the property, and it became the library and museum. I'm proud to say, a Metcalf has owned this blessed piece of earth since 1830."

"It's a beautiful place and so peaceful. I'm glad to have the opportunity to visit."

The library, a large stone and brick two-story building, was in walking distance from the main house. A sign at the front listed tour hours.

"I think you'll be surprised as to what we have preserved," Susie said.

Jennifer was more than surprised when they entered the building. The library consisted of a number of spacious rooms with massive bookcases. In the center hall, two antique mahogany tables gleamed under lamps, elegantly crowned with golden shades. A media room provided computers and printers. At the end of the hall was a walkway that led to the museum entrance where valuable Confederate and Union artifacts were on display.

"This is incredible," Jennifer said.

"It began as a small, private collection," Susie explained. "It grew from there. I don't believe my ancestors ever imagined an expansion of this magnitude that would include a full library and museum."

On either side of the museum's entrance, two large cases proudly displayed the uniforms of the Metcalf brothers: one Confederate, the other Union. A brass plaque told the story of how both were killed in the same battle.

Other display cases exhibited guns, swords, and munitions. A small cannon took aim from the far corner of the room. Bibles, letters, and books—even recipes—were exhibited. It was a treasure trove, and Jennifer knew it would take more than a few hours to study the history of Brandon and its people.

Susie unlocked the door to a private office. It was a large room with two desks, tables, and chairs. "This is where we work when books, family information, or artifacts are brought in.

They sat at a table with a computer, scanner, and printer.

Jennifer held up her pen. "Would you mind if I record our conversation?"

"It's perfectly fine with me. During the war, my family kept records in locked trunks. It was around 1890 when my 2nd great-grandmother, Elsa, implemented the Dewey Decimal System. She made this library and museum her full-time job. I remember hearing stories about how she hid items for fear of being stolen. There was a lot of thievery on both sides. She fancied herself a librarian and curator. All the Metcalf women had a passion for preserving history. I'm glad they did. So, let's find your two families."

Jennifer read off the names given to her by Bradley Taylor.

"I don't recognize any of the names," Susie said. "If John Addison was a pastor here, I think he would have been associated with the Creekside Church, which was destroyed by fire long after the war. The property and cemetery are now owned by Pinelawn Baptist Church. Can't trust my memory, though, as it's sometimes hindered by all the names and requests we get for information."

Susie searched the Taylor family name in the database. Within seconds, a document opened. "Here it is!" she said excitedly. "The doc number is T-235. There are three extensions: A, B, and C. The Taylor household had five family members, plus three other people. There are no slave listings. Unfortunately, there's no current address for this family in Brandon. If the family remained here, we'd have updated listings. But here's something interesting. There's a cross-reference number, A-355, which could indicate marriage between the families. Let's see who married whom." She highlighted the number and a new document opened.

They scrutinized the information.

"This file references the Addison family," Susie noted. "Three family members with no extensions and one cross reference back to T-235. As with the Taylor family, there are no updates. Your two families definitely have a connection beyond friendship. It would appear that a Taylor married an Addison."

A loud knock at the door startled them.

"Sometimes, when I'm here alone, I get spooked," Susie said. "I have an odd feeling that with all these artifacts and records there just might be a couple of spirits hanging around. Silly what the imagination can do. Then again, who knows?" She went to the door and unlocked it.

Marci stood at the doorway and peeked into the room as if expecting to see something out of the ordinary. "Excuse me, Susie," she said, holding up a piece of paper. There's a Mr. Maroni here to see you... something about the pond at the north end."

"I forgot about the pond! Please excuse me, Jennifer, I'll be back, and we'll continue with the search."

Jennifer studied the names on the monitor. She was far beyond the point where it was necessary to be convinced that the Taylor family existed. All the names checked out, and they came from only one source.

The records were well organized. A family chart listed Bradley Taylor's relatives: Matthew B. Taylor and Olivia Jensen Taylor, his parents; Rebecca Alcott Taylor, his wife; and Bradley Taylor Jr., his son. The A, B, C extension indicated Benjamin, Tilly, and Little Ben Jackson as part of the household. The Taylor family tree dated back to the early 1800s when they settled in Mississippi. Prior to that, no records were documented.

Hoping to find the clue that would take her to the next level, she read quickly, scanning the text for keywords. She printed pages showing that Matthew Taylor was a doctor. Bradley married Rebecca in 1857; he was twenty-two, she was eighteen. Their son was born in 1859. Bradley Sr. was missing and presumed dead in 1863. His body was never found, and a sizable estate was left to Rebecca and Bradley Jr.

Matthew, Rebecca, and Bradley Jr. didn't have burial records in Brandon. However, a death record confirmed that Olivia Taylor was buried at Creekside Cemetery. Bradley Jr. was listed as married in 1880. He had no children with his first wife, who died soon after the marriage. A second marriage showed a son born in 1897 and a daughter born in 1900.

Surprisingly, in 1870, Rebecca married John Addison. Addison's first wife died in childbirth, leaving a son, Lewis Addison, born in 1857.

John Addison was an assistant pastor at his father's church when the war broke out. A notation simply stated that in 1873, Pastor John Addison died.

Jennifer glanced at her watch, surprised to see that it was already three o'clock. She was hungry and thought of the sandwiches in her room.

At that moment, Susie rushed in. "Sorry I was so long. The pond needs stocking, and Mr. Maroni is in charge of that. He won't proceed unless my brother gives him the okay. Did you find anything of interest in the bios?"

"Nothing much about the Addison family. I did notice a reference number at the end of each file. Does that mean there's additional information?"

"Yes, most definitely. Events—like birth, marriage, and death— were logged in Bibles or transcribed from church records. Baptism records served as birth certificates in the 1800s. Marriage and death statistics were compiled much the same way. When the war began, local families brought their documents here. In some cases, they even brought money and gold, fearing that Union soldiers would steal it."

Susie went on to explain that just before the war, her family built an underground passageway leading from the main house to the library where valuable belongings of half the town lined the corridor. "After the war," she continued, "much of what was here remained until the Reconstruction. Then, families were able to rebuild their lives. But, oddly, some never returned for their valuables. My grandmother told me that letters were received from families that moved out of state, hoping that their information would be updated for future generations. Once we got our computers, all records were transcribed, and our database grew to what it is today."

"I noticed the same number at the end of the files for both Taylor and Addison," Jennifer said. "But there isn't any additional information to explain what it is."

Susie looked at the two files where the number 656 appeared. "I'm not sure what this means," she said, moving the cursor over the number. "It's not leading to another file. I need to check something because my curiosity is certainly piqued. If it's okay with you, I'll have Marci bring us some tea and sandwiches. In the meantime, I want to check our storage room in the basement. The area is designed to protect our collections from moisture, light, and dust. Much of what was left here is now stored in acid-free boxes. My mother was responsible for that in the 1980s," she said, rushing from the room.

Jennifer continued to search the files, making notes and copies. Before she knew it, Susie came back, holding a large box. Without hesitation, she placed it on the table and sat down. She made no attempt to open it.

"That was quick," Jennifer said.

"Believe it or not, this was the only box with the number 656 written on the top. I've been in that room many times, but I never saw this because it was on a high shelf. Judging from the way the 5 is written, I can safely say it's my mother's handwriting."

At that moment, Marci came in with a lunch tray. She smiled and waited for instructions. Susie thanked her and told her that unless there was an emergency, they were not to be disturbed.

"I'll have to lock the library door," Marci said. "There's a group of visitors strolling the gardens, and I'm sure they'll want to take the next tour. I'll change the time; hopefully, no one will be upset. Will you call to let me know when I can reschedule?"

"Certainly. Thanks for doing this," Susie said. She turned to Jennifer. "There's something strange about all of this. Are you holding back any information? You can trust me, you know."

"It's a very long story. I don't think I can explain it all except to say that what I've learned in the past few days has definitely changed my way of thinking. I'm here to help someone who is caught between two... let's just say that he's in the wrong place."

"That sounds cryptic. I can be a big help to you. I know this town and its people, but no one will talk to you if they think a scandal— even one that occurred during the war—is going to be revealed. My family was careful to preserve the truth and thoughtful enough to keep it from harming someone. That mentality still exists today. The war is long over, but for some, the battle still wages. There are some who would sooner destroy this file than see it exposed. Do you think that any of the information here can bring negative publicity to this library?"

"None that I can think of…but there's something here that is beyond what we know. Are you sure you want to stick your neck out for me and this story?"

"If you use me as a source, do you have to reveal who I am or where you got the information?" Susie asked.

"The short answer is no. But if I come across something questionable, then we'll have to decide how we want to approach it."

"I'll be honest with you," Susie said. "What we found here today leads me to believe that my ancestors knew the real story. I hope they weren't involved in something illegal. This type of information made public could cause serious consequences. I would hate to have anything discredit our reputation."

"I understand what you're saying. We need to be careful. Susie, this has to do with a supernatural event. Before yesterday, I was convinced that I was having a mental breakdown. Happily, what I've since seen and heard confirmed two things: I'm sane, and I'm determined to follow this through…no matter what."

"I'll give you as much help as you need. Can you explain supernatural?"

Jennifer paused, knowing she had to proceed carefully. The people who believed her thus far were those who knew this was not something she'd make up. She decided to trust Susie. "Dr. Bradley Taylor, a Confederate soldier, has contacted me."

The silence was deafening. Even the computer quieted down.

Susie pushed back in her chair. Her eyes widened. "How di-did he do that?" she asked in a shocked voice.

"I don't have all the answers. I purchased a marker that was taken from his gravesite…the site of an Unknown Soldier at the Natchez National Cemetery." Jennifer removed the marker from her tote and handed it to Susie.

Susie studied it carefully. There was no indication that it affected her in any way. "I've seen similar ones, but nothing that looks like this," she said. "A few of the cemeteries here had them removed because they were being stolen."

"This marker is my connection to Dr. Taylor."

"Did you see him?"

"I saw him at the cemetery."

"What's he doing in a Federal cemetery? Wasn't he a Confederate soldier?"

"Yes. And that's the mystery."

"Wow!" Susie exclaimed, taking a deep breath. She handed Jennifer the marker and sighed. "Let's keep this between the two of us. I have to get ready for dinner guests. Please have dinner with me, and we'll talk further. Is eight o'clock too late for you?"

"No, that's fine. If it's okay, I'd like to stay and document some of what we've already found. What do we do with this box?"

"Why don't we open it after dinner? It's quiet here at night, and we won't be disturbed. In the meantime, print whatever you need from the computer files. I'll have my security guard lock up after you leave. Don't be alarmed if you see him walk through."

"You've been so kind. I can't begin to tell you how much I appreciate your help."

"These records are open to everyone, but I'm glad *we* found the box. I'm sure it was never meant for public domain. Knowing what my grandmother told me about the women in my family, they'd go to their graves with a secret. I'll put the box in my brother's safe for now."

CHAPTER 15

Jennifer sat back and stared at the monitor, but her thoughts were on the mysterious box that held a connection to the Taylor and Addison families. She believed there had to be more than just trinkets inside. She printed the remaining documents and left the library. A guard locked the doors and remained positioned at the front, waiting for the tour to begin.

Mental exhaustion set in when she returned to her room. She showered and plumped up the bed pillows. And although the bed was comfortable, sleep didn't come easily. After twenty minutes of tossing and turning, she went out to the terrace to watch the setting sun. Red and orange clouds streaked the sky, revealing that tomorrow was going to be a glorious day. Her view was spectacular, so she snapped a few photos and forwarded them to her dad and Billy.

A kitten walked up the path, and she tapped on the chair to get its attention. The little feline rolled over and stared up at the changing sky. Another photo. This one she sent to Jake with a note suggesting that he get a cat for Elizabeth. *Every child needs a pet*, she wrote.

A police siren ringtone broke the silence, telling her it was Ralph.

"We found the needle in the Taylor haystack," he said in his usual upbeat manner. "His name is Jonathan Matthew Powell. He lives in Atlanta and is the head of Neurosurgery at Emory University Hospital. The connection to him came about by chance when Carl searched a genealogy website. Taylor is a common name, but he was persistent. I'll give you the short story: he found Constance Taylor Powell, Jonathan's mother. Her tree dates back to the Civil War. When he searched the list of people on her tree, all the names we gave him came up. This is an exciting discovery. I'll e-mail the doc's telephone number."

"Well, here's a bit of a juicy find. Dr. Taylor's wife, Rebecca, married John Addison."

"Wow, you're good!" Ralph said. "No doubt there's more here, but I have a feeling you'll fall into it long before I do. I'll continue digging—oops, there I go again."

"There are some other things, which I haven't sorted through yet. I'll e-mail tonight. By the way, you haven't heard from snoopy Sam, have you?"

"Nope, and I don't expect to."

"Great! Don't need him badgering us. Talk later."

At five minutes to eight, Jennifer left the cottage and walked leisurely under twinkling string lights, illuminating the footpath leading to the dining room. The slow tempo of piped in music and the delicate scent of blossoming plants engulfed the serene atmosphere. She thought how great it would be if New York City had music and huge air-fresheners on every street corner.

Marci greeted her and led the way to a table that overlooked the garden. A soft glow of candlelight filled the spacious dining room where an attractive young woman, dressed in period clothing, played classical music on a baby grand piano.

"We have a full bar," Marci said with a smile.

"I'll have a martini with extra olives, please."

Marci rushed off but not before stopping to inspect a dessert cart with an array of delicious confections. Jennifer's attention focused on it, wondering if it would be inappropriate to start dinner with dessert. The notion left her mind when Susie joined her, holding two menus.

"May I boast a little?" Susie asked. "Our specials tonight are really good. I recommend we start with fried green tomatoes. You've got to try the pork chops; they're succulent, and the potato gratin is creamy and delicious."

"I'm so hungry, I could eat a…." She was going to say *horse*, but the thought of the beautiful stallion she saw earlier in the day changed her mind. *I will never eat horsemeat,* she thought, stifling a giggle. "I'll have the pork chops, and I'll definitely try whatever else you recommend, especially the tomatoes."

It was close to ten o'clock by the time they finished dinner. A few guests lingered in the dining room as Susie and Jennifer headed to the library.

Susie unlocked the door and hesitated before turning on the lights. She reached for Jennifer's arm. "Look over there, against the wall," she said in a hushed voice. "Is that a ghost?"

Turning sharply, Jennifer saw a dark silhouette. Her eyes lifted to the overhead spotlights above the tall display cabinet. She smiled, amused and relieved. "It's only a shadow from the showcase. The mind can play funny tricks."

"Guess I'm spooked by all of this. Not to worry, though, I know that spirits can't hurt you…unless they're evil, of course."

Jennifer laughed. "I don't think we have anything like that here."

"Okay then, let's see what else we can find," Susie said, removing white gloves from a desk draw. She handed a pair to Jennifer and got the box marked 656. She placed it carefully on the table and opened it. Inside was a burlap-wrapped parcel sealed under shrink-wrap. A tag with the number 656 dangled from a cord tied around the package.

"Hmm, this is interesting," Susie said. "Plastic film wasn't available in the late 1800s. Someone repackaged this. The burlap is definitely from that era; we've seen it on other items, but not the tie cord."

She untied the knot to free an envelope with a red wax seal of Metcalf Manor. Written across the front were the words: *656 is the property of the Taylor Family and the Curator of the Metcalf Library.*

"As curator of this library, I'm exercising my right to open the envelope," she said. Inside was a note.

The Taylor Family has witnessed my seal, under my hand, Miranda Elizabeth Metcalf, this eighteenth day of October in the year of our Lord

1873. Under the instructions of Rebecca Taylor Addison, I have placed within this package personal letters and documents.

At the bottom were three signatures: Dr. Matthew B. Taylor, Rebecca Taylor Addison, and Bradley Taylor Jr.

Susie opened the burlap, and carefully laid out the contents of the package: a black velvet pouch, a newspaper article, letters, a tattered leather journal, accounting sheets, and a small Bible."

Jennifer opened the Bible. "There's an inscription, but it's faded and difficult to read. The date is 1857, the year Rebecca and Bradley got married. I wonder why they left this here."

"I'm not sure about the Bible, but I think they believed that their documents would be safer here. During and after the war, there were numerous lootings from both Union and Confederate soldiers," Susie said, removing a box of archival-grade sleeves from the drawer. "Now that this package has been opened, we'll have to place the documents and photos into protective sleeves before putting them back into the box."

Susie held up a monochrome photographic image of Bradley, Rebecca, and their son. "What a beautiful couple. I can see by their faces how much in love they were. And look at their son; he looks so much like his dad. How lovely to see them and put faces to all of this." She noticed tears welling up in Jennifer's eyes and quickly touched her hand. "Isn't this the person you saw in Natchez?"

"Definitely. I'm still in shock over all of this. It's a lot to digest."

Susie scanned two accounting sheets, listing deposits made to Creekside Church between 1868 and 1873.

"Rebecca or Matthew must have felt that the dates and amounts were significant; otherwise they wouldn't be in this package," Jennifer said.

"You're right, of course." Susie created a new document in the database, titled *656 Taylor*. "Once I scan everything, you can download it onto your flash drive. I'll also give you copies."

As soon as Susie finished, she placed everything back on the table. The newspaper headline caught her attention. "Take a look at this."

They read together.

Creekside Church Pastor Shot

Brandon, Mississippi, August 26, 1873

John Addison, the pastor of Creekside Church, was found dead in his rectory late last night by his wife, Rebecca. It was reported that Addison was shot once in the back. No weapon was found, and an arrest is pending for thirteen-year-old Ben Jackson, whose whereabouts are unknown.

Addison's son, Lewis, from his first marriage, survives. He was the stepfather to Bradley Taylor Jr. whose father, Dr. Bradley Taylor, was reported missing and presumed dead after a battle with Union troops in the spring of 1863.

Addison lived to be thirty-nine. Services are to be conducted by his father, Jonathan Reid Addison, founding pastor of Creekside Church, Friday morning. Interment will follow at the Confederate Soldier's Park, adjacent to the church.

Susie shook her head in disbelief.

"This is taking an interesting turn," Jennifer said. "The accused is Little Ben Jackson, who was part of the Taylor household. Strangely coincidental."

Susie held up the pouch. "I'm curious as to what's in this." She gave it a gentle squeeze, pulled apart the drawstring, and removed four bundles of Confederate banknotes. "These notes might have some value," she said. "After the war, Confederate money became worthless. Families who were once wealthy found it difficult to survive during the Reconstruction period. The question is, what to do now?"

"Best to do nothing," Jennifer replied. "No one knows about it. Until I find the Taylor family, I think it's better off here. A little more time won't matter."

"Of course, you're right," Susie said, placing the bills back into the pouch. She turned her attention to an envelope containing three letters and handed them to Jennifer.

"This is exciting." Jennifer read the first letter.

Brandon, Mississippi, June 2, 1863

Dear Mrs. Metcalf,

Thank you for your great kindness at this time of our family's bereavement. There are no words to describe the terrible pain we are suffering right now. The news that Bradley was shot during a battle was bad enough, but to not have his remains with us is devastating. My husband and I no longer have our son. Our sweet Rebecca no longer has her beloved husband, and Bradley is devastated over losing his adored father. There is no resting place to visit, which would bring some comfort and strength to all of us. This is just another terrible loss to our family. We will mourn his death every day of our lives.

I will share what happened just this morning, as I was passing along the south meadow of our property. There, in the woods, was a white horse. He didn't move. He watched me. His presence reassured me that someday, my dear, sweet Bradley and I will be reunited.

Your family has been ever so kind. Thank you for sending your own beloved sons to investigate Bradley's disappearance. Unfortunately, those who survived the battle could only report that the last time they saw him was when he was attending to the wounded.

Poor John seems to be grieving the hardest. After Bradley had been shot, he took him into the safety of the woods. When the battle ended, he went back to get him but became lost and disoriented. He carries a terrible guilt that he couldn't find the place where he left him.

We have tried to console him, but he seems to be carrying a burden that is beyond our comprehension.

May God richly bless you and your family and all the generations thereafter. We cherish your friendship and love.

With sincere affection, Olivia Taylor

"Unbelievable," Jennifer said. "On my way here, I saw a white horse, standing alone in the woods. I also knew it was a sign."

"I have the chills," Susie said. "Please continue reading."

Brandon, Mississippi, May 5, 1870

Dear Mrs. Metcalf,

What a sweet gesture for you to offer Metcalf Manor for my marriage to John Addison. We have decided to keep the ceremony small with a light supper to follow at the church. It would have been lovely with the beautiful magnolias in bloom and all the foliage brightly dressed in their spring colors. Please understand our desire to honor Bradley's life and his passing with little fuss about this marriage.

Pastor John has been sick for a long time. I feel he has never fully recovered from his wife's death and not being able to find Bradley and bring him home.

How comforting to know that my caring for him has brought some peace. Although I will never share the love I had for Bradley with any other person, it seems right that John and I marry and give Bradley and Lewis a good home. If it were not for my inheritance, we too would have suffered significant financial hardship.

John has been so attentive to us, even denying his pastoral duties to handle young Bradley's estate and mine.

We must all try to heal now. And although I make this confession only to you, my love for Bradley has never lessened. I do care for John, but not in the way I love my Bradley.

We hope that you and the family will honor us with your presence at our marriage. Please give my best to your lovely granddaughter. I know she will carry on your work with the library you so lovingly built to preserve family histories.

I leave you now with great affection, Rebecca Taylor.

"Maybe this next letter will shed some light on his murder," Jennifer said.

September 3, 1873

My dear Mrs. Metcalf,

Once again, you and your kind family have shown tremendous support during the most dreadful period of my life.

It is with a heavy heart that I record in this letter the terrible three years I've lived as John Addison's wife. As time went on, he became violent and hateful toward Bradley and even more so to me. When he sent his own son away to live with his uncle, we all knew that John was very sick in his mind. From the pulpit, he preached love and mercy. But in private, he was hateful with a vengeful, mean spirit, which manifested after we were wed.

Most of my inheritance is gone, mismanaged by John. We have so many questions as to why he did heinous, unforgivable acts, which I can not mention herein. But I know that John will face it all at judgment. Please know that neither Little Ben nor Bradley had anything to do with his death. They are innocent of any crime. I know this because I was in the office at the time John was shot.

Bradley and I are preparing to leave Brandon within the next few months, the only home we've ever known. We leave for Atlanta and hope that we will be able to return to visit you and your kind family and retrieve our parcel. As you know, the elders of the church have refused to repay the money John took from the Taylor estate and from Bradley and me.

My father-in-law has assured me that Benjamin, Tilly, and Little Ben are safe. He is the only one who knows their whereabouts. We are thankful for that. He has promised that once Tall Oaks is sold, he will join us in Atlanta. Now that Olivia is gone, we are his only living relatives. I hope and pray you will keep him and us in your prayers and that you will watch over him for me.

Thank you so very much for allowing my family to keep our parcel for safe keeping in your library. The contents are rather sensitive in nature, especially this letter, as no one knows the truth about John. I have also placed within this parcel John's journal, which Bradley said he found under a floorboard in his study. He asked me not to read it; I have honored his request. My son also found his father's Bible under the same floorboard.

I can not, and will not, allow hatred to fill my heart any further. Future generations will have to judge the truth.

In closing, my father-in-law and I want you to know that if it becomes necessary for you or your daughter to open the parcel, we only ask that you reveal its contents in a discerning manner, as we know you will.

The people of Brandon owe the Metcalf family a great deal of appreciation. If it were not for your husband's foresight, to provide a secure hiding place for family heirlooms, much would have been lost.

I will not say goodbye, as I hope to see you and your family soon. May God richly bless you for all the kindness you have shown to us.

With great affection, Rebecca Taylor

"I'm speechless and so saddened by what we've read," Susie said, shaking her head. "How do you make sense of this?"

"I filter and sort, push aside personal feelings, and dissect the evidence to produce proof positive. Might sound convoluted but, in reality, it works. Right now, the evidence says that John Addison lived a double life with a tremendous amount of guilt."

"Over what? It sounds like he had a split personality, but guilt over the loss of his first wife and best friend? Questionable. Unless—"

"Unless he had something to do with their deaths. Here's evidence: Dr. Taylor told me he was shot in the back and left to die as a Union soldier. So the question remains: why would someone change his uniform? I think it's because the person who shot him didn't want him to be found or identified. And he also told me that his Bible was in his medical bag at the time he was shot. How did that Bible find it's way into John Addison's office?"

"Maybe the answers are in John's journal," Susie said. "With Rebecca's permission in writing, I think we owe it to Dr. Taylor to find out."

They sat quietly, staring at the small leather journal. So far, everything they'd discovered revealed tragic events in the lives of two families.

"I'm a little apprehensive," Susie said, moving the journal closer to Jennifer. "All the women in my family were mystery buffs and had a passion for puzzles. I feel that if they were here with us, they'd be prodding us on. But I think *you* should read it, and then I'll put it back into the box. Do you agree?"

"It's your decision, Susie. If it makes you feel better not to know what's in here, then I certainly do agree. If it's okay with you, I'll read it later tonight and take photos of the pages."

"That's good. For now, I don't want to know anymore. This way, if I'm asked about these families, I can honestly reply that I don't have the reasons or answers as to what happened so long ago."

"I believe all of this was waiting just for us," Jennifer said. "As for Addison's journal, I think we both know it has to be read. Some secrets need to be revealed."

"I trust your judgment," Susie said.

"If it's okay, I'd like to cancel my reservation for tomorrow. A colleague of mine found a member of Dr. Taylor's family in Atlanta. I would like to get an early flight and see if I can talk to him."

"Things are moving quickly. I think you should take Bradley's Bible to Atlanta. I hope we'll stay in touch. I would like to look into what happened to Tall Oaks. It's very possible the house was demolished when new subdivisions were built. Property taxes and land records will provide that information."

"Wonderful! In the meantime, thank you so much. This could have turned out to be a dead end. You and your family are very much a part of this story."

"I hope what we've found here will act as the catalyst to bring Dr. Taylor home," Susie said. "It's a tremendous feeling of satisfaction to know that, in some small way, I've helped to reunite loved ones."

CHAPTER 16

Later that night, Jennifer propped herself up in bed, reading Addison's journal. Many of his words were difficult to decipher. Loopy *F*s and elongated *S*s looked like *P*s. She took photos of the pages that were legible.

His accounts of events dating before the war were brief, written almost as if to confuse or mislead. At first glance, his words made no sense; however, a second reading revealed that he was an angry man, especially when it came to the death of his first wife and the loss of his best friend. He exposed himself as a person with a tortured soul who vacillated between love and hate, weakness and strength, pride and humility. He wrote of lying, deceitfulness, thievery, and murder but accused no one of these despicable acts. Words scribbled along the margins revealed that his thought process was out of control. And always, there was a definite sense of insincerity, as if he were trying to convince someone of his innocence.

Toward the end of the journal, he became more frantic. It appeared as if a madman had taken control of the pen.

Satisfied with her findings, she closed the journal. She confirmed her flight to Atlanta and booked a room at the Ritz-Carlton in Buckhead.

The next morning, she returned Addison's journal to Susie.

"Would it be possible," Jennifer asked, "to find out who pastored at the Creekside Church after Addison's death?"

"Absolutely. In fact, I thought of that before going to bed last night. I don't think I'll have a hard time finding that information. I'll send you whatever I find and also provide names and telephone numbers if you want to speak directly to the property records department."

"For now, I'd prefer to stay in the background," Jennifer said. "No one would be suspicious if they thought you were updating historical records for the library."

"That's a good idea. Excuse me while I check to see if your bill is ready. I don't want you to miss your flight."

Jennifer called Dr. Powell's office and spoke to his receptionist, explaining that she was writing an article about the Taylor family from Brandon. Without further questions, the receptionist took her cell number.

She went to the front desk, paid her bill, and gave Susie a tight hug.

"I hope to see you again," Susie said.

"I'm seriously thinking of writing my book here...at least part of it. We'll stay in touch." She paused and took Susie's hand. "I couldn't have done this without you."

"It certainly is the most exciting thing to happen here in... forever. I can't wait to hear how this all ends."

By the time Jennifer's plane landed in Atlanta, there was a text from Dr. Powell. *I no longer have family living in Mississippi. If that's what this is all about—I don't mean to sound rude—but I'm really not interested. Thank you anyway.*

She thought about his response. *I'm not going to let this go.* She tried his cell. Much to her surprise, he answered.

"Dr. Powell, this is Jennifer Beasley with News in Review. I got your message and would like to explain my connection to your great-great-grandfather, Bradley Taylor."

"Did I inherit money? Or did the magazine find out that my family was made up of horse thieves?" He spoke in a clear, distinct voice with no hint of a Southern accent.

Jennifer laughed. *At least he has a sense of humor.* "Nothing like that," she said. "But I have information that may be of interest to you."

"Well, Miss Beasley, you certainly have my attention. Tomorrow afternoon I'll be speaking at the Chamber of Commerce luncheon at the Ritz-Carlton in Buckhead. I can meet you in the bar lounge at three o'clock."

"Thank you. That'll work out fine. Strange coincidence, but it happens that I'll be staying at the same hotel."

She clicked off and set the rental car's navigational system for the Ritz.

Were the stars aligned in her favor? Not exactly. She was lucky to get the last room in Atlanta, but paid a hefty price for it. With conventions, concerts, and even a movie being filmed along Peachtree Road, there wasn't enough space for an ant to crawl into. The only consolation was that her suite had a great view and the amenities that went with it were not too shabby.

If all went well, she might give Sam an exclusive and get reimbursed for expenses, including the bottle of champagne and basket of goodies she requested. *While I'm at it,* she thought, *I deserve a facial and massage.*

The concierge was helpful, booking an appointment at the spa for three glorious hours of nothing but being pampered.

On the way to her room, her cell jingled, and she scrambled through her tote to answer it. "Hello!" she yelled, not sure if the caller was still there.

"Whoa! Tone it down. What's going on in the deep South? Are you being held hostage?"

"Couldn't get to the phone quick enough," she said. "What's up, Cohen?"

"We're all missing you at the home office. Sam said he needs you back here ASAP. I told him your latest message was for him to take a long walk off a short pier. Did I get that right?"

"Exact words!" She told him where she was staying with instructions not to share the info with Sam.

"Well, la-di-da," he said, sounding condescending. "Next

time you go away, I'm tagging along as your guest. Any news you want to share?"

"Plenty. But can't right now...going for a massage and facial. I'll try to connect with you tomorrow."

"Okay. By the way, you sound fantastic. There's a change, and I can hear it in your voice. Won't keep you, but I want you to know that the cat suggestion was a good idea. Elizabeth told me to thank you. Any idea when you'll be back to the real world?"

"Not sure. I might not come back...I like the South, seems to do me good. Got to run—talk later."

She unpacked and lowered her cell's setting to vibrate. *I won't answer it,* she thought, knowing full well that if she felt its rhythm, the promise would be broken in a heartbeat. She took a relaxed breath, secured all her valuables in the guest safe, and headed to the spa.

A petite, perky blonde greeted her at the entrance with an offering of spring water in a crystal goblet. A sliver of lemon floated happily inside. She was escorted to a private room where she put on a robe and slippers. If there was a thought in her head about the last few days, it didn't have time to surface. Instead, the spa treatments—enhanced by calming music and soothing scents of essential oils—made her feel serene and rejuvenated.

She returned to her room, relaxed and ready to sip champagne and nibble peppered crackers topped with Fromage de Monsieur. It didn't take long before a dinner she'd ordered earlier arrived. Broiled scallops, wild rice, grilled asparagus, and a glass of Chardonnay were a delicious ending to a perfect day.

Before long, she scrunched under a fluffy duvet and slipped quietly into a deep sleep.

By morning light, the breakfast she'd ordered the night before arrived, and she attacked it with gusto. She dressed and perused the photocopies tucked into the Taylor family folder. With notations marked in red along the margins, she categorized birth, marriage, and death dates and meticulously logged and snapped photos, transferring them to respective computer files. Normally, recording research findings was a boring task. This project, however, took on a life of its own: the more she investigated, the more she found. She worked past lunch, deciding that she'd have a salad in the lounge.

She backed up her work and went to the hotel's business center where she made two sets of copies. Placing one into a manila envelope, she wrote her name and home address on the front, and gave it to the concierge for mailing. She stuffed the other copy into her tote and headed to the lounge, famished.

Three o'clock came and went. She finished a Cobb salad and a glass of wine. After ordering dessert, she checked her phone, but there were no new messages.

By a quarter to four, she was visibly aggravated. *He's not coming. What do I do now?*

Her cell rang, and she thought it was Dr. Powell. To her disappointment, it was Sam. She ignored the call when she saw a man staring at her. Her heart raced, and the hum of chatter around her went silent as if someone muted the lounge.

He didn't speak. Instead, he studied her face, remarking to himself that she was quite stunning. He forced himself not to smile, but his face softened. He refused to accept that his pounding heart was because of her. *Two cups of caffeine,* he thought and left it at that.

She continued to stare at him. The resemblance to Bradley Taylor was striking. He had the same facial features, but his thick, curly hair made him look charmingly scruffy. Her gaze remained fixed on his blue, penetrating eyes.

He's adorable, she thought and then laughed to herself because she sounded like a silly teenager. She said his name, and he nodded. She liked the way it sounded in her voice and wanted to repeat it.

He finally sat across from her and placed his cell on the table.

"I don't have much time," he lied, knowing that had the circumstances been different he would've stayed.

"This won't take—"

He cut her off. "I checked you out on the Internet, to make sure you're legit. And you are."

"Well," she said, sounding relieved. "That's good to know."

"Then, I called your magazine and spoke to Sam Baldwin."

"Oh, boy," she moaned.

"Exactly. He told me you're on the verge of a mental breakdown… slightly off the vertical is how he described you. He said, and I quote, 'If she's applying for a job in Atlanta, call the police and have her arrested.' Those were his exact words."

All Jennifer could do was to laugh. "Good old Sam," she said, shaking her head. "He's true to a fault."

With one eyebrow raised, he watched her curiously. He stretched his hand toward his cell phone, and her immediate thought was that he was going to call the men in white coats to take her away.

"Please let me explain," she said, holding back another round of laughter. "Sam Baldwin does silly, stupid things because he's an insecure person and afraid I'll leave the magazine. I'm not crazy, and I'm not here looking for a job." She held back the whole story, knowing that he'd think she *really* was a mental case.

And so, she weighed her words and placed the folder on the table in front of him. "I have proof that Dr. Bradley Taylor is your 2nd great-grandfather," she said.

"I know the history of my ancestry. Bradley Taylor fought for the Confederacy, and, yes, he was a doctor."

So far, so good. But before she could answer he said, without emotion, "Both my parents and my fiancée died in a plane crash last year. I have no family left, so what's the purpose of this?"

She offered condolences. *Now for the hard part.* Her hand trembled as she removed the marker and handed it to him. He read its inscription, turned it over, and shrugged. "Where did you get this?"

She rattled off the details.

A smirk of disbelief crossed his face. "Did I hear you right? You spoke to my deceased relative at a cemetery in Mississippi where he's buried? This might come as a shock, but my relatives are buried here in Atlanta. And anyway, I find it interesting that he didn't come and speak directly to me."

"I know how this sounds. I've gone over this a thousand times in my head. I had no prior knowledge of your family or the town where they came from. Bradley provided the information that led me to Brandon. I have documents that came from the Metcalf Library," she said.

"I'll say this again...my entire family is buried here. Furthermore, I don't believe in ghosts, and I certainly don't believe that the person you think you saw is related to me. What's the con here? You want what? Money? Publicity?"

She took a deep breath before answering. "I don't believe in ghosts, either. At one point, I was ready to have myself committed. But I can assure you that every word I've spoken is true, and the proof I have speaks volumes of that truth."

He handed her the marker and stood. "You're a beautiful woman; too bad you're slightly off the vertical—not my words. Evidently, you're under a great deal of stress, and you're using your vivid writer's imagination to eke a story out of a few facts that, in my estimation, add up to nothing. Your information is worthless to me. Any genealogist could have done the same."

"Dr. Powell, I'm here to ask for your assistance to help Bradley find his rightful resting place."

"His final resting place? You haven't heard a word I've said. And you certainly don't see how ludicrous this sounds. Why would a dead man want to get out of one cemetery and into another? And please don't tell me that it's because he's buried with Union soldiers...as if the dead care about the person lying next to them. Seeing as you're into cemeteries, and my family history, you should visit Oakland Cemetery here in Atlanta. My family mausoleum is there, as well as many Civil War soldiers. Who knows, maybe another soldier will reach out to you. I'm sorry if I sound rude. If it's a matter of inheritance, please contact my office, and they'll give you the name of my attorney. Sorry, I have to go help the living now."

And with that, he was gone.

On the way back to her room, Jennifer thought about calling Sam and resigning. But for some strange reason, she wasn't really angry with him. If truth were told, she'd found the whole incident amusing.

She called Jake and told him what happened.

"I know all about it. Sam just told me how he tried to foil your plans when Dr. Powell called asking about your credentials. Then, he asked me why you were in Atlanta."

"What did you tell him?"

"Told him you were on vacation, and he should mind his

own business."

"Doesn't matter. I don't think Powell would have believed me anyway. In the meantime, I've got to try and find the Jackson family. I'm not sure if they remained here, but I owe it to Dr. Taylor to give it a shot."

"Still don't know when you'll be heading back?"

"Might be sooner than later. I don't have a clue as to where or how to begin finding the other families. Thank goodness Ralph is spearheading much of this stuff."

"Does Sam know that Ralph's helping you?"

"Heavens no! How are things at the mag?" she asked.

"Amazingly, Missy is still with us. I like the way she stands up to Sam, and I honestly believe he likes it. Everyone misses you, and…so do I."

A long, silent pause told him that they either got disconnected, she wasn't listening, or she didn't like what he'd said.

"Jennifer, are your there?"

"Huh? Oh, sure, Missy's great with Sam. I'll call you later."

Without another word, she disconnected. Something she saw last night in Addison's journal flashed in her mind. She opened the photo file on her laptop and studied the journal pages. Why didn't she see it before? It was right there, clearly written at the bottom of the last page she photographed: PRYOR STREET, ATLANTA.

A search in Google, and there it was. She called Ralph, and the sound of ruffling papers at the other end meant that he found something.

"Bad news first," he said with a sigh. "There's nothing, and I mean nothing, leading to the Jackson family in Atlanta or anywhere. I've hit a wall, and I don't like hitting walls."

"I think I may have found something; although, I'm not sure if it has anything to do with the Jacksons." She gave him the name of the street.

"I'll get right on it," he said.

"Wait! Before you go, what's the good news?"

"Oh, yeah! I found property records from 1873 for the Taylor family and up came the original deed of a house owned by Bradley's father, Matthew, on Peachtree Road. And the really good news is that the property is still owned by our very own Dr. Jonathan Matthew Powell. The house was torn down years ago. Get ready for this little nugget. There's a medical building, belonging to Powell Medical Associates, on the same property. Did you know that?"

"No, and that's interesting because I saw Dr. Powell earlier today. Because of Sam's foolishness, he thinks I'm a mental case. Long story short, he wasn't interested in anything I had to say. Anyway, I'm not sure if he could have provided any new information. I didn't even get a chance to ask. I wonder...." She paused, and her mind drifted.

"Yeah, I'm thinking the same thing. Most people from that era kept records of family events, which were noted in Bibles. Do you think he'll speak to you again?"

"Right now, he thinks I'm a crazy woman."

"Truthfully, if I didn't know you as well as I do, I'd probably feel the same way. Don't get discouraged. I'll check out that address and get back to you."

Across town later that night, in a stately house on West Paces Ferry Road, Jonathan Powell sat alone in his study, flipping through the pages of a medical journal. Every few minutes he lifted his head to stare at framed photographs of his parents on the fireplace mantle.

They were too young to die, he thought. *I wonder what they would have made of this woman's story. Perhaps they know why she's here.* He laughed, knowing that he didn't believe one word of what he was thinking. However, his mother would have fallen in, head first, believing every single word. But not his father; he would have wanted proof. As for Susan, she would have believed whatever he thought was true or false.

He tried to concentrate on an article about the Affordable Care Act, but the gorgeous woman who sat across from him earlier today occupied his mind. He shook his head, rejecting her words, but not dismissing the attraction he felt for her. This feeling took him by surprise.

His cell rang, and the number that came up had a New York City area code. Without hesitation, he answered the call.

"Dr. Powell," Sam Baldwin began in a meek voice. "I owe you an apology. It was a stupid joke, and I can assure you that Miss Beasley is not crazy. In fact, she's the only woman I know who's sane. Not sure what she's doing in Atlanta, but whatever it is, I hope my stupidity didn't mess things up. She's certainly one person whom you can trust. Please accept my apology."

Jonathan eased back in his chair. "I appreciate the call. I was a little harsh with her today. I owe her an apology as well."

"Thanks for understanding. By the way, does she know what I said?"

"Sorry, but I told her your exact words."

"Oh boy! What did she say?"

"She laughed, and quite heartily I might add."

"What a relief. When she laughs like that, it means all is well."

Ten minutes later, Jonathan opened a file drawer in his office and removed a folder marked Taylor-Powell Mausoleum. He checked the number of tombs and reviewed the family names. But a piece of vital information caught his attention. "Why didn't I see this before?"

He quickly drafted a text to Jennifer, apologizing for his rudeness and added that perhaps they'd gotten off on the wrong foot. *How about dinner tomorrow night so I can apologize in person. And I also have something to tell you,* he wrote.

When Jennifer heard the ping of a text message, her first instinct was to ignore it and go to bed. It was a long day, and she didn't want to speak to or text anyone, no matter who it was. But curiosity got the best of her when she saw the message was from Jonathan Powell. She stared at his words, wondering what initiated his change of heart.

She messaged back that she was free for dinner, and went to bed happy.

That night, Jonathan dreamed of Jennifer standing in a cemetery in front of a headstone. When he saw the marker in her hand, he felt a searing pain in his back.

Meanwhile, at Metcalf Manor, lights flickered as flashes of lightning streaked across the sky. In the dark stillness of the library, two eerie shadows crossed the wooden floor, blocking the entrance.

At the Natchez National Cemetery, a strong gust of wind snapped a dead tree limb, causing it to fall directly onto tombstone 1186. The force of the blow split the stone down the middle.

CHAPTER 17

In the light of a new day, sunshine blazed down on Atlanta. The weatherman on the morning news promised a beautiful day with clear skies and warm temperatures. Jennifer had a good feeling that this was going to be a day of endless possibilities.

She called Ralph, and he picked up the excitement in her voice when she mentioned Powell's name.

"It certainly was a surprise to hear from him," she gushed.

"One step forward," he said, slurping his morning cappuccino. "Carl's friend at the Department of Archives and History in Atlanta found that in 1870, Dr. Taylor's father purchased a parcel of land on Pryor Street. It appears that Addison found that out because of his journal entry."

"Who owns the property today?"

"It's a parking lot in the Lakewood Heights section of the city. A man named Cameron Belinger currently owns the property. I'm trying to track him down; however, I have a feeling that this property was bought and sold many times. We keep running the name Jackson, but nothing's coming up. It's a dead end. The only good news is that Carl won't give up. We lit a fire under him, and he's determined to find this family."

"Give him my thanks, and tell him I owe him dinner when I get back."

"He'll hold you to that; so will I. A dinner with us will be a lot more costly than my fee."

Jennifer laughed. "I'm not worried. Anything else?"

"One more thing…not important, but it'll help make clear what happened to Powell's parents. Last year, they were on their way to Georgia for his wedding to Susan Bland when their plane crashed in the Everglades. Everyone perished. Tragic story. I have nothing on Powell; he's squeaky clean…not even a traffic violation. Don't ask me how I know this because if I tell you, well, I might have to make you a pair of cement shoes. That's it for now. If I find anything else, I'll give you a call. What's your day looking like?"

"I'm off to Oakland Cemetery in downtown Atlanta. It says in the brochure that it was founded in 1850 and is the final resting place of Civil War soldiers and a few notables, one of which is Margaret Mitchell. It's also the site of the Taylor-Powell mausoleum."

"You seem to be very comfortable around the dead these days. Why are you going to another cemetery?"

"Not sure. Jonathan mentioned it. Anyway, it's not the dead we have to worry about."

She grabbed her tote, picked up the morning paper outside her door, and went down for breakfast. Georgian pecan waffles with pure maple syrup and a pot of steaming coffee awakened her senses. She delighted in the fact that food took on a whole new, exciting meaning, giving credit to Bradley Taylor. *He definitely changed the colors of my life.*

She calculated expenses for the trip thus far and found she was way off budget. She laughed, thinking that if her life hadn't changed, she could have blown a bundle on a shrink. *Nah! This is far better, and I'm having one hell of a good time.*

She lingered over another cup of coffee, content to do some people watching. One of the many things she enjoyed about the South was seeing the cultural diversity. Hospitality existed, and it was real.

She glanced at the time and paid the check. Within an hour, she was at the cemetery, walking along a wide cobblestone path. She caught up to a group of tourists, following a guide. She listened as the guide mused about mausoleums and the dearly departed. It seemed that most of the people were more interested in ghosts, rather than the history of the cemetery.

When they came to Margaret Mitchell's grave, the guide explained how the famed writer of *Gone with the Wind* died.

One young man ignored the account. "Did you ever see her haunting the cemetery?" he asked.

"I haven't," replied the guide with a grin. "But who knows? Maybe she'll appear today."

The tour moved on, but Jennifer decided to sit on a nearby

bench that offered a view of the Atlanta skyline. *I like this city. I also like the quiet beauty of this place. How strange is that?*

She was completely immersed in her own thoughts, unaware that an older gentleman was standing near the bench. He held a single red rose in his hand.

"May I sit here?" he asked. "Or are you waiting for someone?"

"I'm alone," Jennifer answered, moving over to make room.

"Sobering place, huh?" he said.

"It's really quite lovely here," she replied. "It doesn't feel like a cemetery at all, more like a park for the living to enjoy...if that makes sense."

"I agree. My Sarah is buried over there." He pointed to a freshly dug grave covered with a large spray of yellow, orange, and purple rosebuds. An abundance of floral baskets, wreaths, and crosses circled the site.

"My deepest condolences." Jennifer's voice revealed compassion.

"Life will never be the same without her. Been together since high school. Would have celebrated our wedding anniversary today. What do I do now?"

Without thinking, she lightly touched his hand. "Life will never be the same, but you go on as best as you can until you meet again."

He smiled. Not a smile of sadness but more like a knowing, peaceful acceptance. "That's exactly what she'd told me before she slipped into eternity. She had such great peace about her illness, and never once complained. She was one in a million."

"I'm sure she was."

"Please forgive my rudeness; I'm Ronald Aguda."

She introduced herself, and they shook hands.

"Do you live here?" he asked.

"No, I'm visiting. I'm from New York."

"I grew up in Manhattan," he said. "Went to NYU, studied law, and practiced there until I was offered a partnership with a growing firm here. And so, Atlanta became our home, raised our children, and now…."

"Now, give yourself time to grieve and time to remember all the wonderful things you shared and cherished with your wife. Are you still an attorney?"

"I'm a Superior Court Judge. I love what I do, and that's a good thing."

And so, they talked for more than an hour as the busy world revolved around them. They were comfortable, sharing details about their families and careers. There was something unique about their meeting, but neither could explain it.

Jennifer shared her account of how she came to be in Atlanta.

He seemed intrigued but wasn't intimidated. "What a fascinating story. I would love to see the marker," he said.

She removed it from her tote and watched closely as he studied the piece. There were no signs that it affected him.

"I don't know much about Civil War artifacts, but this appears to be genuine," he said. "I'm glad you're going to return it to its proper place. Not many people would do that."

"Do you feel or sense anything strange about this piece?"

"No, should I?"

"Just wondering. Some people claim it has healing powers."

"The mind is a complex thing. But for some…who's to say. You stumbled onto this and through it found details about a family you wouldn't have known otherwise. If you're telling the truth, and I'd stake what I know about human nature on the fact that you are, then you must follow this to the end. Do you think our meeting is by chance?"

"Before all this happened, I might have brushed it off as a pleasant encounter, but nothing more than that. The amazing part is that you believe the story without reservation."

"Just before my wife passed, she saw angels descending and ascending to heaven, explaining that one was holding her hand. Sarah looked radiant. Her peace gave me hope. Then, in a blink of an eye, she was gone. I so want to see her again, but my pastor explained that her spirit returned to God and that I'd never physically see her until I die."

"How then did I see and hear Dr. Taylor so clearly?"

"Well, according to Scripture, angels take human form when there's a message from heaven to share. Perhaps you saw an angel in the person of your soldier. Does that make sense?"

Jennifer nodded. "Probably the most sense I've heard since all of this began. Thank you, Judge."

"I believe that what was revealed to you is meant for this generation as opposed to those in the past. Can't change what has happened, but we certainly can change today and even tomorrow, especially when it comes to protecting the innocent. I have no doubt that all of this fell into your hands for a reason. So, with that in mind, please continue your journey. There's another side here. You're going to need hard evidence to prove his identity. My son took a DNA test some years ago. He traced our lineage back to West Africa in the 17th century. It's interesting to learn that we're a mixture of many cultures. Please don't hesitate to call me for assistance. Some of our agencies don't act quickly with requests, so perhaps I can speed things up," he said, handing her his card.

"It was such a pleasure to meet you and spend this time together," Jennifer said. "I hope we can meet again before I return to New York."

He nodded in agreement. "I'd like that. Call me anytime."

She walked to her car feeling melancholy. She called her dad, and his upbeat voice lifted her spirits.

"I've been reading your e-mails and helping Billy with research. We're not finding too many things, but we're sure having fun trying. I want to thank you for this; it's been quite an experience. Guess what? Billy and Carolyn are coming for dinner tonight, and they're bringing Morton to stay until you come home. Not sure what to make of this new relationship, but Billy seems happy."

"That's terrific news; especially that Morton will be spending time with his grandpa. Miss you all. We have so much to talk about, particularly the judge I just met at an Atlanta cemetery." She explained it all and her dad listened in amazement.

"When will you be coming home? I miss you."

"It depends on what I find in the next few days. You know, Dad, I need real hard proof that the remains in Natchez are that of Dr. Taylor. I've been trying to wrap my brain around this, but I keep coming up empty. I have hunches, but they don't mean much in my line of work. I need facts and evidence to back it up."

"Always the consummate journalist. But you did find Dr. Taylor's relative, and that's a plus. And of course, you're right, it's not enough. I think you're getting close to something major. Keep on going, and I'll keep having positive thoughts. Got to dash, making grilled salmon tonight."

"You've just succeeded in making me hungry. I'm having dinner with Dr. Powell."

"Perhaps he can shed light on some of the unanswered questions. I don't know of a single family that doesn't have some old papers hidden away in a box somewhere."

CHAPTER 18

Not a day passed that Jonathan Powell didn't think about his parents and what he'd lost when they perished. There was no consolation in the fact that they died instantly. Their deaths were a continual reminder that he lost the only family he'd ever had. And in that loss, he often thought about how he neglected them. He blamed it on his career, especially after he accepted the residency at Emory. Long hours and medical emergencies took precedence over family.

Even now, nothing seemed to change. In fact, he made sure that he'd have little time for anything but work. And as much as he thought about them and his mistakes is as little as he thought about life after death. He was raised to think for himself, to believe in what his heart told him was true. But he didn't trust his heart because it revealed nothing.

As soon as he arrived home from the hospital, he showered and dressed for his dinner date. He took special care to pick the perfect shirt and tie to match his suit. The thought of dinner with a woman he barely knew excited him and worked wonders for his ego.

Before leaving, he remembered a family tree that his mother worked on when he was in high school. He went to the attic, hoping to find it so he could show it to Jennifer. His parents' personal belongings were stored in sealed boxes. Until now, he never had the desire to open them. He flicked on the light switch.

As he stared at the stack of boxes holding a treasure trove of family memorabilia, he realized that had it not been for Jennifer, he'd have no interest in the contents.

He took a box and opened it. It was filled to the top with photos. He set it aside. He opened another with holiday and vacation videos. He smiled, remembering how creative his mother had been when it came to gift giving. She never gave a gift that didn't have a specific meaning.

He took out a video wrapped in a silk scarf. Holding the scarf to his nose, he inhaled deeply. A mild scent of his mother's favorite perfume sent a memory sailing through his mind. The video was labeled 1969, the year he was born. A photo was taped to the back of the cassette. It was his grandfather, Matthew J. Taylor, holding him up in front of the church where he was baptized. Ten years later, Jonathan said farewell to his beloved grandfather when he was laid to rest in the family mausoleum.

His thoughts strayed to Susan and the anxiety he felt as their wedding day grew closer. He was having doubts. The day of the crash was the day he'd decided to tell her that they should postpone the wedding. And now, he carried this guilt and built a fantasy of her and what their relationship actually meant to him.

Jonathan wanted what his parents had: the kind of love that

endures. In his heart, he knew that he and Susan didn't have that.

His cell rang, and he immediately dreaded that it might be the hospital with another emergency. He was relieved to see Jennifer's number.

"I'm sorry to bother you," she said. "I forgot what time you're picking me up."

He thought for a moment, not sure if he'd mentioned the time. "Is seven o'clock good for you?"

"Perfect," she said.

"My schedule was so busy that I didn't have lunch. I'm starving."

She laughed. "It looks like both of us will enjoy dinner tonight."

"Did you have a good day?" He was surprised that he actually cared what kind of day she had.

"Actually, I would have to say that I had the best day ever. I took your advice and went to Oakland Cemetery. My only disappointment is that I didn't get to pay my respects to your family."

"It's not easy finding a burial site there. I should have given you the location."

"I would like to see it before I return to New York."

"I can arrange my schedule to take you there."

"I'd like that. Just before leaving the cemetery, I met a judge… perhaps you've heard of him, Ronald Aguda?"

"My gosh, not only do I know him, I treated his lovely wife. I've seen far too many deaths, but Sarah's passing hit me hard. He sat back. *I don't want this memory.* "Anyway, yes I know the family very well. How is Ronald doing? Today is their anniversary."

"He's doing as well as can be expected. I'll share more with you tonight."

He left the attic, but not before thinking about the family history yet to be disclosed.

By the time he reached the hotel, Jennifer was already waiting for him. The moment she got into the car, a delicate scent surrounded him. Although he wasn't a big fan of perfume, the fragrance was pleasing.

"I've made reservations at one of my favorite Italian restaurants. I think you'll like it. The food is authentic."

"Right now I can eat everything and anything. I'm thrilled that my appetite is back."

"Have you been ill?"

"No, it's just, well...I kept anger and resentment a little too long in my life over a bad marriage and divorce. It caused a loss of appetite. But that, I'm happy to say, is a thing of the past."

"I won't ask what happened because sad memories are not something either of us needs to discuss right now."

Jennifer agreed. "I like Atlanta, especially the casual, laid-back style of living. And I like Southern food and the warm hospitality."

"I've lived here all my life. Never thought of leaving, never thought of doing anything else but being a doctor. Is that the way you feel about writing?"

"Exactly. By the way, my dad's a doctor."

"What's his specialty?"

"General practitioner. He's retired now. His patients adored him. He even made house calls." She told him about Billy and how they were raised as brother and sister.

And, in turn, he told her about his parents. He was surprised that he went into details he'd never shared with another person. He spoke freely about the plane crash and how their bodies were found still strapped into their seats. "They were holding hands," he said. "I made the decision to remove a separating wall in their tombs. I didn't want them to be apart."

She looked at him through misty eyes.

"So much has been lost over the last year," he said.

"But there's also joy and hope."

He looked puzzled.

"There's sorrow over the loss, joy in the memories, and hope for the future," she explained.

"You're right," he said, pulling up to the valet attendant.

The owner of the restaurant greeted them with a big smile.

"Thank you, Elyse, for fitting us in tonight," he said.

"There's always room for you. Your table is ready." She led the way out to the patio where wicker chairs and tables were nestled in cozy nooks between the trees. "Would you like to start with drinks, perhaps a bottle of wine?"

"I'll have an Aperol on the rocks," Jennifer said.

For a moment, Elyse studied her. "Lei è bellissima," she said, giving Jonathan an approving smile.

"Grazie," Jennifer said.

"Ah, prego," Elyse replied. She handed them menus.

Jonathan cleared his throat. "If anyone's interested, I'll have an Aperol too."

Elyse laughed and walked away.

"Do you have a favorite dish?" Jennifer asked.

"Everything's good," Jonathan replied. "I'd like to hear the specials, but we can certainly start with a few appetizers. They make the best lasagna, and the roasted artichokes are fantastic, so is the cold or hot antipasto."

"If I were to say that I want it all would that be piggish of me?"

He laughed heartily. "Piggish? That's an interesting word. I doubt if there's anything piggish about you."

They ordered, and when the food arrived, they ate slowly as if not wanting the evening to end. There was no lull in the conversation or lack of agreeing on most of what they'd discussed. They talked about careers, schooling, and childhoods but didn't approach the subject of Bradley Taylor.

Three hours later, they sipped a complimentary cordial of Limoncello. Inside the restaurant, the lights dimmed, but neither noticed that they were the only two left.

Jonathan leaned forward in his chair. "Tell me again about Natchez and Brandon. Start from the beginning."

Jennifer was taken aback with the sudden reversal in the conversation but was quick to respond. "No matter how I say it, I don't think you're going to believe it."

"Try me, I'm eager to hear what you have to say."

"Ok," she said, taking a deep breath. "Before my trip to Natchez, I could only hear his voice. But at the cemetery, I was able to see him. He told me that he was shot in the back and left to die as a Union soldier. I don't doubt a word of what he said. The letters and documents I read at Metcalf Manor revealed startling facts." She waited for his reaction.

He remained silent, eyes focused on her. She spoke with passion, and he could see the honesty in her discourse.

She went on to explain that whoever did this to him would be revealed. "But that's a small part of this story. Finding you opens the door to having his remains confirmed by DNA…albeit a difficult process. His only request was to bring him back to his family. But I believe that there's a greater purpose here. Unfortunately, at this time, I have no clue as to what it is."

His demeanor was composed. "If that's the case, then there must be many spirits trying to rectify the past."

"I don't think so," she said, explaining Judge Aguda's account about angels.

"I accept his explanation," Jonathan said. "When my grandfather died, I desperately wanted to talk to him, but my mother made it clear that it was impossible and that someday I would understand why. I believe that today is that *someday.* I'm going to keep an open mind. So, I'd like to help in any way I can. I have an attic full of family photos and documents. You're welcome to review what I have, and perhaps you'll find what you're looking for."

"You were easy to find because the information was given to me. As for the other two families, they've become a challenge."

"What are their names?"

"Addison and Jackson. But these families are not related to you. Benjamin, Tilly, and Little Ben Jackson were born into slavery. They lived with your 3rd great-aunt, but she never treated them as slaves. She wanted to keep them together as a family, so she gave them her last name and educated them. When she died, they went to live with Bradley and his family until after the war."

Jonathan pushed back in his chair. "That's good news. Thank you for telling me."

"There's more," she said. "Your 3rd great-grandfather, Matthew B. Taylor, made sure the inheritance to Benjamin and his family was protected and given to them when they all lived in Atlanta. Isn't it interesting to see how everything has evolved? Each step brings me closer to the truth. Even meeting Judge Aguda was not a coincidence. These are things I can't explain, so I won't even try. I can only thank you for giving me the opportunity to review your family documents."

"Let's go to my house, and we can look through the boxes. I think it might also help me to remember the wonderful times I had with my parents, rather than always focusing on their tragic deaths."

"My life has taken a dramatic turn, and I owe it all to Bradley. I won't even go into *my* issues and how far they took me in negative thoughts."

"How long will you be staying in Atlanta?"

"I'm not sure. Besides my family, a few close friends, and a private detective, I've hit a brick wall finding those two families. I'm running out of vacation money, and the Ritz is not exactly my affordable cup of tea."

"Do they all believe this story?"

"Yes, because they know I wouldn't make this up. Until I visited the cemetery, I was the hardest one to convince. When I saw Bradley's pleading blue eyes, I knew. And here's something remarkable. Before he went off to war, he dreamed of a young woman, holding a marker. And I was that woman."

"He told you this?"

"He did. But I don't think I'll ever see him again—except when I look at you. You have his eyes, features, and even his voice. He appeared gentle in nature and soft-spoken, much like you. But he didn't smile or show any emotion."

"That does sound like me."

"Perhaps it's because of what you've lost. We change when we grow up and discover that the fragility of life is surrounded by the reality of death. And while I can't explain everything, I now know that what I saw and heard is important in my life and for all those who have been touched by this phenomenon."

"You certainly got my attention. I'm going to keep an open mind. I've been carrying around a lot of old, musty baggage for a long time. Let's go and look in the boxes."

Jonathan's willingness to help delighted her. Just twenty-four hours ago, he had written her off. Now, his enthusiasm to share family information was going to be enormously helpful.

Jennifer gazed out into the darkness as he steered the car along West Paces Ferry Road.

"Almost there," he said.

Most of the houses were set back from the road and were quite large.

He turned into a private road and pulled up to a wrought iron gate. He pushed a button above his rear-view mirror. Within seconds, the gate opened to a brick-paved driveway, leading to a brightly lit Georgian-style colonial.

Beveled-glass mahogany entrance doors presented a warm welcome to an interior that was as remarkable as the exterior. The center hall Italian marble floor led to a double staircase that spiraled up to a balcony.

The house was tastefully decorated. But it was the kitchen that took center stage for her. It was a cook's delight, spacious and spotless, trimmed in English oak cabinetry.

"It's a beautiful home," she said. "And I love this kitchen."

From a built-in side-by-side wine cooler, he removed a bottle of sparkling wine. He uncorked it, grabbed two long stem glasses, and led the way to the attic.

On the second level, the spacious master bedroom caught Jennifer's eye. She peeked in and laughed inwardly when she thought about her small apartment.

The finished attic was roomy and neat. He offered her a seat on a rocker next to his mother's desk and pulled a chair over to join her.

"Where do we begin?" he asked, pouring the wine.

"Any box you want to start with is fine with me," she said excitedly.

He pointed at the boxes he'd already opened. "Just photos and boring home movies in those. We'll have to go through each and every box, as none of them are labeled."

He opened a box. "More photos," he said, holding up one of himself, his parents, and his grandfather.

He went to get another box, and she watched the way he walked. *How remarkable that even his stature is that of Dr. Taylor,* she thought. When he turned to walk back, she stared up into his eyes, and her heart pounded. She lowered her head and blushed slightly.

As the evening wore on, they opened box after box. Most of the contents belonged to his father's side of the family. With just one box left, they felt disappointed.

"Well," Jonathan said with a shrug, "at least we had a good time opening everything."

"It's a good thing we're down to the last one as you still have to drive me back to the hotel, and the wine bottle is almost empty."

"Let's see what's in this last box," he said, cutting through the tape. "Wouldn't you know it, this is the one we should have opened first."

Jennifer looked at the items stored in protected plastic sleeves. At the very top of the box, a family tree traced the lineage from Jonathan to his 3rd great-grandparents, Matthew and Olivia Taylor.

They each took a stack of papers and went through them slowly.

"What exactly should I be looking for?" Jonathan asked.

"Deeds, property tax records, letters, baptism certificates, marriage licenses, death records…stuff like that. I can take photos of whatever we find that's important."

"Take whatever you need, Jennifer."

"That's kind of you. But if we do find something, I'd be more comfortable with photos. I never realized how important family documents could be. It's safeguarding one's history for future generations. The first thing I'm going to do when I get home is to make sure my family records are in a safe place. I know that my dad has kept everything together, but I want to check it out. Who knows, I might find something interesting about *my* ancestors."

"Look at this; it's my fifth-grade report card. I failed PE," he said with a chuckle. "I think that was the year I had pneumonia."

"I didn't know someone could fail PE," she said with a straight face.

He shrugged.

She held up a plastic sleeve with a letter inside.

Jonathan's eyes widened. "Open it. Let's take a look at the date."

"Oh, my gosh! We've hit gold. Here's a letter from Mrs. Metcalf to Rebecca. The address on the envelope is Peachtree Road, dated 1878."

"That's the same address of my medical center. Did you know that?"

"Yes, I did. That much I found out. I think *you* should read it."

Jonathan carefully opened the envelope and unfolded the letter.

October 15, 1878

My dear Rebecca,

It was wonderful to receive your letter and to know that you, Bradley, and Matthew are settled into your new home.

Much has happened since you left Brandon. Lewis returned to collect his father's belongings. I have never seen him so distraught.

He did not speak of you or your family, nor did he mention his father. He said he was going to Atlanta. He seemed bitter, distraught, and resentful, all the attributes you saw in his father. It was a different Lewis, and it frightened me.

I got the feeling that he does not know where you live. Except for my family, no one knows where you are. I hope he does not find you.

I am very pleased and proud to say that my grandmother has been instrumental in helping many of those emancipated to safety up north. No one here knows what happened to the Jackson family. The search for Little Ben has ended. Hopefully, this news brings comfort to all.

Please let me know if you want your package mailed to you.

Our love and warmest regards, Elizabeth Metcalf

Jonathan continued to stare at the letter. "Can you give me a timeline on this? Who is this Lewis person, and why were the authorities looking for Little Ben?"

"I don't have all the answers," she replied, filling him in on what she did know.

He listened intently. "So, let's see if I got this right. John Addison stole money from my family and possibly murdered Bradley Sr. But no one actually came out and accused him of that crime. Right?"

"Right. And when Addison was found dead, the authorities went after Little Ben. I have no proof, but I think John's guilty of two murders: his first wife and Bradley Sr. From all accounts of the letters I've seen, he suffered what appeared to be a mental breakdown. He returned home after the war, married Rebecca and, according to a letter she wrote to Elizabeth Metcalf, his behavior after the marriage was abusive and cruel. He misused her money and property for his own gain. Your 3rd great-grandfather saved the family's fortune, including

Benjamin Jackson's inheritance, by converting much of his holdings to gold before the war. And he also brought the Jackson family to safety in Atlanta. Now, you know as much as I do. As for the Jackson family, we keep coming up empty-handed."

"Perhaps the Jacksons changed their name, or there were no male heirs."

"If that's the case, finding this family is going to be impossible."

"Have you considered the possibility that perhaps Lewis became a pastor like his father?"

"It's possible. I could check every church in Atlanta, but I don't have that kind of time. If I don't find something within the next two days, I'll have to go back to New York and do research from there."

"I'd like to help. Would you consider staying here? I certainly have enough room. I don't live alone."

Jennifer's heart sank.

"Mrs. B has been our live-in housekeeper since I was a young boy. But she's more than that to me. Tonight, she's visiting her sister," he said. "Anyway, most of the time I'm at the hospital, so we won't be bumping into each other."

"That's very kind of you but—"

"This would certainly solve your money problem."

"Yes, but accepting your offer might create problems of another kind." She looked unsettled, and he picked up on it.

"I think you're close to finding the other families. And unless

I'm mistaken, if they're here, then you need to be here to follow wherever that road leads."

She didn't want it to appear that she'd be using him in any way by accepting his offer. She turned to him and said, "I'll seriously consider it."

"Fair enough. Either way, I'm here to help."

She sipped the last of her wine and continued to peruse the stack of papers resting on her lap. There were personal letters between his parents, which she didn't open. She passed them to him and looked at the last item in the box. Not thinking much of it, she handed it to him.

"Let's see what we have here," he said, unfolding a newspaper article. Finding nothing on the first page to indicate any importance, he turned it over. "Whoa!" he said, holding it up. "First Fellowship Church of Atlanta opens its doors in Brentwood and…Lewis Addison was the founding pastor! The first service was May 10, 1907."

"Lewis founded his own church!" Jennifer said with excitement. "Dare I ask where he got the money to do that?"

Jonathan reached for his cell phone and logged into the Internet. He typed in the name of the church and the address popped up, complete with names and telephone numbers. "It's still there," he said. "What say we take a ride? I know exactly where it is."

Jennifer jumped up, reached for his hand, and squeezed it. "This is incredible!"

He agreed, but not because of the newspaper article. The touch of her hand in his sent his pulse racing. "Let's have some coffee before we go," he said. "I don't want a DWI at this stage of my life."

An hour later, they drove off like high school kids on a date. The mood was jubilant, and Jonathan didn't want it to end.

"This is all because of you," Jennifer said.

"There it is," he said, pointing at the church.

The sign at the front displayed the name of the current pastor: Francis A. Rhodes.

"I think it's time for me to pay a visit to Reverend Rhodes," Jennifer said.

"Then you'll be staying?"

"Looks that way. Does your offer still stand?"

And there it was, the widest and sweetest smile she'd ever seen.

CHAPTER 19

Early the next morning, Jennifer packed her suitcase and sent a text to Ralph that she was checking out of the hotel. Within seconds, her cell rang, and she excitedly told him what she and Jonathan had found.

"We went to see the church, and it's definitely the one Lewis Addison founded. Not sure if the current pastor, Francis A. Rhodes, is related. Hoping you can find that out," she said.

"Hey, this is good. Now, I have something to go on. Are you heading back to New York?"

"Ah, no. Jonathan has invited me to stay at his home to continue my research. I know what you're going to say before you say it: I don't know him, he could be a serial killer—"

"I wasn't going to say anything like that. First of all, I know who he is and where he lives. I have eyes and ears all over the place. I can assure you that you're on my radar." He laughed heartily and asked if there was anything else.

"You're so practical, which is one of the many reasons why we're good friends."

"Tell that to Alice next time you talk to her…the friend part. She's a tad jealous. I take it there's nothing on the Jackson family yet?"

"Nothing, but I'm confident you'll find something before I do. It's possible they moved away to escape the bigotry."

Ralph agreed, and her cell announced another call coming in.

"Gotta take this," she said, switching the call.

"Miss Beasley!" The person on the other end tried to disguise his voice. "What's going on in Atlanta? You promised to call back; it's not like you to break a promise."

"I also said I'd marry you—"

"You what? What's happening?"

"Oops! Sorry, Jake. I thought you were someone else."

"I know things are moving quickly on your end but…marriage?"

"More importantly is the fact that I've found the Addison connection."

"Great news. Does that mean you'll be coming home?"

"Not exactly, but I'm leaving the Ritz…a little too pricey for me. After this trip, I doubt if I'll be able to afford another vacation. I've had an idea for an article, which may keep me here a little longer. I'm sending a text to Candy to see what she thinks of it."

"Does it have anything to do with the soldier and his family?"

"Yes…in a way. Still in the planning stages, but there's a church here, and I'd like to do a story about its roots and how it grew."

And so, she recounted what happened the night before. The only news she left out was the offer to move into Jonathan's house.

Jake remained quiet, but it didn't take long for him to realize that Jonathan Powell had a lot to do with her cheerfulness. His silence caused her to stop talking.

"Where will you be staying?" he finally asked. His voice sounded strange.

"There's so much going on right now. I'll explain everything soon." She wanted to tell him the truth but decided against it. He'd ask too many questions and could never understand how important this was to her. A confrontation with him would take her off the high she was on.

"You never answered my question. Where will you be staying?"

"I have lots of research to do, so I'll sign off for now and get back to you."

He was glad she couldn't see the disappointment on his face. She didn't trust him enough to say what was really going on. "Okay," he muttered. "I'll be here if you need me."

And with that, she breathed a sigh of relief and sent the text to Candy.

She called Billy. "Pick up, it's me," she said hurriedly.

"I'm here, waiting to hear from you. Any news?"

"Yes, but first I need to talk about something else. I can't afford to stay at the Ritz any longer. I'm way over my head—"

"Not to worry. How much do you need? Whatever you want I'll put it into your bank account."

"No, you don't understand. I have another place to stay.

Jonathan invited me to his home until I finish my work here."

"Oh? That's a thoughtful gesture…I think. How old is this man?"

"He's in his late forties. But what does that have to do with anything?"

"Don't get defensive. Are you considering this offer because of money? Or is it something else?"

"Oh, boy, here we go. I don't want to second-guess my intentions, but it's an open door, and I need all the help I can get while I'm here. I could work the research from New York, but it'll take much longer, and you know how I like to be in the thick of things. I could also find a cheaper hotel—"

"But you don't want to—do you?"

"No, smarty pants."

"You're a big girl. But okay, you want to hear me say it: get the rest of the story, and then come home."

"Don't tell Dad about this, just yet. I don't want you to lie, but I'd rather tell him myself."

"Fair enough. I have some news to share. Do you have time to listen?"

"Of course I do. What is it?"

"It's Carolyn and me—"

"Did you have a disagreement?" she interrupted.

"No, not at all. A lot has happened since you left. I…we need to take our relationship to the next level."

"Relationship? What's the next level?"

"We're dating and…."

"And? By the next level, do you mean sex?"

"Sex? Oh, cousin, we're beyond that. I'm talking commitment."

"Commitment? Are you insane? You've only known each other—"

"We've known each other for years. And the best part is that we really like one another."

"I'm going to go out on a limb here: do you think you're falling in love?"

"It's headed in that direction. We're not talking about marriage, but we are discussing a commitment not to see anyone else."

"Oh, well that's good. Did you mention this to Dad?"

"I did, and he's happy about it. Now, don't get all crazy on me, but I have a feeling that Dad and Kathryn are more than fond of each other."

"I'm gone a short time, and my whole family is making commitments? Have you all gone nuts?"

Billy laughed. "This is all positive stuff."

"You're right. I need to keep an open mind."

"You're not angry, are you? Do you feel left out of the loop? It's just that…with everything that's happened on your end, it proved to us that life has to be lived. I won't speak for Dad, but for us, our lives have been anything but complete. What I mean is that we, as a family, love each other, and that will always be. But I want children before I'm too old to enjoy them."

"I understand. I think it's because I'm not there to be a part of it. And now I'm missing you all. I'll give Dad a call and tell him the latest on this end. And we'll wait and see what happens."

The call ended when a text came back from Candy. *I like the story idea. Run it by Sam, and I'll bring it up in the editorial meeting later today.*

Jennifer dialed room service, ordered a big breakfast, took a hot shower, and dressed.

Mid-way through her breakfast, Ralph called. "You hit the mark!" he said. "Rhodes is a descendant of John Addison. He has a large congregation, a school from K to 12th grade, and a TV ministry. I'm going off the record to tell you something that needs to stay between us. There are rumblings around Rhodes, nothing confirmed, but tread lightly with this one. Let's move on to finding the Jackson family."

"Wow! I knew there was a story here."

"What's your next move?"

"I think I'll pay a surprise visit to the church today. I've already sent a text to Candy, and she's on board for an article. I'm going to call Sam to confirm."

"Are you going to lie to him?"

"Of course," she said with a loud laugh. "But really, I don't have to. I just have to tweak the story idea a little to make it more palatable.

I need to stay here and have our expenses covered."

"Okay. Plant the seed, and I'll get back to work."

Jennifer felt new motivation stirring within. She composed a text to Jonathan: *Is today too soon?*

A minute later, he called. "I'll be in surgery all day," he said, sounding rushed. "Mrs. B will be home; she'll let you in. The guest suite is on the first floor, down the hall, next to the library. You won't have to worry about anything because she'll want to mother and smother you. Please feel free to take another look through the boxes in the attic. If you have any problems, send a text, and I'll try to get back to you."

"Perfect. Thanks again for opening your home to me."

"This is my pleasure. After all, if Bradley Taylor approves of you, then we're practically family," he said with a spontaneous laugh that made her heart skip a thousand beats.

She called Sam. "Good morning, handsome," she said sweetly.

"Ah, the prodigal child finally calls. I take it you've forgiven me?"

"Of course. I found it amusing and rather sweet of you to try and protect me." She rolled her eyes. *Protect me? That's a laugh.*

Sam paused, confused. "Who are you? And what have you done to my favorite writer?"

"Your favorite writer is doing what she does best. I've been working a story idea for the past few days, did a lot of researching, and I'd like to run it by you. There's a mega-church here with a school and television ministry. My sources tell me that there's something hidden underneath all the nice-nice stuff. Anyway, I'll approach it from the bottom up. Where they came from, how they grew, blah, blah, blah."

"It's the blahs that have my attention. Well, there's no doubt that you have the best nose for news of anyone I know…so why don't you go for it. I'll get with Candy and see which issue will work best for this type of story. Is there anything you need on this end? You'll do your own photos, right? We don't need added expense—like sending Jake down."

"Jake's not needed," Jennifer responded quickly.

"Sounds great. Do you need anything else?"

"I'll be on your clock starting—"

"When did you start pursuing the idea?" Sam interrupted.

"When I came to Atlanta. My biggest expense, thus far, is the hotel bill. But I won't be incurring any additional charges as I'll be staying with a friend."

Silence at the other end told her that Sam was thrilled by this news.

"But everything else will go on my corporate card." She waited for his reply.

"Of course," he answered. "Just keep me posted. I'll tell Candy to call you if she has any questions. You know how finicky she gets when you and I decide on an assignment without her in the loop."

"I'm not sure when I'll be contacting the church. Please don't make any jokes about the magazine or me when they call to check my credentials."

"What do you take me for—an idiot? I'm very professional. It just so happened that on the day the doctor called I was angry because I hadn't heard from you. However, I really thought you were looking for a job down there. I will admit it was stupid, and I won't let that happen again. Should have known you had a story idea brewing."

"For the record, I'm not looking for a new job."

"Wow, I'm relieved."

"Oh, and one more thing. I can't tell you why, but I'll need additional help from Ralph. Do I have your approval?"

"I'm going to ask this again: who are you and what have you done with Jennifer Beasley?"

"Very funny."

"By the way," Sam said, lowering his voice. "This is rather delicate news, and no one else knows about it. Henry Marshall left his wife and—"

"Not my business, Sam," she said quickly. "I already know who he is and…well, let's just keep it at that."

She ended the call, checked out of the hotel, and followed the commands from the car's navigational system as it directed the way to First Fellowship Church of Atlanta.

CHAPTER 20

Your destination is on the left.

Low-hanging tree branches crossed over the two-lane road that led to the church, administrative office, and school. Just beyond the building complex, behind a stone wall, headstones and mausoleums occupied acres of pristine land that rendered a somber reminder of life's end.

She eased the car into the last available visitor space and turned off the ignition. She rummaged through her tote and found the valuable, unobtrusive item that proved to be her best tool: the pen recorder. Although she was careful to mention that her interviews were sometimes recorded, very few realized that her pen was the actual device.

A young man, holding a clipboard, approached her car. A photo ID was pinned to his shirt. In a squeaky, adolescent voice he welcomed her to First Fellowship Church. "How may I help you?"

Jennifer introduced herself. "I'd like to see Reverend Rhodes."

He stared at a list of names on his clipboard. "Your name is not on the list for today. Do you have an appointment?"

"I don't, but I was hoping to see him before I leave Atlanta."

"I need to see some identification, please."

Jennifer handed him her driver's license.

"Wow, you're from New York! Welcome to Atlanta. Come with me," he said, walking to the front door. He pushed an intercom button and waited.

"Yes, Bobby," a voice responded.

"Miss Jennifer Beasley is here to see Pastor Rhodes."

"Bobby, you know that he's not here today."

Jennifer tapped him on the arm. "Please ask if it's possible to see his secretary," she whispered.

The young man asked, and the church door unlocked with a buzz. He guided her through the main reception hall. They passed a large sanctuary where television cameras were aimed at the pulpit. Technicians in the control room on the second level tested sound and camera angles. Soft organ music filled the air.

The church administrative offices were at the end of a long corridor. Bobby opened the door, and Jennifer approached a reception desk where an attractive woman, void of any expression, extended her hand.

Botox. Definitely! Jennifer thought.

"Good morning, I'm Joan Collier, Miss Carmine's assistant. What can I do for you?"

"She's from New York!" Bobby squealed.

"Thank you. You can return to your post now."

"Okay. Bye, Miss Beasley. Have a great day."

"I don't have an appointment," Jennifer said, handing her a business card.

Joan looked warily at the card. "Let me call Miss Carmine. Please have a seat, I'll be right back."

Jennifer eased into a Queen Ann style chair. At the back of the reception area, sunshine poured through tall windows, highlighting the warm patina of judges paneling and expensive furnishings. Two large portraits on the wall between the windows captured her interest. She got up to take a closer look, aware that cameras observed her every move. Affixed to each portrait frame were bronze plaques bearing the names of the two individuals: Lewis Addison and Reverend Francis Addison Rhodes.

And there's my connection, she thought, pleased that the camera couldn't read her mind.

She returned to her seat.

"I found her," Joan said, a slight bit flushed. "If you don't mind waiting a few minutes, she'll be happy to talk to you. Would you like something to drink? We have bottled water."

"Thank you, but no. This is a beautiful church. How many parishioners do you have?"

"About two thousand attend services in our main sanctuary, and thousands more in satellite churches around the country." She parted her lips in a stiff, half smile.

Jennifer replied with the two words she was expecting: "Very impressive. How long have you worked here?"

"Since I graduated college. I grew up in this church. My father is a deacon, and my mother plays the organ. You probably heard her when you came through the main hall. She's well known, travels the world, and even has a music program on cable."

The phone rang, and Joan hurried to answer it. She turned away as if trying to hide the caller's identity. "Yes," she whispered. "She's still here. No, she's very pleasant. Please hurry."

If one were to compare Joan Collier to Agatha Carmine, it would be to say that they were night and day. Agatha was unattractive and dowdy. Her unkempt black hair frizzled around her chubby face.

Before meeting Jennifer, she logged into a computer in the media center to get a first-hand look at the magazine. When she saw Jennifer's name on the cover story about adultery, she trembled at the thought of why she was there. She knew better than to trust a journalist. She clicked the link to the magazine's staff photos. Up came Jennifer's profile page. *This is not good,* she thought. *She's far too attractive.*

She wasted no time calling the magazine. A cheerful voice at the other end of the phone said, "Good morning, this is Missy. How may I help you?"

"I'm inquiring if Jennifer Beasley currently works at the magazine."

"Yes, she does. But she's out of the office on assignment.

Who is this?"

Agatha placed the receiver into its cradle. It took every ounce of strength for her to walk downstairs. She entered the office with a forced smile. "Good morning, I'm Agatha Carmine. Welcome to our church. How may I help you?" she asked, trying to steady her nerves.

"Thank you so much for seeing me without an appointment," Jennifer said, wanting desperately to wipe Agatha's sweat from the palm of her hand. "I'm working on a human-interest story about churches across America and the tremendous, positive influence they're having on our youth. There's a definite movement of young people attending church today. I don't have much time, as I'm on a tight deadline."

Agatha felt a slight tinge of relief, and it showed on her face.

We're off to the races, Jennifer thought.

"Let's talk in my office," Agatha said.

Unlike the rest of the opulence, this room appeared to be functional rather than showy: one plain desk, a grouping of chairs, and a row of file cabinets. Photographs lined the walls, showing the church, school, and cemetery in various stages of development.

"What information do you need for your article?" Agatha asked.

"May I record this conversation?"

She hesitated, wanting to say no. *I'll be careful with my answers*, she thought, and reluctantly gave approval.

Jennifer clicked the pen. "For now, I need some basic background info. I see that Lewis Addison founded the church in 1907."

"Pastor Lewis came to Atlanta after his father, the pastor of a small church in Mississippi, was tragically killed in the Civil War as he heroically tried to save the life of his best friend."

"How sad," Jennifer said. *And how untrue,* she thought, holding back the fact that John Addison was murdered long after the war.

"But heaven works in strange ways," Agatha continued with a reassuring smile. "The church elders in Mississippi bequeathed Pastor Lewis a large sum of money to start a new church home in Atlanta. Unfortunately, he came upon hard times and lost all the money. He had to work as a farm hand for Augusto Larson, the original owner of this property. Within a year, Mr. Larson passed away and left his entire estate to his only child, Augusta. At that time, Pastor Lewis acquired five acres from Miss Larson. He was not called to ministry work at that point."

"When you say acquired, was this a gift or did he purchase the land?"

"Oh, it was a gift. It wasn't long after that he decided to enter the ministry," she continued with her scripted account. "His decision precipitated Miss Larson to donate over twenty additional acres to include a school and cemetery. Pastor Lewis got to see the completion of the school but passed away soon after. You can see from the beginning, how this ministry has had favor upon it."

"Yes…it's evident that something here is beyond our understanding."

Agatha shot her a quizzical glance.

"It's indeed…heavenly," Jennifer blurted. She believed in miracles but felt that heaven had little to do with all of this.

Agatha pushed back in her chair. "It's a wonderful story of how a small ministry grew into what we have now. We came from such humble beginnings."

Jennifer felt a prickly sensation on the back of her neck. She shivered at the thought of murder and stolen money as playing a humble role in church prosperity. *But of course,* she reasoned, *the sins of the past have nothing to do with the present. Or do they?*

Agatha sensed a change in Jennifer's manner, and it confused her. She lowered her eyes and opened a leather datebook.

"I'll have to check with Pastor Rhodes first, but he does have some time tomorrow morning if you'd like to interview him and have a tour of the school."

"That would be perfect. What time should I be here?"

"I can schedule you for an eleven o'clock meeting and perhaps lunch in our school cafeteria with our wonderful students. But I will have to confirm this via text later today."

Jennifer smiled. "I certainly appreciate this."

"How did you come to pick *this* church?" asked Agatha with a hint of concern in her voice.

"The bigger the church, the greater the possibility that there would be both an elementary and high school. I have to say that yours is impressive."

This remark brightened Agatha's demeanor.

"I noticed the cemetery as I was coming in. Is Lewis Addison buried there?"

"Oh, yes. The family has the largest mausoleum in the cemetery." We also have a small Civil War section. The Addison-Rhodes mausoleum is not far from there. If you like, I can show it to you before you leave."

"Perhaps tomorrow. I have another appointment, and I'm already late. I won't keep you any longer. Thank you so much for your time. I look forward to meeting Reverend Rhodes. By the way, I assume Lewis Addison was married and had children as Reverend Rhodes is his descendant."

"He married Augusta Larson, and they had a son. Their son had three daughters. Reverend Rhodes is the child of one of their daughters."

"Thank you so much," Jennifer said.

"My pleasure." Agatha wasted no time in escorting her to the parking lot. She gave her a limp handshake, and then joined a group of students.

In the distance, happy children romped in a playground oblivious to the reality of what lay in the cemetery beyond the stone wall. *From the cradle to the grave, life is short; make the most of it,* Jennifer thought.

She got into her car and turned on her cell. A text message was waiting for her. *Our sunny-side is up! Call ASAP!*

She hit #5, and Ralph answered quickly. Before she could say a word, he told her that he had exciting news.

"I gathered that from your sunny-side up idiom," she said.

"The search is over! We tracked the Jackson family. Everything is in my e-mail, so you just have to listen. After arriving in Atlanta, Benjamin Jackson changed his surname to James. Records indicate that James acquired the property on Pryor Street in 1873. He built a house and operated a small tailor shop. By the time of his death, the business had expanded. This is when his son, Little Ben, took over the company and moved the operation to a dress factory on Montgomery Street. It remained at that location until 1945. The business grew into a mega fashion house, known as Little B's Fashions. They're still in business, and still family owned. I don't have to tell you that this discovery is thrilling. Even Alice is cheering! And it only gets better. Let me bring this up to today. Mitchell James, a United States Senator from Georgia, is a direct descendant of Little Ben. He and his wife, Carmella, had two daughters. Lucille, the oldest, had two sons who still own the business. Their younger daughter died during childbirth. She wasn't married; thus her child's name is Teresa James. No big whoop in finding her. Hold on, because this will blow your mind. Teresa not only lives in Atlanta but she works for the FBI. Does it get any better than this? YES!"

"You're incredible!"

"Hold the accolades for one more unbelievable goody. Teresa's boss is...wait for it...Mike Mancuso, my nephew—"

"Get out! You're teasing, right?"

"Dead serious."

"Wow! Talk about everything coming full circle! Am I living in a dream?"

"Well, if it's a dream, I'm thrilled to be in it with you. I love surprises, don't you? I suggest you speak to Mike first, as Teresa might find this whole story a bit crazy. His number is in the e-mail. I'll give him a heads-up on how trustworthy and fabulous you are."

"I'm ecstatic! I have an appointment tomorrow to talk to Reverend Rhodes. Not sure what, if anything, I'm going to learn that I don't already know. It's not likely he'll say anything negative about his family or the church."

"You can count on that. But it's also possible he knows nothing about the past— other than what he was told."

"By the way, I spoke to Sam. He'll be covering my expenses and your bill."

"Just between us, I don't care if I ever get paid for all of this. Not much changes my life or way of thinking, but this has made a very positive impact. Have you moved in with the good doctor yet?"

"I'm not moving in with him, I'm his guest."

"Well, of course, isn't that what I meant? Anything else you need me to follow-up on?"

"Nothing right now. I still don't know how I'm going to get the proof needed for anyone to believe that the soldier in Natchez is Bradley Taylor."

"You'll need a court order for that. I've heard of cold cases, but this one is colder than all those happy penguin feet dancing in Antarctica."

"That's funny!" Jennifer said. "But remember, we do have a judge on our side."

"And that's your ace in the hole!"

CHAPTER 21

An hour later, Jennifer glanced at her watch. She'd stopped to get a bouquet of flowers, and by the time she got back on the road, lunchtime traffic was in full force and a bit daunting.

Her heart quickened as she steadily moved along West Paces Ferry Road. When she pulled up to the intercom camera at the front gate, she adjusted the rearview mirror to check her appearance. A wisp of hair curled over the frame of her sunglasses, and she tucked it behind her ear. After giving her parched lips a swipe of strawberry flavored lip gloss, she pushed the intercom call button, making sure whoever was watching had a full view of her face.

"Been waiting for you, my dear," a sweet voice answered.

The gate opened, and Jennifer slowly eased the car to the front of the house. Before she could turn off the ignition, a plump, older woman with hair the color of salt and pepper hurried down the front steps. "I hope you're hungry because I prepared a special lunch for you." Mrs. B spoke with a soft Jamaican accent.

"Thank you so much. I'm always hungry. These are for you," she said, handing her the bouquet.

Mrs. B lifted the flowers to her nose and thanked her. "Nothing like spring flowers to brighten the day." She squinted in the brilliant sunlight and waved to a man supervising the landscaping crew. "Thomas, please help with Miss Beasley's suitcases!" she called.

Without hesitation, he rushed over.

"You can put everything in the guest room on the first floor," Mrs. B instructed.

"Will do, Aunt B. Nice to meet you, Miss Beasley." He turned and went up the front steps.

Mrs. B took Jennifer by the arm and together they went into the house.

"I made a delicious salad with strawberry dressing, and a chicken is roasting in the oven. Your room is ready. One of the nicest rooms in the house, I might add. Dr. Powell called to say he'll be home for dinner and hopes you could join him if you have no other plans." Her dark eyes sparkled when Jennifer said she was free for dinner.

"Would you like to have lunch outside?" Mrs. B asked. "The gardener and pool people should be finished soon."

"Sounds lovely."

As they crossed the front hall, Thomas walked by, and Mrs. B. told him to come back for lunch. "I'll wait for you in the kitchen," she said.

He rushed off, and she explained that he's one of two nephews working for Dr. Powell. "My other nephew is Oscar Benson. You may have heard of him; he's a retired Atlanta Falcons linebacker." She lowered her voice. "Had a bit of bad luck during his career. Living in the fast lane caused him to almost lose his life. But it was Dr. Powell's help that literally saved him. After rehab, Oscar started his own business…very successful limo service. He's remarried now and has two lovely children. But one thing he didn't forget was what Dr. Powell did for him. I'm very proud of them."

"I can see why you would be." Jennifer smiled and gently touched her arm.

Mrs. B opened the double doors leading into the guest room and stepped aside. "I hope your stay with us will be a pleasant one. This is my favorite room in the entire house. I'll leave you to settle in."

The room was beautifully decorated in an English country motif. French doors opened to a covered slate patio. A brick path circled a garden leading to a pool and guesthouse. On one side of the room, a king four-poster maple bed, topped in creamy colored linen bedding, looked comfortably inviting. On the far wall, a stone fireplace, between floor-to-ceiling windows, overlooked a private garden area with comfortable outdoor furniture.

Jennifer unpacked, filled the drawers of a double dresser, and hung her clothes in a walk-in closet. She placed her toiletries in the bathroom and strolled out to the patio where Mrs. B was busily setting a wrought iron table for lunch.

"Another perfect day," Mrs. B said as she waved to get Thomas's attention. As soon as he noticed her, she motioned for him to stay away from the patio with his loud equipment. He quickly obliged.

"Please enjoy your lunch," Mrs. B said. "It's lovely here at this time of day. And now that the gardening chores are almost done, it will be quiet enough for you to work. Dr. Powell left instructions that you're not to be disturbed."

"There's nothing here that could possibly bother me," Jennifer said, smiling. After lunch, she pondered how to approach Rhodes. *Carefully*, she thought. *Very carefully.* She was well aware that celebrities and dignitaries were often on guard when it came to the media, in particular for writers associated with renowned publications.

Her cell jingled a message. It was from Agatha Carmine. *Your 11:00 a.m. meeting with Reverend Rhodes for tomorrow is confirmed. We look forward to your visit.*

She called Ralph. "Appointment with Rhodes is on for tomorrow."

"Great. FYI, he's married with children and a bunch of pets... lives in a big multi-million dollar house and drives expensive cars. I'm in the wrong profession. Gotta run, Alice is giving me her lunch scream."

In the silence that followed, Jennifer stared out at the pristine gardens. A cloudless sky offered brilliant sunshine, filtering through pale green leaves. The property felt like a secluded park. It wasn't as if she hadn't witnessed other glorious seasons, but this was different. Dare she wonder why?

She poured a glass of sweet tea, leaned back, and closed her eyes. *It's amazing how everything has led me here. But what happens now?* And a small voice in her head answered: *Time to call the FBI.*

Special Agent Mike Mancuso picked up on the second ring. "I was just getting ready to give you a call," he said, sounding as if he'd known her all his life. "My uncle told me all about the story about the marker and of Teresa James's ancestral connection. I'd be happy to introduce the two of you, but I'll have to break the story to her gently. I know her, and she's probably not going to buy any of it. But, *I'm* intrigued."

"It's been an exciting journey. Without Ralph's help, I'd probably be back in New York getting ready to return the marker to the cemetery."

"I commend you on that, most people would try to sell it. I'd like to hear more about the other families connected to the soldier, but I'm getting ready to go into a meeting. Teresa and I will be at Starbucks at four o'clock this afternoon—if that works for you?"

"It does. Thanks so much. Which Starbucks?"

"I'll text you the address. See you later."

She sat back, closed her eyes, and inhaled the refreshing air of spring.

Mrs. B came out to the patio. *I like her,* she thought, nodding. *And I think Jonathan does too.* "Can I get you anything?" she asked.

"Nothing right now. Dr. Powell said it would be okay if I went through the boxes in the attic."

"Of course, you go right ahead. I have baking to finish, but if you need anything, just give me a holler. Hope you like peach cobbler?"

"One of my favorites."

"Well, look at that. It's also Dr. Powell's favorite."

The first word that popped into Jennifer's mind was *delicious,* but she wasn't referring to the peach cobbler.

On her way to the attic, she stopped to take a peek into the master bedroom. The hunter green walls were tastefully decorated with paintings of English hunting scenes, and the rich mahogany furniture was impressive. A loveseat faced a fireplace where French doors opened to a balcony. When she realized that this room was right above the guest room, she smiled. *Well, Jonathan,* she thought, *you'll be sleeping right over me.* A delightful laugh escaped her mouth when she realized the double connotation of her statement.

She climbed the steps to the attic and opened the door. Daylight filtered in from all sides. The boxes they'd looked into the night before were now neatly stacked against the wall. She noticed a small wooden case on top of his mother's desk that wasn't there before. She lifted the lid and looked in. A gold locket with a glass cover rested on letters yellowed with age. She could clearly see a wisp of sandy-colored hair tucked inside the locket. Then, she remembered the pair of white gloves Susie had given her. She rushed to her room to retrieve them.

From the kitchen, she heard Mrs. B's cheerful singing. A rich, sweet aroma filled the air, and she licked her lips. The thought of peach cobbler gave her pause.

"How are you doing?" asked Mrs. B as she passed Jennifer in the hall. "Would you like a cup of tea?"

"Thank you, but not now. I'll be handling family documents, and I don't want to take a chance of spilling anything on them. I'll be down shortly. I have an appointment at four o'clock at Starbucks. Is there a local taxi I can call? I'd rather not drive."

Mrs. B nodded and looked at her watch. "I'll have a car pick you up; hopefully, traffic won't be too bad."

"Mrs. B, you're wonderful!" Jennifer said with a wave, rushing back to the attic.

She slipped on the gloves and gently picked up the locket, wondering whose hair was inside. Placing it down on the table, she took a photo. She removed two envelopes dated 1873. One was from Atlanta; the other from Brandon.

She decided to read the letter from Atlanta first. It was to Rebecca from Matthew, confirming his safe arrival. Jennifer scanned down to the last two words at the bottom, *I found….* She quickly turned the letter over and finished reading the sentence *…the locket of my beloved son's hair when I unpacked a box of Olivia's personal belongings. It is yours now.*

Her heart pounded, and she fought back the tears. "Here it is," she whispered, clutching the locket. "Bradley's DNA."

She carefully opened the letter from Rebecca to her father-in-law. The letter began with the simple words, *I will wear the locket until I die, at which time it will be given to Bradley's first born.*

"Your ride will be here in five minutes!" called Mrs. B.

Jennifer placed the locket and letters back into the box. She went down to her room and got her tote.

Outside, a black limo was parked in front of the house. A tall, husky man, in his late forties, wearing a black suit and dark glasses greeted Mrs. B with a hug.

"Thank you for being on time," she said with affection. She turned to Jennifer. "This is my nephew, Oscar Benson."

"It's nice to meet you, Oscar," she answered, shaking his hand.

"Likewise, Miss Beasley." He looked at his watch. "Better leave now, or you'll be late for your appointment."

He navigated the busy streets like a pro, weaving in and out to avoid traffic. Jennifer found that she liked him right away. Within fifteen minutes, they were in the front of the coffeehouse.

"That was quick," she said.

"I took the back roads; otherwise, we'd be in the thick of it. My aunt said it was important for you to arrive on time. Been told to wait for you. And trust me, when my aunt speaks, we all listen."

"That's great. Where will you be?" Jennifer asked, looking around the crowded parking lot.

"No need to worry. I'll see you when you come out."

CHAPTER 22

A strong scent of fresh coffee permeated the air in the coffeehouse. The line was unusually short, and it wasn't long before a tall, lanky young man took her order for a grande mocha Frappuccino. She paid, gave her name, and waited patiently amid the familiar ambient sounds of the espresso machine and milk frother.

The barista called her name, and Jennifer eagerly took her coffee. One sip confirmed the dependability of her favorite blend.

As expected, there wasn't a place to sit. Almost everyone had electronic devices and used them while sitting alone or with someone. As she maneuvered around comfy leather chairs and crowded tables, bits and pieces of loud, lively chatter distracted her. A melding of faces confused her until she finally saw a man resembling Ralph. He gave a friendly wave.

"I'd know you anywhere," Jennifer said with a bright smile. She sat across from him. "The family resemblance is remarkable. But how did you know me?"

"My uncle sent a photo. You know that man is thorough; once a cop, always a cop. He filled me in on some of the details of the marker, your soldier, and Teresa's family connection to all of this. I have to tell you that she's a straight shooter and a no-nonsense woman—one of our best field agents. But when she heard the story, I could see that she was skeptical."

"I felt the same way. But the overwhelming evidence changed my mind." She placed her cell on the table. He looked at it and laughed. "That's a popular phone cover. My wife has the same one. It's an exact match to our cat."

"Yeah, mine too."

"My uncle's e-mail mentioned three names: Dr. Jonathan Powell, Judge Ronald Aguda, and…." He raised an eyebrow. "Francis Rhodes. Is this the same Rhodes who's the pastor of First Fellowship Church?"

"Yes, do you know him?"

He paused a little too long. "Yeah, I've heard of him."

Jennifer picked up on something in his voice but didn't pressure him. This was not her first time sitting across from an FBI agent.

"How is Rhodes involved in all of this?" he asked.

"His 3rd great-grandfather, John Addison, was a good friend of Bradley Taylor. I have an interview with Rhodes tomorrow, but he knows nothing about this story, and I don't intend to share why I'm really in Atlanta. He thinks I'm doing an article for my magazine, and I'd like to keep it that way for the time being."

"Do you suspect him of any wrongdoing?"

"I don't know him. Actually, I'm not sure if I even need any additional info from him. I pretty much know who did what and where the money came from to build the church in 1907."

And then, there was silence—an uneasy break in the conversation that felt like a forewarning.

Mike fiddled with his phone. He had a peculiar look on his face, as if he wanted to say something but decided against it. He looked at his watch. "I think Teresa is stuck in traffic."

Within a few minutes, a doorbell chime on his cell signaled a message: *I'll be there in a few. You're buying: tall latte and a toasted bagel with cream cheese. Don't forget to leave a tip! TJ*

He lifted his head, letting out a robust laugh that was reminiscent of his uncle.

It wasn't long before a silver sports car pulled into a space in front of the coffee shop. Mike dipped his head slightly, motioning with his eyes that Teresa had arrived.

Like a breath of fresh air, Special Agent Teresa James emerged from the car, her short skirt exposing long, shapely legs. A strong gust of wind tousled her perfectly coiffured jet-black hair, causing it to swoop across a flawless mocha complexion.

With an air of elegance, she slung a designer handbag casually over her shoulder. Her stiletto heels gave her petite frame the appearance of height as they tapped steadily across the pavement. There was a spring of confidence in every step she took. Eyes lifted in her direction as she made her way into the coffeehouse. No one would have taken her for an FBI agent.

"I could have walked here faster," she said, in a strong but feminine voice.

"Not in those shoes," Mike said. "How do you balance on those things? They should be classified as dangerous weapons."

Teresa threw back her head and laughed. "Now that's funny. And where may I ask is my coffee and bagel?"

"Right on it," Mike said with a salute.

Teresa offered Jennifer a firm handshake. "How long have you known Mike?" she asked, tugging at her skirt to try and cover her knees.

"We met today. I'm glad he told you about the marker." Jennifer handed her a business card. "I'm hoping you can fill me in on your family history…in particular, Benjamin, Tilly, and Little Ben Jackson."

"I'd be happy to help, but I don't know much about them, except that they were slaves."

"They may have come here as slaves, but they weren't treated as such in the Taylor family."

"How do you know that?"

"The research material I found confirmed it."

"I remember hearing that their overseer left an inheritance, which I know they used wisely. When I was a little girl, my grandparents told me that Jackson was the family name of the overseer."

"Jackson was the name of Bradley Taylor's aunt."

"I'm not sure if anyone in my family knows why they changed

their name."

"Do you know the name of the family that helped them?"

"I believed it to be Jackson. I don't remember hearing the name Taylor. Apart from that, I have no knowledge. I'm sorry I can't be more helpful. Your story is fascinating, but some of it, especially the part about the seeing a ghost, sounds like fiction. But I'm sure Mike believes it all, as he loves this kind of stuff. My cousin, Anton Fulbright, might be able to help you. I'll give him a call and let him know you'll be contacting him." She took a notebook out of her handbag and wrote Fulbright's address and business number.

Mike returned to the table holding a bagel in one hand and coffee in the other. He set them down. "What do you think?" he asked Teresa.

"I'll keep an open mind," Teresa replied. "This might be an interesting diversion from the latest intelligence regarding the case file we're working on."

Mike gave an understanding nod. "Jennifer has an appointment to see Reverend Francis Rhodes."

Teresa widened her eyes. "Really! What does *he* have to do with all of this?"

Before Jennifer could answer, Mike looked at his phone, hastily got up, and offered an apology. "Teresa, we have to leave. Nice meeting you, Jennifer. Let's keep in touch."

"Please feel free to call me if there's anything else you need,"

Teresa said.

Outside the coffeehouse, the two agents huddled in an animated conversation. Jennifer had a distinct feeling that something was brewing, and it wasn't coffee.

That evening, Jennifer came into the dining room and placed Bradley's Bible on the table near Jonathan's dinner plate. "This belongs to you," she said, explaining how it was found in a box at Metcalf Manor.

He was visibly moved. "What a lovely surprise. I'm going to keep this on my desk in the library."

Later, he asked about her meeting with the two agents. "Did they believe your story?"

"Mike did, but not Teresa. It's okay, though. I'll call her cousin tomorrow morning and go from there."

"What's your strategy for the interview with Rhodes?"

"One thing I won't be asking about is church finances or hint that there might be hidden improprieties. I'm going to steer him into telling me what I want to know. His demeanor and body language will be a good indicator of the direction my questions will take."

"How do you go about that?" Jonathan asked.

"By first making him feel comfortable. He already knows the reputation of the magazine. Once he's convinced that I'm not the enemy, he'll be relaxed, not guarded with his answers."

"Do you think he'll buy it?"

"Can't see why he wouldn't. He has nothing to be suspicious about, and I don't intend to give him any reasons. I'm treating this like any other assignment. I'll explain why we're doing the story and why his church was selected. I've already prepared questions and will be able to give him definitive answers to anything he throws my way."

"Sounds as if you're going in well prepared. I'm impressed."

"But there's a caveat here," said Jennifer with a slight frown."

"What exactly?"

"Even one small error on my part and I'm sure he'll close up quicker than a clam. If there's anything amiss in his life or ministry, he'll be on guard. One wrong question and I could end up with nothing."

Jonathan put his fork down and took a sip of wine. "Do you think he might have something to hide?"

"It's possible. Everything on the outside looks good, but...."

"Ah, it's always the nagging *but.*"

"People who get away with things are usually smart, and they rarely trip up, unless someone comes along and rats them out. I'm banking on his ego, though, and the need for attention. I'm not looking to expose or depose him. I just want to get additional information and, with your approval, have Bradley's body exhumed for DNA proof."

"And what if the DNA doesn't prove your theory?"

"Then I'll have myself committed, and you can sign the papers," she replied with a laugh. "But you see, I know the truth, and I'm willing to stake my reputation on what I've found thus far. Everything from the past has led to this moment in time. For now, I have to count on learning something more from either Rhodes or Teresa's cousin."

"Do you think you're going into this with a preconceived notion that because of Rhodes's ancestry, he's guilty by association?"

"That's a good question," Jennifer said, shaking her head. "I'd like to think I'm fair, but facts are facts. As a writer, it's my job to report the facts and let others decide what the truth is."

"I understand. But you agree that it's possible Rhodes doesn't know anything about Lewis Addison, his father, or the misuse of money? And it's also possible that he's nothing like them."

"Yes, of course."

"Churches today face a whole different set of financial issues. Television and PR budgets could easily run into tens of millions of dollars annually. And the church can pay him as much as they want. There's nothing that says a pastor has to live in poverty."

"I'm not implying that anyone should live in poverty, least of all someone in ministry. But there's a limit. My opinion is that when people are donating to a religious organization, they expect their contributions to help the poor and encourage outreach in the community. I'm not sure if building bigger churches and buying expensive houses and cars is the answer to serving God."

"Let me play the devil's advocate for a moment," Jonathan said. "Big churches bring in lots of people. The more people, the more money received. The more money, the more the church needs to keep up with the overwhelming costs of promoting the ministry. Doesn't that work for the betterment of furthering the message?"

"The premise is right, but history has proven that some are weak when it comes to money and how it's used."

"So then you believe the root of all evil is money?" Jonathan asked.

"No. I believe how it's used can produce either a root of good or of evil. In our lifetime alone, we've seen countless downfalls of corporations, politicians, and ministries that have crumbled in disgrace because of the inappropriate use of funds. Let's take your family's estate as an example. They left a sizeable legacy to the people they loved and wanted to protect. Their faith and moral principles were founded on a strong belief in God, which led them to do the right things with their money. They were people of good conscience, who used their assets wisely. But the person who stole from them was not of good conscience, and the money was not used for good. Oh…my…gosh! How could I forget! I have Bradley's DNA! Earlier today I found a locket on your mother's desk with a small treasure in it. A letter from Rebecca's father-in-law confirmed that it's Bradley's hair."

"I found it this morning when I went to the attic to straighten up. It was in the bottom drawer. I saw the locket, but didn't have time to read the letters."

When Mrs. B stuck her head into the dining room, their conversation ended.

"Jonathan," she said in a sweet, motherly voice. "Would you

like to have dessert on the patio by the pool? It's a lovely evening."

Jonathan nodded in Jennifer's direction.

"I think that sounds perfect, Mrs. B, as does the smell of your peach cobbler," Jennifer replied.

For the rest of the evening, Jennifer steered the conversation away from her interview. Instead, she asked Jonathan to tell her about his childhood.

"It was good…really good. My parents were kind and fun to be around." His eyes lowered, and he shook his head in disbelief.

"I'm so sorry," Jennifer said, touching his hand. "I didn't mean to upset you. I still can't get past my mother's death. She was young and vibrant and gave everything she had to her family. The loss of a parent is bad enough, but to no longer have their unconditional love and support to sustain us through difficult times is a sadness that endures."

As the evening wore on, they talked about school and career choices. Neither of them spoke of previous relationships.

"I can't recall a time when I've enjoyed a quiet evening like this," Jonathan said. "My life is so hectic, I rarely have time to socialize."

"This was enjoyable, and I appreciate your hospitality."

"You're welcome to stay as long as you want."

Early the next morning, Mrs. B served Jennifer her breakfast on the patio. "You're spoiling me," she said.

"Jonathan told me to take care of you, and it's my pleasure.

You're a refreshing change in our daily routine, and I know he's happy to have you here."

The familiar siren announced a call from Ralph, and Mrs. B. walked away to give her privacy.

"Are you still on for today's interview with Rhodes?" Ralph asked.

"Nothing's changed. Has anything come up that I should know?"

"Yes. It appears that Rhodes was involved in something. Let me rephrase that—he was accused by one of his staff of being too much of a hands-on person."

"Clarify, please."

"As in touchy-feely. She issued a complaint to the church board, which was later dismissed as a misunderstanding on her part. This would have never come to light had she not taken it to her brother-in-law, who's a trial lawyer in Atlanta. He didn't take action through the courts, but he did threaten to take action against the church unless a settlement was offered. The woman later gave a signed statement to the church board that Rhodes was only trying to help her after she tripped, coming into his office. Her statement was that he grabbed her and, perhaps, she misunderstood it."

"Wow! Where…how did you find this out?"

"It's all about who you know, my dear. But really, this is off the record…just between us."

Jennifer sighed. "You amaze me. But you do know that it's suspicious at best."

"There's something else. The woman took the money and left Atlanta. No name was given, but my source is reliable."

"She vanished?"

"Yep. Gone…no sign of her anywhere. No missing person issued by anyone, so it's assumed that she went off and started another life with a bundle of cash. Other than that incident, which happened last year, nothing else has come to light. You don't have to rely on your instincts on this one, though. If it were a simple case of misunderstanding, this woman wouldn't have disappeared into thin air."

"You're right," Jennifer said with a sigh. "We can bet if there's one instance of inappropriate behavior, there's more."

"I've known you a long time, so I know your instincts are right on target. What's the next move if you can't find proof?"

"I guess I'll be stuck doing a really boring article on the success of his church and outreach programs. But I'm sure, once Candy sees that there's no real story here, it'll be trashed. I think the public is bored with church gossip. We'll leave that kind of reporting to the tabloid press."

"What about Teresa James? How did she handle all of this?"

"Doesn't believe a word of it, but she gave me her cousin's number, which I'll call as soon as we hang up."

"Great. Keep me posted."

She tried to reach Anton Fulbright, but the call went directly to message.

Within seconds, her cell rang. It was Susie Metcalf.

"Susie, what a pleasant surprise. How are things in Brandon?"

"All is well here…hope the same on your end."

"Yes, a bit of a slow go getting info, but we're chugging along."

"I found something too involved to text, so I decided to give you a call."

"That's great. It's nice to hear your voice," Jennifer said brightly.

"I didn't want anyone here to get suspicious about my inquiries regarding Creekside Church, so I decided not to stay close to home. The research librarian at the Jackson Library is a good friend of mine. She confirmed the sale of the church property, but nothing else. There's no information about who took over after Addison died."

"Another dead end."

"On that front, yes. But last night, I found something we completely missed when you were here. I didn't think to look in the storage room file cabinets where we keep miscellaneous records not connected to any particular person or place. It's a good thing I went through all the folders, or I'd have missed a sealed envelope addressed to Lewis Addison. Can't tell you how excited I was when I saw his name."

"Did you open it?" Jennifer asked.

"Not yet. There's no postage, which indicates that it was never mailed. Someone brought it here for safekeeping, but it was misfiled. I checked the handwriting on the letters and envelopes we have from both families. I'm not an expert, but the classic style shows that it's a match to that of John Addison's journal entries. I think the only person who would have brought it here was—"

"Rebecca Taylor!"

"Exactly!" Susie exclaimed. "If you have time, I'll send the photos to your cell now."

"Of course," Jennifer said.

Susie took a photo of the envelope. She opened it carefully, and gently removed the letter. Laying it on the desk, she snapped another photo and forwarded both to Jennifer. "I'm right about it being from John Addison," she said.

A ping told Jennifer that the photos arrived. She uploaded them to her laptop and studied them carefully. "The letter is written on Creekside Church stationery. Oh, my gosh!"

"What is it?" Susie asked, reaching for a magnifier.

Jennifer enlarged the letter. "There are three dark impressions on the left-hand side of the paper."

"I see that. It looks like...could it be? Fingerprints? But why would fingerprints be on the paper?"

"He must have pressed down with his left hand to hold the paper as he wrote. I think the smears could be...blood. But there aren't any similar markings on the envelope."

"If his hand was bloody, then there would also be some staining on the envelope."

"Not necessarily," Jennifer said. "It's possible he addressed the envelope before he—"

"That's right!" Susie yelled. "The date on the letter is August 25, 1873...the same day of his death."

"The letter appears to be written under duress. As you can see, the words are barely readable; his handwriting is all over the place. Let's see if we can make sense of this.

"Well," said Susie. "The letter is addressed to Lewis...we know that much."

"It's difficult to read, but it appears that John refers to himself as doomed to spend eternity in hell for the sins he committed."

"And he admits that he deliberately set his hand against two people because they got in the way of his ambitions. That's a powerful statement of guilt."

"Ah, near as I can read, he wrote that his journal is missing and something about it falling into the hands of his enemies. I can't make out the last sentence except for the words *Georgia* and *inheritance*," Jennifer said. "As you can see, his pen trails off the paper at that point."

"I can see that. It's as if his life came to an end at that precise moment."

"I think I'm right in saying that Lewis never saw this letter. I have no clue or theory as to who was in his office at the time of his murder...except that Rebecca wrote that neither Bradley nor Little Ben killed him. The only way she'd know that is if she were there. If I find out anything new, I'll call you. I have to leave now for an appointment with a descendant of John Addison."

Susie wanted to say that this was exciting news, but an odd, fearful chill came over her. "Be careful," she murmured.

Jennifer forwarded photos of the envelope and letter to Ralph with a short explanation. As soon as he acknowledged receipt of it, she made another call to Anton Fulbright before leaving for her meeting with Francis Rhodes. Once again, the call went to his voicemail.

CHAPTER 23

Francis Rhodes sat quietly at his ornately carved mahogany desk. He picked up his pen and began doodling on a sheet of paper. His mind raced with thoughts of how he would handle the interview with Jennifer Beasley.

Agatha stood at his door, observing his incessant scribbling. She knew him well enough to know that his anxiety level was over the top.

He looked up at her and eased back in his chair. *Relax,* he said to himself. *Don't overreact or become defensive.*

"She's no ordinary journalist," Agatha said in a small voice. "She's a shark."

"Agatha, please! A shark? Let's not go over the deep end here. You checked her out, and this is a legit story."

"I don't trust anyone in the media," she hissed. "And neither should you."

"I'll handle Miss Beasley. You just make sure that all goes smoothly while we tour the school."

"Why are you doing this? We don't need publicity—especially at this time."

"Don't be overdramatic," Rhodes said, gesturing for her to

leave his office. When she didn't, he crossed his arms and waited. "Your concerns are based on nothing more than insecure jealousy. Every time an attractive woman enters my office you overreact."

Agatha stood her ground. She clenched her hands and drew a deep breath. "I have a bad feeling. We've had to put out far too many fires in order to protect this church."

Rhodes glared at her. "Crazy fool," he hissed. "I should have gotten rid of you years ago."

"That's not a wise thing to say, Francis. I know where the skeletons are buried. Don't ever force my hand."

His cell rang. "What is it?" he asked harshly.

A deep voice at the other end said, "She's here."

Rhodes picked up a stack of folders and stomped over to Agatha. "These need to be filed," he said, shoving them into her chest. "I believe Miss Beasley is here; please show her in."

"Be sure to keep your intercom on," Agatha muttered under her breath.

"I'll do no such thing!" Rhodes moved ahead to greet Jennifer.

Without another word, Agatha rushed out and slipped into her office.

"Thank you, Reverend Rhodes, for seeing me on such short notice," Jennifer said.

Her beauty took him by surprise. He reached for her hand and cradled it, not wanting to let go. She eased it from his grip, and he told himself that she also found him attractive.

To the contrary, though, Jennifer's initial impression was that he was not good looking, and his apparel was equally unattractive. The buttons on his three-piece custom pinstriped suit bulged over his paunchiness. With an air of superiority, he casually strolled to his desk, and the elevated heels of his black patent leather shoes clacked hard against the wooden floor.

He pointed to a chair, and she sat down. She removed her notebook and pen. With a click, the recorder was set, waiting for voice activation.

"As you might know," he said, "I seldom take interviews, but I have a lot of respect for your publication."

"That's good to hear. And I'm very impressed with your church and school."

"Well, thank you. Since I've taken over, the church has expanded. You probably know that I've been married for over forty years—to the same woman, I might add. My wife and I believe in the sanctity of marriage. We have two children, both working in ministry. We are a family dedicated to serving our church and community."

Jennifer wrote in her notebook that he sounded like a politician running for office. *There's no doubt that he perceives himself as charming, charismatic, and believable.*

"We're one of the wealthiest churches in the state," he said. "I don't have to tell you what that means. While other ministries are going bankrupt, ours is flourishing."

She furrowed her brow but said nothing.

He noticed the change in her demeanor. "Well, you know," he added quickly, "no ministry could grow to this stage without divine intervention. I can't speak for all churches, but, as for this one, we continue to grow, and our donations are at an all-time high."

"My article will focus on the resurgence of young people returning to the church and the reasons why. I have no interest in the financial matters of your organization."

He smiled, convinced that she wasn't on a witch-hunt to discredit him. "I'm happy to hear that this article is about our young people. So often, the bigger the church, the more of a target they become."

"I haven't seen any negative press about your ministry."

"That's because we're careful to follow all the laws regarding church and state. Like other big churches, we have a security staff. Can't be too careful these days."

"I didn't see any security people when I came in."

"Oh, I assure you, they're here. The fact that you haven't noticed means they're doing their job. It takes a tremendous amount of money to operate a ministry of this magnitude. But I don't concern myself with the amount that's spent, only that the job gets done and we're protected."

"In what sense do you mean that?"

"Well, for one thing, the media is relentless to get news—

whether it's accurate or not. Nothing sells better than bad news and sex."

"How is your church protected?"

"We retain one of the top PR firms in the country. It's their job to make sure our image doesn't get tarnished. I mean no offense when I say the media is just waiting to discredit churches. One of the reasons I agreed to this interview is because your publication is not a gossipy rag sheet. You know, I'm a subscriber."

Jennifer nodded, knowing that if she stayed quiet his train of thought wouldn't be interrupted and he might venture into another topic.

"Your article on adultery was, in my estimation, award-winning. Very fair; although I feel it missed the mark by not mentioning that it's a sin."

Jennifer offered an apologetic shrug. "I'm sure you understand that some editors don't share the same belief system that…." She paused to weigh her next words carefully. "That we have."

"Oh, of course," he said, sounding pleased. "I'm happy to hear that your beliefs coincide with mine. But I, as a reader, would have liked to see a verse…you know, to affirm that point."

"There was biblical text in the article," Jennifer said, holding back a smile of vindication.

"I must have missed it," he said, narrowing his eyes.

"Let me see if I can quote it correctly…if *anyone* looks at a woman lustfully, he has already committed adultery with her in his heart."

Rhodes fixed his cold eyes on her. His mouth twitched, and she could see that he was uncomfortable.

He grabbed the armrests of his chair and pushed back. "Right, of course. It was a well-written article, and I enjoyed it."

"What are some of your goals for the future?" she asked.

"My biggest goal is to ensure that no improprieties upset my ministry or my private life. I've seen far too many preachers topple off their pulpits because of...well, how shall I say...because of minor indiscretions."

"I'm not sure I understand. Can you give me an example?"

"Well, there's always an issue with misappropriation of funds or misinterpretations of one's actions by others. Ministries and their leaders are always under a watchful eye. I always make sure to hold myself to a higher standard. I provide full and comprehensive disclosure of donations, my salary, and staff compensations. We are, after all, responsible for showing our congregants and world partners that we're good and faithful stewards of their money."

"I totally agree," Jennifer said, knowing that he was avoiding any mention of the accusation against him from a former member.

"If you like, Agatha will take you on a tour of the school now," he said. "I have a lunch appointment with the mayor, so my time is limited. We can certainly continue this interview...." He paused and flicked through the pages of his datebook. He looked up and shrugged. "I'm in meetings most of tomorrow, and I have a dinner engagement. I'll be free on Friday…but…it will have to be at six-thirty in the evening. That's the only time I have available. Anyway, fewer interruptions and no school events are planned because it's the start of spring break."

"I'm on a deadline, so I'll have to make it work. Thanks so much for doing this on such short notice."

"May I ask why this interview wasn't scheduled in advance?" he asked.

"Internal problems with scheduling. It happens all the time in publishing. I was actually assigned to another story with two interviews here in Atlanta. So when the senior writer assigned to this article up and quit, I was the logical one to complete the assignment. Not professional, but these things happen."

"Wonderful. And I'm glad *you're* doing it. I hope I can help you meet your deadline." He pushed a button on his phone, and his secretary rushed in.

"Agatha, please join us for a tour of the school," he said with a pleasant smile.

Jennifer noticed an expression of relief on his secretary's face. But it wasn't until the end of the tour that her countenance brightened.

Thank goodness, it's over, Agatha thought with a relaxed sigh. *I guess I did overreact.*

CHAPTER 24

Jennifer had mixed thoughts as she pulled out of the church parking lot. She couldn't shake off the feeling that something sinister was hidden underneath Rhodes's religious exterior.

She stopped at a red light and tried Anton Fulbright's number. A cheerful voice boomed through the car's Bluetooth.

"Sorry for not calling you back," he said. "Teresa explained a little about why you're here. I have some family documents…not many, but you're welcome to take a look at them. I'll check with my brother later and see if he has anything to share. If you like, I'll be in my office tomorrow. You can drop by in the morning, anytime after eight, as it's usually quiet then."

"That's perfect," Jennifer said, and the call disconnected. *I'm closing in*, she thought, hoping that her words reached Dr. Taylor.

Later in the day, Jennifer changed into a pair of capris and tank top. She went out to sit by the pool. No one was in sight. She held her head up to the sun and embraced the warmth, the serenity of the garden, and the feeling that she belonged in this place. Before long, she heard footsteps along the pathway.

Jonathan walked toward her with a child's shoebox in his hand, followed by Mrs. B, carrying a tray with sweet tea and cookies.

As soon as Jennifer saw him, her face brightened. This did not go unnoticed by Mrs. B. She placed the tray down and rushed away with a grin on her face. "*Privacy*, she thought. *That's what they need.*

Jonathan poured two glasses of tea and handed one to Jennifer.

"Another great find?" she asked, gazing at the box.

"I remembered something my mother said many years ago. I think it was before I graduated high school, actually. She told me that when I found the love of my life—those were her exact words—she would give me my great-great-grandparents' love letters. I was to read them with the person I was going to marry."

Jennifer had a disappointed look on her face, believing that he was talking about Susan.

"I went crazy trying to find them," he said, shaking his head. "We already looked in every box in the attic, so I didn't go there. I was about to give up when I remembered that my mother loved to sit and read in the back guest room upstairs, which has a window seat facing the greenhouse at the south end of the property. I searched every bit of that room, going through the closet, dresser drawers…I even looked under the bed. Then, by chance, I lifted the window seat and found things she'd obviously held close to her heart. There were her favorite books, an e-reader, various pieces of baby clothing, which I assume are mine." He laughed and held up the little box. "And then I saw this Buster

Brown shoebox. I honestly thought there was a pair of my shoes in here. Imagine my surprise when I found letters. Of the ten letters, my mom singled out only two, which she placed in a separate envelope with my name on it."

And together, they stared at the envelope.

"Did you read these with your fiancée?" she asked and then regretted the question.

"My mother never gave me these letters."

Jennifer looked into his eyes and what she saw melted her heart. Her face softened, and her mouth opened to say something comforting, but words eluded her. They looked at each other, and a bolt of electricity passed between them. She didn't care if the expression on her face revealed her tender feelings for him.

"I'd like to read them...together," he said.

"Do you want to do that now?"

"We can, or we can wait. It's up to you."

"Let's wait," she said. "You'll know when it's the right time."

"Before I met you, I never gave any thought to my ancestry. I know this will sound terrible, but apart from my parents and my work, nothing mattered to me. I lived in the moment and drowned myself in the many duties of being a doctor. But that was before I met you." He stared at her, wanting to reveal his true feelings but thought that it was too soon. He changed the subject. "How was your meeting with Rhodes?"

She gave him a full account. "He seemed straightforward but…."

"So basically, you didn't learn anything new?"

"No, but at times he seemed a bit odd; although, it's too early for me to put my finger on what it is. There's definitely something amiss with that man. I have another meeting with him Friday night at six-thirty. He said it's the only time he has available."

"I have a charity function that night, and I was hoping we could go together."

Jennifer couldn't hold back her enthusiasm. "I'd love it!" she said quickly. "What time?"

"We'll have to leave here no later than eight-thirty. But it's formal—black-tie. Will that work?"

"I'll make it all work. But I'll need to go shopping."

"We can go to Phipps Plaza…great shopping there. I have a staff meeting tomorrow morning, but I'll be back by noon. If you like, we can spend the afternoon shopping and have a late supper." He moved forward. "There's definitely something between us. I think we need to find out what it is, and I hope you feel the same way too."

She nodded happily. "I do, and I think time together is just what the doctor ordered. I'll be seeing Fulbright in the morning. And, for the rest of the day, we'll definitely get to know each other."

He didn't hide his excitement. "Oscar will take you to Fulbright and then pick me up at my office; this way we won't have to fight traffic. I have to check in on a patient now. If you're free, you could come with me…I won't be long. After that, I'm going over to Oakland Cemetery. Sarah Aguda's headstone was set, and I wasn't able to be there with Ronald and his family this morning. I want to pay my respects and also take you over to *my* family mausoleum."

"Dr. Powell, you sure know how to turn a girl on."

And, for the first time in over a year, joyful laughter spilled across the Powell property.

Upstairs, in the master bedroom, Mrs. B giggled as she secretly watched from the window. "It's about time," she whispered.

It was late afternoon when they reached the cemetery. Tombstones and mausoleums crowded their range of vision, but neither felt melancholy. Their thoughts centered on each other.

Jennifer allowed herself a brief moment to think of her family back in New York. *Dad and Billy would adore Jonathan,"* she thought, sneaking a glance at his handsome profile.

They felt comfortable walking together. It was as if they, and this solemn place, were in a protective bubble where the chaotic clamor of the outside world couldn't penetrate their peaceful reality.

He reached out for her hand, and the moment she felt his touch, she obligingly took hold, as if it were the most natural thing to do. At that moment, a strong bond was forged that neither could deny.

They walked silently to a majestic stone angel. A simple inscription at its base— *Till we meet again in our heavenly home—*

marked Sarah Aguda's gravesite.

"What was she like?" Jennifer asked.

"She was grace and beauty and love. She filled a huge void for me this past year. All who knew her adored her."

He never let go of her hand, explaining that Sarah was to be the chairperson of the charity event. "Ronald will be there, as will the rest of her family. I think they'll be a tribute to her."

"I'm looking forward to it. What a great way to mark our first date," she said.

He looked deep into her eyes. "I'm not sure this is our first date. I feel as if we've known each other for a very long time."

He caught the sparkle in her warm eyes and knew that his optimism mirrored hers. If either gave thought as to how this all happened, they certainly didn't articulate it. But when their eyes locked, a silent agreement of *this was meant to be* was understood.

Jennifer didn't give a thought that things were moving quickly between them, as she did when Jake tried to pressure her. Her wait was over, and this was now her time to find happiness.

Jonathan glanced at his watch. He took out his cell and called Mrs. B. "Jennifer and I will definitely be home for dinner," he said.

Home for dinner! His words resonated in all three minds and the reaction of delight was evident.

Reaching again for Jennifer's hand, he led the way to his family mausoleum where two stone benches offered visitors a place to rest and meditate. Above the bronze door, the bold etching of the Taylor-Powell names stood out.

Jonathan unlocked the door. As soon as it opened, they felt the coolness of the sealed tomb. The setting sun cast its glow through a stained glass window, and a hue of colors streaked the granite floor.

On the right side were the Powell family vaults, but only two names were inscribed on the marble: James Powell and Constance Taylor Powell. Along the left wall, the Taylor family vaults bore the names of Matthew B. Taylor and Olivia Taylor, Rebecca Taylor and Bradley Taylor Sr. Underneath, were the names of Bradley Taylor Jr. and Elizabeth Cumming Taylor, and Matthew J. Taylor and Susanna Perkins Taylor. No other vaults were available on that side.

In her mind, Jennifer questioned the Taylor names, while Jonathan looked lovingly at his parents' side.

"Something isn't right," she whispered. "How could Bradley and his mother be here when Olivia is buried in Brandon, and Bradley is in Natchez?"

To her surprise, he put his arm tightly around her. "I'm so sorry. I kept reminding myself to tell you, but there were so many things happening at once that I forgot. Matthew B.," he said, pointing to the top vault, "had the mausoleum built in 1895. At that time he must have thought that Olivia and Bradley's remains would someday be brought to Atlanta. When we first met, you said that Bradley was buried in Natchez. That's why I was so adamant about you being wrong. But something gnawed at me, so I looked at the original documents regarding the mausoleum. It clearly stated that two vaults were empty. That's when I knew—even though I had a difficult time with most of the story—that you were telling the truth. I hope you're not angry with me."

"Absolutely not. If nothing else comes out of all of this, I know we've done our best. Standing here, I feel as if they've all come to life. I want to tell Bradley that I found them."

"I have a feeling somebody already did that."

"There's more," Jennifer said. "I want to tell him that I found... *you*. This is going to sound strange, especially coming from me, but I feel as if I've been waiting for you all my life."

At that moment, in the middle of the family mausoleum, they shared a passionate embrace. When their lips touched, it not only cemented their feelings but also their passion for one another.

Later that night, Mrs. B served dinner in the kitchen. She was pleased that they wanted to eat there and that something had changed between them. She even noticed how relaxed they were and how much laughter surrounded their conversations. They sat close, as if not wanting to be apart. At times, Jonathan touched Jennifer's hand and she sparkled.

When Mrs. B overheard their plans for the next day, a smile of happiness filled her face. And that's when she knew that she had to do something.

"These lamb chops are delicious, Mrs. B," Jennifer said.

"Jonathan's favorite. He likes almost everything. A little too picky, though, when it comes to breakfast. That is the most important meal of the day."

"You're right, Mrs. B," Jonathan said, raising his eyebrows in approval.

Mrs. B excused herself, saying she had to make a call.

"Speaking of calls, I left my cell in the car. I'll be right back," he said.

Jennifer sat back and closed her eyes. *What an absolutely beautiful day. Okay, tomorrow is Thursday; Fulbright in the morning. Friday night Rhodes, and then the charity event.*

"No messages," Jonathan said, sounding relieved.

Mrs. B rushed in, wrapping a sweater tightly around her shoulders. "Oscar's coming to get me…so I can visit my sister. She's not feeling well; I'll bring her some chicken soup. I might stay over…not sure. I prepared a delicious dessert but—"

"I think Jennifer and I can take care of dessert. You go on ahead. Let me know if you need me."

"Thank you, both. Enjoy the rest of the evening. I'll see you in the morning."

"I'll make coffee," Jonathan said, carrying the dishes to the sink.

"And I'll load the dishwasher. This kitchen is a cook's dream."

"Do you like to cook?" he asked.

"In this kitchen, I think I'd like to do just about everything." As soon as the words spilled out, she threw back her head and laughed.

The sound of her laughter hit him like a wave—softly at first and then, as he moved toward her, it crashed into him, leaving him breathless. He reached out and pulled her close.

She didn't resist.

"What's for dessert?" she asked in a low, sexy voice.

"You are," he whispered. His breathing grew heavy as his lips gently brushed against her hair, and he pulled her closer. "You didn't answer my question. Do you like to cook?"

"Yes, I do," she answered, melting into his embrace.

"That's all I need to know." His lips traced her face, stopping when they reached her mouth. And as if they were standing above the epicenter of an earthquake, their bodies trembled in waves of passionate desire. He gently moved his finger across her lips, around her face, and down her neck. He kissed her eyelids and then her nose. He purposely avoided her lips, which she parted, waiting for his kiss.

She trembled as he moved his hands across her back and around to her hips. His touch sent the blood rushing through her veins. The warmth of his mouth against her skin sent lightning bolts through her.

"I don't want you once, I want you for the rest of my life," he said. "And when I make love to you, I'm not walking away. I won't be able to."

"I don't intend to ever let *you* go," she whispered.

CHAPTER 25

Early the next morning, Jonathan kissed the sleepy face that nestled close to him. "Don't get up," he whispered. "I have to call my office. I'll be right back."

A deep feeling of contentment followed him out of the guest room. Before closing the door, he turned and looked at the one person he'd been waiting for all his life. "I'm never letting go of you either," he said softly.

He went into the kitchen and found it just the way they'd left it the night before. Realizing that Mrs. B wasn't home, he let out a sigh of relief. After picking up his phone by the coffee machine, he sat at the country table facing the French doors where a view of the garden gave him pause. *It's really lovely looking out from here,* he said to himself.

He called his office and spoke to his partner. "Jim, I'll be a little late for our meeting this morning," he said. "And, by the way, I'm going to take a few days off." He didn't give a reason why.

The silence at the other end was not surprising.

Finally, he heard Jim laugh. "It's about time. Never thought I'd see this day."

"Me either."

"There's nothing pressing here. Actually, it's unusually quiet this morning. See you later."

Just as Jonathan was getting ready to plug in the coffeemaker, he looked out the window and saw Mrs. B and Oscar coming up the rear path, heading to the back door. He darted upstairs and sent a text to Jennifer that Mrs. B was back. He felt like a schoolboy who got caught making out in the backseat of his dad's car.

Jennifer looked at the time and scrambled out of bed. She showered and dressed in record-breaking time, excited about her meeting with Fulbright and spending the day with Jonathan. *Today is the beginning of endless possibilities,* she thought. But her mind and heart centered only on Jonathan. She couldn't wait to see him, to touch him, and to love him. She sent texts to her dad and Billy with the simple words *I found my soul mate.* And instantly, the two most important men in her life knew it was Dr. Jonathan Powell. Emojis—from corks popping, to bouncing hearts, to streamers flying in the air—filled her message app.

By the time Jonathan came downstairs, Mrs. B already had the kitchen in motion. The rich aroma of coffee, the sizzling of sausage patties, and country biscuits rising to a golden brown in the oven made him surprisingly happy.

Oscar was standing at the counter, checking the traffic app on his cell. "Are we still on for today?"

"What's your schedule, Oscar?" Jonathan asked.

"The new cars are being detailed…should be ready later today. Apart from that, I'm available."

"You can take me to the office and then pick me up after Jennifer's meeting." He turned to Mrs. B. "I'm starving! Everything smells delicious."

Jennifer bounced into the kitchen. "Good morning! It smells delicious in here."

And then, as if he'd been doing it for years, he poured her a cup of coffee and set it down on the table. He sat beside her and marveled at how comfortable it felt to be near her. He couldn't remember the last time he had breakfast in the kitchen. Usually, he'd pass through, grabbing a cup of coffee or a muffin, and didn't take notice of anything else "You know," he said, to no one in particular, "this kitchen has a pulse. Can you feel it?"

"That's because it's the heart of the home," Mrs. B said with a bright smile.

"And look at the beautiful view we have," he said as if seeing it for the first time. "I think we'll have breakfast right here, every morning, from now on."

No one noticed the smile on Mrs. B's face or heard her thoughts that staying out last night turned out to be a good thing after all. "I'm happy to see that everyone is starving this morning. And that a particular someone is not only hungry but has also finally noticed the lovely view."

"I notice things, Mrs. B," Jonathan said with a wink.

"Will wonders never cease?" she replied, shaking her head.

"Join us, Oscar," Jonathan said. "How's traffic this morning?"

"We'll be okay. But we'll have to leave soon."

Mrs. B looked out the kitchen window that faced her herb garden. "Dinner at home tonight?" she asked without turning around.

Jonathan looked at Jennifer.

"Yes," she answered. "We'll be dining in."

And at that moment, Mrs. B knew that her wish came true.

Thirty minutes later, Jonathan was sitting in a meeting going over new plans for three satellite healthcare centers in the surrounding Atlanta suburbs. Although the meeting was intense, his thoughts were not far from Jennifer. He had no doubts that from the moment his eyes met hers he fell in love. He didn't ponder the whys of it; he accepted that a greater plan existed long before either of them met. He fought to keep himself from laughing out loud or, worse yet, uttering her name to everyone in the room.

Across town, Jennifer had the same problem. She was glad that Anton Fulbright gave her a tour of Little B's factory and that the incessant humming of sewing machines and chatter from garment workers drowned out the urge to shout that she loved Jonathan Powell. Saying it last night was natural as if she'd loved him all her life. She had no problem expressing it, repeatedly.

Fulbright took her up to the second level where designers and stylists were busily working on dress forms and live models. "We're finishing our line for the New York Fashion Week this September," he explained.

The realization of Little Ben's legacy was remarkable, and she was filled with new excitement as Fulbright led her to his office.

They sat at a table. "I hope you can make sense of this," he said, laying out a few documents and a tattered notebook. "The documents are nothing more than land deeds and my grandparents' marriage certificate. Much of the information in the notebook is sketchy. Seems to me there are a lot of innuendoes and none of it makes sense. Even my father and grandfather didn't understand it. And why the name change? It's all rather confusing, but I'm grateful for the little we have and that it's been preserved. Please feel free to make copies of what you think you'll need for your research."

"That's very kind of you," Jennifer said. She explained some of what she'd learned about Benjamin, Tilly, and Little Ben and how they came to be with the Taylor family. She purposefully left out the part of seeing Dr. Taylor at his gravesite in Natchez. If he knew anything about it, he didn't say.

Ralph's discoveries were confirmed by what she reviewed. Disappointment at not finding anything new, however, didn't dampen her spirits. She carefully opened the small, fragile notebook that was badly yellowed with age.

A woman knocked on the office door and told Fulbright that he was needed in the cutting room.

"Please take your time, Miss Beasley," he said. "I'll be right back."

Jennifer clicked her pen to record what was legible and also interject her own comments so she wouldn't forget.

"This notebook," she began, "was definitely written by Benjamin James. There's no date and its title, The James Family, indicates that he wrote this after they moved to Atlanta and changed the family name. Although some of the words are difficult to decipher, there's no indication in the tone of any stress in their lives. Benjamin noted that they lived in the Great House, which I think was in Mississippi, and that they didn't have slave quarters. He wrote that he would never forget his best friend but didn't give a name. There's no mention of John Addison or the incident surrounding his death. Interestingly, nowhere in the text does it refer to the surname Jackson."

Jennifer was about to close the notebook when she noticed three folded pieces of paper under the last page. She opened them carefully and laid them on the table. "Each one has child-like drawings and scribbled words that are difficult to read. The text is written with the sweet innocence and imagination befitting a child."

She snapped a photo and recorded that Little Ben liked to fish every day at the Creekside pond behind the church with his friend. "The drawing at the bottom of the page is of two stick people, fishing. The names Bradley and Ben are scribbled underneath.

"The second drawing is of a book and the same little stick people. I can only make out a few words…it appears that they looked into Pastor John's office and saw him hide a book under the floor. They also saw a gun and sword on the desk.

"At the bottom of the last piece of paper, there's a big stick figure holding the sword. I'm going to paraphrase this as best as I can. Miss Rebecca needs help…Pastor John killed Bradley. Little Ben's final words were that there was a loud sound that hurt their ears."

Jennifer was convinced that Rebecca, Bradley, and Little Ben were in Addison's office at the time he was shot. The only thing she didn't know was who pulled the trigger. *I don't think we'll ever know the truth, and that's okay,* she thought sadly, believing that whoever it was, did it in self-defense against a lunatic.

The office door opened abruptly, and she nearly jumped out of her chair.

"Sorry. I didn't mean to scare you," Fulbright said. "Did you learn anything?"

"Yes, I did. The notebook is a treasure, and I'm very grateful that you've allowed me to see it. Your ancestors were remarkable people. They left a legacy of love and kindness. It has been a pleasure to meet you and Teresa. Thank you for taking the time to show me your family history."

"It's my pleasure. I will tell Teresa that you came by today. Have a great weekend, and I hope to see you again." He accompanied her outside, and she introduced him to Oscar.

"My wife loves your clothing," Oscar said.

"You're Oscar Benson. Wow! I'm a fan. What a pleasure to meet you."

"The pleasure is all mine," Oscar replied.

As they drove out of the parking lot, a wave of sadness filled Jennifer's heart. *Addison killed Bradley, and the reasons why are no longer important.*

Oscar looked in the rear view mirror. The look on Jennifer's face concerned him. "The doc called and said he's ready when we are. Shouldn't take us long to get to his office. Did you have a good meeting?"

"Yes, it was very good." Her mind drifted. *The last piece of the puzzle is Rhodes. And then, Jonathan and I can....*"

"You know, Miss Beasley the doc saved my life."

She didn't let on that she already knew. Instead, she asked him to call her by her first name.

"Thank you, I'll do that from now on. The doc was the first to recognize that I was about to lose everything. My manager, accountant, and first wife ravaged my finances. I began drinking heavily. I was once a multi-millionaire but ended up so deep in debt that I didn't have enough cash to buy a cup of coffee. The doc took me in, got me into rehab, and his accountant took over what little was left of my finances. It was a long road back, but I found my way, and the doc played a significant role in making it all possible. There he is now!"

Jonathan rushed into the car and gave her a passionate kiss. She melted into his arms.

Oscar turned his eyes away. *Oh, wow! Wait till I tell Aunt B.* He cleared his throat. "Where to now?"

"Home," Jonathan said. "I'll be using my car for the rest of the day. We've got shopping to do. But we'll need you tomorrow night if that's OK?"

"Whatever you say," Oscar answered with a smile.

"Jennifer has a 6:30 interview at First Fellowship Church, and then we're off to the charity event at the Georgia Aquarium Ocean Ballroom. The good news is that we won't need you for the rest of the weekend."

Oscar laughed. "Not sure if that's good news or not. Between Aunt B and my wife, they'll have me running all over town with errands the likes of which you can't even imagine."

Before leaving for Phipps Plaza, Jennifer went to her room and quickly inserted her pen's flash drive into her laptop. She watched as her words scrolled down the screen. She saved her work, forwarded a copy to Ralph and Susie, and went to look for Jonathan. When she saw him and Mrs. B heading toward the pool, she decided to wait for him in the house.

"You know, Mrs. B," Jonathan said quietly. "I loved Susan, but I wasn't in love with her."

"I've known that for a long time."

"After the accident, I convinced myself that I'd never fall in love again. But then, I met Jennifer."

"I saw from the beginning how you looked at her. This is an answer to my prayers."

"Your approval means a lot to me. You're the only family I have."

"You found your destiny," Mrs. B said quickly. "And I couldn't he happier. Make your plans and don't let her get away."

He hugged her.

Now, with his mind and heart in sync, life took on a whole new look and meaning. And so, for the next few hours, he and Jennifer did something that neither of them had done in years: they shopped. And like two kids in a candy store, everything looked sweet and exciting.

He helped pick out an evening dress, shoes, and a satin clutch.

She gave her opinion about a new suit for him. She picked out a tie and even a French coffee press he wanted to buy for over a year.

Every time she pulled out her credit card to pay, he pushed his forward.

"You can't buy everything," she said.

"Oh, yes, I can," he said. He looked deep into her warm eyes and saw his present and future with only her.

"Dr. Powell, you don't want to begin this relationship by spoiling me."

"I don't see it as spoiling; I see it as loving. And by the way, before we take another step forward, I want you to stay. You can write your book here and we can—"

"I need to clear something up right now! I have no intention of leaving."

And for the rest of the day and night, he enjoyed being loved in a way he'd never dreamed possible.

CHAPTER 26

Friday morning began as a perfect spring day in Atlanta. Bluebirds and sparrows sang in harmony as balmy breezes rustled the leaves in lofty trees, casting shadows that danced along the paths and flowerbeds.

Jennifer noticed everything as she inhaled the sweet scents of the morning. The rich aroma of coffee and the smell of freshly mowed lawn gave her pause for thought. *I want to live here forever.*

Mrs. B was nearby, humming happily, setting the table for breakfast. "Miss Jennifer, this is going to be a most spectacular day. Are you almost finished with your work?"

"Tonight is the last interview and then…."

"And then your book? Dr. Powell told me you're going to stay with us. I'm beyond delighted."

"Thank you. But I haven't told my family or my boss yet."

"You'll find the right time," she replied gently. "Everything in life has its own time and place. You've found your place. The rest will happen in its own time."

"You're very sweet. And thank you for accepting me into Jonathan's life and yours too. You mean the world to him."

"My dear, I can now breathe easy knowing that he will have a life with you. I wish his dear, sweet mother were here to see it."

"I wonder if she'd be happy for us. He was with Susan for such a long time."

"Being with someone you love like a friend doesn't make for a strong marriage. Mrs. Powell knew that, but she had faith that her son would find the right person. And he has. We should never second guess what is meant to be in life."

"A woman in New York had a dream and said I was going to meet a man and we'd fall in love. At first, I brushed it off as nonsense. But she was right."

"Who's right?" Jonathan asked, walking into the kitchen.

"Someone told me I was going to fall in love with a handsome, kind, and gentle man," Jennifer answered.

"Oh, no," Jonathan said without a trace of a smile. "That's not going to happen. You're already in love with me."

Both Jennifer and Mrs. B expressed amusement at his serious face. He finally burst into laughter and asked, "What's for breakfast?"

Mrs. B widened her eyes. "Your favorite when you were a little boy. Chocolate chip pancakes!"

"Could this day get any better?" he asked.

She nodded and turned back to preparing the batter.

He leaned forward and took Jennifer's hand. "Have you told your family...about us?"

"Yes, but I'm not sure how they're going to take the news that

I'm staying."

"How about we fly up and tell them together?"

"I'd like that," she answered.

"I'll make reservations for tomorrow afternoon, and we can stay until Wednesday."

"Perfect. As soon as you have the schedule, I'll text my dad. He and Billy will be thrilled."

"By the way, Oscar will be here at a quarter to six," Jonathan said.

"I'll be ready. I have everything laid out for tonight. All I have to do is slip on the dress and the shoes, and we'll be good to go. I'll be home…love the sound of that…by seven fifteen, no later."

The day slipped by gloriously slow for them. Jonathan made the airline reservations, while Jennifer spoke to Ralph.

"How's it going with y'all in Atlanta?" he asked in a deep Southern drawl.

"Not a very good accent. But then again, you're Italian."

"Come va con tutti voi a Atlanta?"

"Ah, now that's authentic. Things are happening at a fast pace. Jonathan and I are flying up to New York tomorrow, and I'd like you to meet him if you have time."

"You're planning to stay in Atlanta, aren't you?"

"You are too smart for your own good. Do you have a tail on me?"

"Don't need to. I can hear it in your voice. I'm thrilled for you. And yes, Alice and I will make time to see you both. Just let me know when and where. Are you still on with Rhodes?"

"Yes. Any advice?"

"Cancel. He's not going to reveal his true self or tell you anything about his church, finances, or inappropriate involvements. Remember the Mafia hit man?"

"I still have the scar on my leg from that lunatic. You don't think—"

"I do!" he interrupted. "Look, we've been working together for a long time. Much of what we've seen turned out to be harmless, but a few were potentially dangerous. If you're still bent on this meeting, don't trust him. Take mace or, better yet, carry a big stick."

Jennifer laughed. "If it makes you feel any better, Oscar will be driving me and will wait outside. He's not someone to mess with, so I think I'll be okay."

"What's our distress code?"

"Pasta fagioli. I could never forget it, or its delicious taste. Will you make it for us when we visit?"

"Will do. Give Jonathan my house and cell numbers. I expect a text from you later, right after the interview. Don't forget!"

"You can count on that."

Jonathan glanced out to the patio and saw that Jennifer was off the phone. He took the letters written by Bradley and Rebecca over to the table, sat down, and looked at his watch. "We have time to read them," he said.

She pulled her chair closer to him. "Before we begin, Ralph told me to give you his contact numbers."

Jonathan added both numbers into his cell. "Does he anticipate a problem?"

"I don't think so. He's the type of person who covers all his bases and doesn't leave anything to chance."

"I understand that. Let's get into these letters. Remember, they're the one's my mom wanted me to read with the woman I'm going to marry."

"Say that again."

"Which part?"

"The woman part."

"Sorry, haven't asked for her dad's approval yet."

Jennifer laughed. "Well, in that case, let's read."

They sat close and read the first letter dated 1857 from Rebecca to Bradley.

My dearest Bradley,

I am counting the days until we shall become husband and wife. With all the many preparations, time will pass quickly.

My family and I are very grateful that your parents have graciously offered to host the reception at Tall Oaks. I can not think of a better place for us to share our love and happiness with family and friends.

When my father and I came to visit Brandon four months ago, I never dreamed that we would meet and fall in love. Nor did I know that he would have wholeheartedly given his approval. The joy and overwhelming support we have received from both our families has made our temporary separation almost bearable.

I know it has been difficult for you to understand why John is opposed to us marrying, and why he has refused to perform the ceremony at your church. Please try to forgive him, as he is quite distressed over the news that his wife is seeking a separation. I can never imagine how I would survive being apart from you. It is truly sad that their union has been destroyed by vicious rumors and no doubt lies about his handlings of church matters.

I am especially grateful that my cousin has agreed to marry us at his church in Jackson. In just two short weeks we shall be standing before God and family to unite in holy matrimony. I am counting the days.

I have loved you from moment our eyes met. In you, I have found the person I have been waiting for all my life. If you ask how long I will love you, I will say for eternity. If you ask how much I need you, I will say until the end of time. You are my beginning and end. I love you beyond my frail human understanding, and it thrills me that our love will soon make us one flesh before God. I pray that our generations will someday know this kind of love.

Good night, my beloved. Rebecca.

Jonathan took hold of Jennifer's hand. "Rebecca's prayer has been answered," he said. "I would never have met you had it not been for the marker. I hope there are no doubts in your mind."

"None whatsoever," Jennifer said, nestling in his embrace.

Together, they read Bradley's letter to Rebecca, dated 1863, just prior to his death.

My darling, sweet wife,

Much of my time has been spent tending to the wounded. It is quiet now, and I am relieved not to hear agonizing voices crying out for loved ones.

Every hour of every day you and Bradley are in my thoughts. The both of you have been my salvation through this long and terrible war. Although miles separate us, our love bridges the gap and keeps me strong.

Your constant love, and my decision not to allow this dreadful war to rob me of faith in my fellow man, has protected me. So many have been deprived of life, home, and loved ones. I refuse to allow the hatred I've seen on the battlefield take one tittle away from what we have and what we will accomplish in our lives when I return home.

And now, my love, I bring news that I am coming back to Brandon to assist at Metcalf Manor hospital in less than two weeks. When I return home, I will devote my life to you and our son. I will always honor my oath as a doctor, but family will come first.

I close for now, as my eyes are heavy with sleep. And yes, my love, even in sleep you are with me. I embrace the image of you in my mind and hold your beautiful face close as my beating heart waits for the time we will be together.

Your loving and devoted husband, Bradley.

"I now understand why my mother told me about these letters. It feels as if my great-great-grandparents' words were meant just for us; especially Bradley's vow that his family would come first in his life."

A feeling of joy swept over Jennifer. "The letters are Bradley and Rebecca's final message to us. But how sad that he never made it home. Addison had to know that he was leaving. That's why he murdered him."

"Excuse me, Jennifer," Oscar called from the other side of the patio. "We have to leave soon. Friday traffic is heavy at this time of day."

Jennifer tucked her pen inside her pants pocket and checked her tote. Her cell, marker, and LED flashlight were there. She swung the tote over her shoulder and walked with Jonathan to the front of the house.

"I'll see you in an hour," he said. "Please don't take any chances with Rhodes. You have all the proof you need to get a court order of exhumation; you don't need anything else."

At a quarter to six, Oscar and Jennifer left for First Fellowship Church.

CHAPTER 27

A black Bentley occupied a space in the driveway in front of the church. Sitting in the car were two men, wearing Aviator sunglasses.

Oscar pulled up in front of them and turned off the ignition. "Do you want me to come in with you?"

"No, thanks. I'm going to make this quick. I'm glad you're here."

"Do you anticipate a problem?"

"I don't think so…not with you here."

"You have my cell number. Call if you need me."

She nodded and got out of the car.

The two men exited the Bentley, but only one walked over to Jennifer. His confident gait and tall, bulky frame almost equaled that of Oscar.

"My name is Crawley. I'm security here at the church. That's my partner, Edwards. The church door is unlocked," he said to her. "You can go right in. Reverend Rhodes is in his office."

"I'll be waiting here for Miss Beasley," Oscar said with authority.

"That's fine," Crawley replied, stepping aside to let her by.

As Jennifer passed the Bentley, the other man seemed to ignore her, but she was sure that his hidden eyes were fixed on her.

It was eerily quiet inside the lobby. The sanctuary doors were closed, but the door to the reception office was open. She walked in and allowed herself to pause and glance at the paintings of Lewis Addison and Frances Rhodes. Rhodes's eyes appeared cold and intimidating. An unnerving chill ran through her. She shivered and thought of leaving. *I don't have to do this,* she said to herself. *I have enough information. And if Rhodes is a fraud, who cares?*

His office door was slightly ajar. She heard him talking to someone and moved closer to listen. "Just take care of it," he grumbled, slamming down the handset.

She pulled her tote closer and tapped against the marker. *I just want to see his reaction when I hand it to him. And then, I'm out of here.*

Outside, Oscar leaned against his car and watched as Crawley beckoned to his partner.

"We're going to have to ask you to move your car off church property," Crawley said.

"Sorry," Oscar answered. "Can't do that. I'll be waiting right here for Miss Beasley. She won't be long." He tucked his cell into his jacket pocket and straightened his six-foot-two frame.

Crawley grabbed Oscar's arm. "I'm not sure you understand," he said gruffly. "You *will* move this car."

Oscar looked down at Crawley's hand. "I'm not sure *you* understand," he replied, taking a tight grip on his wrist. "First, get your damn hand off me, and second, I'm staying right—"

Edwards rushed forward and rammed his fist into Oscar's side. It knocked the wind out of him, but he was still able to strike a hard blow into Crawley's gut.

The three men wrestled, but Oscar wasn't a match for the two of them. That's when the butt of a pistol struck the back of his head, and he fell forward into Edwards waiting arms.

"Get in the driver's seat of his car," Crawley hissed at his partner, clutching his stomach.

Edwards pushed Oscar into the passenger seat. "What do we do with him now?"

"Rhodes has a bottle of vodka in the trunk of the car. Get it!" Crawley yelled. "Follow me to the 14th Street parking lot. We'll leave him there for the cops to find drunk."

Jennifer knocked on the office door and waited for Rhodes to acknowledge her arrival. He sat behind his desk, doodling. When he saw her, he jumped up. "Right on time," he said with a grin.

"Other than the two men outside, there doesn't appear to be anyone here. I find that unusual for such a busy church."

"Spring break. Most of the staff is away, and my senior pastor and a few deacons are having a meeting in the conference room upstairs. Not quite deserted," he said with a lying tongue.

"I don't have much time," she said. Slipping her hand into her pocket, she clicked her pen. "I came tonight to tie up a loose end. Not so much for the article, but more so out of my own curiosity."

"I'm happy to help."

"Did you know that Lewis Addison's father, John, stole a great deal of money from his best friend's family in Mississippi? As it turns out, the money was given to Lewis. He squandered much of it when he came to Atlanta and was penniless until he met Augusta Larson."

"I honestly don't know what you're talking about," Rhodes said, shaking his head. "I know very little about the Addison side of my family. Now I understand why my parents kept me away from them."

"On the outside, it appears that your personal life and conduct are above reproach. But, as we know, history has shown that appearances can be deceiving. Some churches have misused funds, and incidents of sexual misconducts have increased." She waited for his reaction.

He forced a smile. "No black eyes here."

"Well, thank you for your time."

His jaw tightened, and he clenched his fists. He was about to rebuke her and knock her off her high horse. But calm prevailed within him. He realized that he was in control. Her driver was gone, as were his security people.

"How about a drink before you leave? There's something I remember about Lewis and his wife."

"Perhaps a glass of water," Jennifer said.

"I only have soda."

She nodded approval, and from that moment his persona changed. He believed her reason for staying was that she was attracted to him. He walked over to a credenza and dropped two ice cubes from an ice bucket into his glass of Scotch. He swirled the glass and took a few big gulps. A tingling of lust rushed through his body. The potent liquid gave him a false sense of control. His back stiffened as he opened a bottle of soda and poured it slowly into a glass where a pill rested at the bottom. As soon as it dissolved, he stirred it and carried it over to her.

Excitement rose within him, knowing that the drink would produce a slow euphoric state of mind and then, she'd be immobilized. He'd done this before, and the thrill of it made him feel powerful.

She noticed that his demeanor seemed relaxed and confident. She took the drink and sipped it.

He downed his Scotch and returned to the cabinet to pour another. When he turned, she was still holding the drink, sipping it as she wandered around the room, gazing at his bookshelf.

Her first mistake is to perceive me as being uninformed and naïve, he thought with a smirk. He moved toward her, hoping she didn't notice his trembling hands. She excited him, but he didn't dare expose his feelings, as this would give her the upper hand.

"You're beautiful," he said. "I imagine that this could be a hindrance in your line of work."

"A hindrance? Not at all," she said, turning around to find him a little too close for comfort. "I'm a professional, and don't allow or encourage any misunderstandings about my interests." She moved to the other side of the room.

"I have no doubts that many men must come on to you. But I can see that you're all business, and that's a wise way to be." He followed her, this time keeping a slight distance between them. "Would you like something else to drink?" he asked softly.

"No, this is fine," she said taking another sip. She placed the glass on a table next to the couch, reached into her tote, and removed the marker.

Before he had the chance to ask what it was, she held it out and offered for him to take it. He backed away, refusing.

"What's wrong?" she asked sweetly.

"What is that thing? It looks evil."

"Evil?" she questioned with a laugh. "It's nothing of the kind. It's a grave marker. Take it!" She pushed it into his hands.

He took hold of the marker and immediately screamed out in pain. His hands turned bright red. "That evil thing burned my flesh," he said, flinging it across the room. "What kind of witchcraft is this?" He hurried to the credenza and immersed his hands in the ice bucket.

Jennifer picked up the marker and stuffed it into her tote. By now, the effects of the pill were taking hold. She reached into her tote for her cell and stumbled toward the door.

Rhodes grabbed her before she could get out and pulled her to the couch. She resisted. In the scuffle, her cell fell to the floor. He threw her down and dropped on top of her. Her arm was still locked tightly in the straps of her tote. She screamed, and a strange numbness settled over her like a warm blanket.

"You bass-stard! You drugged me!"

"It's not nice for a lady to curse," he said, covering her mouth with his.

The bitterness of Scotch and his vile, foul saliva on her lips sickened her.

She felt herself drifting. "No!" she cried. Her heart raced. She was succumbing, and there was nothing she could do.

"Don't fight it," he said calmly. "Just lay back and enjoy the feeling. I've been through this many times, and I always enjoy myself. So will you."

She fought to stay conscious, struggling to keep her eyes open. *He's trying to suffocate me*, she thought. *Oh, my God, I'm going to die. Oscar! Where are you? Help me!*

She felt herself falling into a dark, deep hole. She tried to push him away, but the drug rendered her unable to resist his powerful hold. He crushed against her, and a pitiful cry escaped her mouth.

With both his hands now free, he ripped her blouse. His mouth was all over her face, neck, and chest. His hands groped hungrily at her breasts. "Oh," he moaned. "You're going to be the best of all of them."

Meanwhile, miles from the church, Edwards found a secluded spot in the parking lot. Crawley stopped the Bentley a short distance away. By the time he approached Oscar's car, Edwards had already doused him with vodka, making sure he poured some down his throat.

"I think he's coming around now," Edwards said frantically, tossing the bottle in the backseat. "We'd better get out of here!"

They rushed away, forgetting to close the driver's side door.

Crawley turned on the ignition and blasted the air conditioning. Just as he was steering to make a U-turn, Edwards spotted a squad car pulling into the parking lot.

"Wouldn't you know it? Damn luck. I'll do the talking," Crawley said through clenched teeth. He stopped the car and turned off the ignition.

The patrol car pulled behind the Bentley. A sergeant and an officer got out and slowly walked toward the car.

Crawley lowered his window.

"What's the problem?" the sergeant asked.

"We saw that car weaving in and out. When he turned into this lot, we pulled in to see if he needed help," Crawley said calmly. "That's when you came along. Didn't even have a chance to get out to see what was wrong."

"License and registration, please," the sergeant said.

Crawley smiled and handed over his credentials. "We just got off work. We're security at First Fellowship Church."

The sergeant nodded and returned to his vehicle but not before instructing his officer to check out the other car.

"We'd better get out of here," Edwards hissed.

"Don't panic," Crawley snapped. "Who they gonna believe? A drunk or two security people?"

"I don't know about you," Edwards said. "But I'm not going back to jail. Get us out of here now!"

"They've got my license and registration, you idiot! I have no violations, and I'm not a convict. And there's no need for them to run a check on you."

"What if Rhodes messes up with this Beasley dame. She could call the cops. Don't forget, we're connected to that last girl. And what about the proof Rhodes has on us that we helped arrange her disappearance? He'll turn his back on us so fast, we'll spend the rest of our lives in jail for a murder we didn't commit."

Crawley ignored him. Instead, his attention was drawn to the officer at Oscar's car. "Think smart for a minute, Edwards. There's a drunk in that car. As soon as my license and registration come back, we're out of here."

At Oscar's car, the officer placed one hand over his gun and aimed a flashlight into the backseat. After seeing the bottle of vodka, there was no doubt in his mind that the man in the car was drunk. He heard a moan and shined the light on him.

"Sir, can you hear me?" the officer asked, tapping him on the shoulder.

Oscar moaned and turned his head. His eyelids fluttered. "Where am I? What's happened?"

"What the heck? Sarge! Come take a look!"

The sergeant went to Crawley's car. "Thanks for trying to help," he said, handing back the registration and license.

"Thank you, officer. Hope everything's okay with that guy." Crawley made a slow U-turn and left the parking lot.

As soon as the sergeant approached Oscar's car, the officer stepped aside. "Take a look," he said, raising his eyebrows.

"Oscar Benson? What happened to him?"

"He's drunk! The car reeks of alcohol."

"Impossible. Oscar doesn't drink…he's been sober for years." The sergeant shook him. "Oscar, what happened to you?"

Oscar moaned and rubbed his head. "Where are those two guys? They hit me on the head and…where are they?"

"I let them go!" The sergeant turned to his officer. "Call in for an APB on the two suspects."

"Send help to First Fellowship Church!" Oscar yelled. "Jennifer Beasley is in great danger. Hurry!"

Oscar reached into his pocket and pulled out his cell. He pressed speed dial, and Jonathan answered.

"Oscar, it's late, are you on your way back?"

"Doc…get to the church…Jennifer's in trouble. They knocked me out…lucky for me, the police are here, but I don't know where I am.

They're dispatching help…she's alone in the church. Hurry!"

Jonathan rushed from the house. He called Ralph. Within seconds, he answered.

"Ralph! This is Jonathan Powell. You have to get in touch with your nephew. Jennifer is in great danger at the church. Oscar's injured, but I don't have all the details. He's with the police now, and they're on the way to the church."

"Stay on the line with me…I'll call Mike on my other phone."

Jonathan sped across town.

Mike Mancuso answered with a cheerful greeting.

"Mike!" Ralph yelled into the phone. "You need to get over to First Fellowship Church ASAP. Jennifer is with Rhodes, and she's in danger. I have Jonathan Powell holding on my other phone. His driver was waiting for her outside the church, but it appears that there's been some kind of foul play. He's no longer at the church…he's with the Atlanta police."

"I'm on my way," Mike said, taking his ID and gun. He bolted from the house. "I'll call Teresa now. Sorry, but I couldn't tell you before that Rhodes has been on our radar for quite some time…on-going investigation…can't discuss what it is. Tell Powell to stay away from the church. We're on the way."

The call ended, and Ralph knew that the situation was far worse than his nephew let on. He picked up his cell to tell Jonathan to stay away from the church, but the call was disconnected. He tried his number; it went immediately to voicemail. He placed a call to Jennifer, but a recording instructed him to leave a message. And so, he anxiously paced—frustrated and unable to help. All he could do now was wait. And waiting was not one of Ralph's strong points.

CHAPTER 28

From inside First Fellowship Church, a blood-curdling cry for help reverberated through the hallowed halls of what was supposed to be a sacred place.

"Your screams, Miss Beasley, won't be heard by anyone," Rhodes said with a scowl. "Although I like it when a woman screams."

"Oscar…help," she moaned in desperation.

"Oh, dear. I'm afraid Oscar can't hear you and has met with an unfortunate…accident. There's no one here to help you."

Jennifer felt his fumbling hand slide clumsily down her hip and around to the front of her trousers. He pulled at the top button and ripped it off. She tried to wiggle free, but he clasped her neck and began to squeeze.

"If you stop squirming, you'll enjoy the ride I'm going to take you on," he said, whispering in her ear.

The numbing effects of the drug still rendered her somewhat helpless. And even though her voice was weak, she managed to mumble that the FBI knew where she was.

"Nice try. But you see, I've been cleared of any wrong doings. There's no one coming to your rescue."

"I…Mancuso and James…they—"

"How do you know those names you little bitch? You and your magazine tricked me. Damn you! You've been working with them all this time. No one is going to bring me down! I've gotten away with three murders, and you're going to be next." He released the hold on her neck when she passed out. He ran to his desk, removed a gun and a set of keys from the top drawer, and returned to the couch. He lifted her lifeless body and pulled her to the double French doors facing the back of the church. He kicked them open and continued dragging her toward the gate leading into the cemetery.

Jennifer was regaining consciousness and tried to break away from his firm hold. Her shoe slid off as she squirmed to free herself from the tight grip around her waist. In the scuffle, her tote fell to the ground.

It was dark by the time Jonathan reached the church. In the distance, he heard the blare of police sirens. He ran into the lobby, shouting Jennifer's name. He tried her cell and waited. The familiar sound of her call tone gave him hope as he dashed into Rhodes's office. But his heart sank when he saw her cell on the floor. Muffled screams caught his attention. Rushing out, he saw two figures in the cemetery.

He raced ahead and tripped over her tote, almost falling flat on his face. He snatched the tote, locked his arm through the straps, and skirted around tombstones, catching Rhodes by surprise.

Instead of knocking him off his feet, he reached for Jennifer with the intention of whisking her away. But Rhodes reacted quickly and shoved Jennifer to the side. Before Jonathan could break her fall, Rhodes pushed him, and she tumbled down, bashing her head against a gravestone. The pain was unbearable, and she cried out.

Jonathan lunged forward and grabbed Rhodes by the neck. They fought.

Jennifer managed to pull herself up and staggered over to Jonathan, falling hard against his back. She wrapped her arms around him.

Rhodes broke free and ran. He reached into his pocket, pulled out the pistol, and turned to face them.

Without thinking twice, Jonathan turned and hugged Jennifer, acting as a shield. A single shot rang out, and the bullet struck him in the back. His face contorted in pain, and he dropped to his knees. Clutching his chest, he slumped to the ground.

Jennifer lost consciousness and fell beside him.

Rhodes rushed to a mausoleum hidden behind dense shrubbery. He knew exactly how to weave his way through the thick foliage. After unlocking the large bronze door, he returned to get Jennifer. She offered no resistance as he pulled her into the darkened mausoleum. He ran back, retrieved the tote, and dragged Jonathan in, placing him next to Jennifer. He threw the tote across the marble floor. Looking down at them he uttered the words, "Many of them that sleep in the dust of the earth shall awaken, some to everlasting life, and some to shame and everlasting contempt."

He left, locked the door, and returned to his office.

FBI and police swarmed the driveway in front of the church. Agents, wearing hidden earpieces and neck microphones, spoke quietly to one another.

Jonathan's car still had the motor running, and the driver's door was opened.

An agent cautiously approached. "The car's empty," he said.

"Check the glove compartment," Mike replied, as he and Teresa entered the church.

"Registration is in the name of Dr. Jonathan Powell," the agent said.

With guns drawn, law enforcement officers spread out. Instructions were given for a team to go to the second level balcony of the sanctuary. Mike directed a police captain to have his men cover all entrance and exit doors. "No one comes in, and no one goes out," he said.

From the lobby, police and agents had a clear view of the sanctuary, where overhead lights and cameras were aimed at the altar and pulpit only. The church was empty.

"Check to see if anyone is directing the cameras and lights," Mike said. He instructed everyone to stay away from the sanctuary doors.

"There's no one in the balcony area," reported an agent. "The control booth is empty, too. Monitors are on, and I have a clear view of the altar and pulpit. There's no sign of…wait…someone's coming into view from the right side. Do you see him?"

"Yes," Mike replied in a hushed voice.

And there, in a black robe trimmed in purple, was the Reverend Francis Rhodes. Clenched fists hung by his sides as he moved calmly toward the pulpit. He took his place behind it and stood quietly, facing empty pews as if getting ready to preach a sermon. He eased one hand into the pocket of his robe and removed the gun, placing it on the pulpit.

Mike and Teresa inched their way down the center aisle into the sanctuary, guns pointed in his direction. Agents and police followed, filling the aisles leading to the altar.

"Reverend Rhodes, lift your hands and step away from the pulpit!" Teresa called.

"Who are you?" Rhodes asked, squinting. The bright lights overhead prevented him from seeing into the darkened sanctuary.

"Teresa James, FBI."

"Ah, Miss James. I believe my attorney's provided your agency with everything you've asked for. This intrusion now borders on harassment. I will call my solicitors and issue a statement to the press of unfair treatment to an upstanding man of the cloth."

"Reverend Rhodes, this is Mike Mancuso. Raise your hands and step away from the pulpit," he ordered.

Rhodes showed no emotion, nor did he honor the command. He turned his head from side to side. "I'm afraid I can't do that," he answered calmly. He slowly lifted his right hand to the top of the pulpit and eased it over his pistol. "Why are you here?"

Mike took a few steps and aimed his gun squarely at Rhodes's forehead. "Where's Jennifer Beasley?" he asked.

"Now how would I know that? She was here, we spoke, and she left."

"What about Dr. Powell?" Teresa asked.

"I don't know anyone by that name. Please leave my church. I have a sermon to rehearse."

"Dr. Powell's car is parked in front of your church," Teresa said.

"Just a coincidence, I'm sure. Perhaps someone had car trouble and left it there."

"I'm going to say this just once more!" Teresa shot back. "Put your hands above your head and step away from the pulpit!" Her voice echoed.

Rhodes smiled and looked into the overhead camera that focused on his face.

"He's smiling into the camera," the agent in the control booth reported. "I can't see the rest of him, only his face."

"Stay at your post," Mike instructed. He turned and nodded to Teresa as she cautiously moved forward.

"Reverend, we need to clear up a simple matter," she said in a non-threatening voice. "Then we'll be out of your church."

Rhodes sighed heavily and closed his eyes. He knew the remark was to trick him. *They know*, he said to himself. And then he uttered the words, "Until we meet again, I bid you all farewell."

The blast of a single gunshot resonated throughout the sanctuary as the Reverend Francis Rhodes took his own life with a single bullet to the heart. He slumped over the pulpit as officers rushed forward.

""I've called for an ambulance! Can't find a pulse," said an agent.

Another agent hurried over to Mike, holding a cell phone. "Found this on the floor in his office."

Mike took it and immediately recognized the cover. He instructed his agent to contact church administrators. "I want them here ASAP! Break up into groups. Agent James and I will lead the search in the cemetery."

Jennifer stirred on the cold, black floor. Her vision was blurred, and her head pounded. For a moment, she couldn't remember what happened or where she was. She sat up and tried to take a deep breath, believing it would make her feel better. Instead, it made her dizzy and nauseous. She tilted to the side, bumping into something. It was a body. She screamed.

It didn't take long before she realized that it was Jonathan. Believing him to be dead, she sobbed uncontrollably, calling his name. She gently touched his face, his lips, and took hold of his wrist to feel for a pulse, but she couldn't find one.

"I can't see!" she yelled. "Where's the light switch? I need light!" And that's when she remembered the flashlight she'd always carried in her tote. "Where's my tote? A wave of panic swept over her. *Stay focused,* she said to herself. *Jonathan had it…where is it?*

She pulled herself up into a sitting position and felt all around his still body. It wasn't there, so she pushed across the floor, using her feet and hands to explore the marble. When her foot hit something, she panicked. At first, she thought it was another body. Much to her relief, it was her tote. She reached inside and found the flashlight. Turning it on, she then placed it into her mouth, aiming it downward. She slipped her arm into the tote strap and crawled back to Jonathan.

He was lifeless, pale, and unresponsive as he lay on his side. She opened his tuxedo jacket and aimed the flashlight at his white shirt. There was no sign of blood anywhere.

She shook her head, dazed and confused. She turned the tote upside down, and the contents spilled out, clanging against the floor. She grasped the marker and shined the light on it. A deep indentation in its center revealed where the bullet hit. This discovery gave her a sudden rush of adrenalin, and she had hope.

"Jonathan!" she cried, kissing his face. "Oh, my gosh! You're going to be okay. The bullet didn't hit you…it hit the marker. Can you hear me? It was the impact that knocked the wind out of you. You probably have a collapsed lung or maybe even a broken rib." She stroked his head and kissed him again. "I love you! Please…wake up."

Jonathan struggled to breathe. He coughed, and it hurt. His eyes fluttered open. "Who's the doctor here?" he said in a weak voice.

"By the way, will you marry me?"

Jennifer's sobs, mingled with joyful laughter, filled the somber burial chamber.

"You bet your sweet life I will!"

Outside, thick clouds separated, and moonlight aided in the search.

Law enforcement gathered around Mike and Teresa.

"They've got to be somewhere," Mike said. "I don't believe Rhodes had time to bury either of them. But he probably had time to stick them in a mausoleum. Bang on every door and shine your lights into windows. I want this entire cemetery turned inside out. Wake up the dead if necessary! Did someone call the church administrators? Why aren't they here with the keys?"

"Already done," said one of his agents. "We're just waiting for them to arrive. We also got the street blocked off to keep the media and curiosity seekers back."

"Does anyone know how many rounds are left in the chamber of Rhodes's gun?" Mike asked.

"His gun has three rounds," said an agent within the church.

Mike's cell rang.

"Agent Mancuso, this is Detective Pilcher of the Atlanta police. Oscar Benson is on the way over to the church with one of my men. He has Miss Beasley's sweater so the search dogs can pick up her scent. We got the two men who allegedly kidnapped him. One of them has a record. He's antsy and sweating like a pig."

"We're looking for Dr. Powell and Miss Beasley. Time might be running out for them…it's possible Rhodes shot one of them. See what Edwards knows. Did you read him his Miranda rights?

"Yes, but he doesn't want a lawyer…said he just happened to be in the car, hitching a ride from Crawley. But he'll talk if he gets a plea deal."

"Put your cell on speaker, but don't let him know I'm listening. Tell him kidnapping is a federal offense and murder brings the death penalty."

"Murder? There's been a murder?" Pilcher asked.

"We're not sure, but tell him that. And also, there's no plea deal. Scare him."

The detective went to his office. "Listen up, Edwards. We're turning you over to the FBI. The charges are kidnapping, which makes this a federal offense and murder."

"I'm not going down for what that slime Rhodes did to that poor girl!" Edwards yelled, banging his fist on the table. "We just got rid of her…we didn't kill her."

"Who's we?" Pilcher asked.

"I…don't know!"

"Do you have a name for the girl?"

"Katie Bentley. She worked for Rhodes. Pretty little thing… wouldn't hurt a fly. He drugged her and well, you know, had his way with her. She told her brother-in-law, and they got money to keep quiet about it. But then, she decided that it wouldn't be right cause he did that to other women. I don't know anything about the others, but I can tell you one thing's for sure, there's been a lot more."

"Where's Katie Bentley?"

"In the cemetery, where else do you bury someone?" Edwards said, wiping the sweat from his brow.

"What cemetery?"

"The cemetery behind Rhodes's church."

"Did you bury her?"

"I didn't put her anywhere. Somebody else did that. I just brought her there and left her by those big houses where they bury the stinkin' rich."

Mike disconnected and quickly placed a call to his uncle. "Did Jennifer call or leave you any messages after six-thirty this evening?"

"Nothing. My last conversation with her was earlier in the day. I advised her to cancel Rhodes. I'm worried, Mike."

"Rhodes killed himself," Mike said, and his nephew's heart sank.

"Where's Jennifer?"

"She's missing...so is Powell. The Atlanta police found Oscar Benson. He's okay."

Ralph felt a shiver of fear. "Do you have any idea as to what happened to them or where they might be?"

"We're searching...." Mike left out the fact that it was now down to the church cemetery.

"She had a function...a charity dinner tonight. Maybe they went."

"I...don't think so. Powell's car is here. I'll keep you posted."

And with that, the line went dead. Ralph closed his eyes and began to pray.

Police and agents, walking in parallel lines, searched the cemetery. Flashlights beamed across the grounds, and the panting of search dogs resonated through the silence of the night.

Teresa and Mike retraced their steps along the main path.

"Over there!" called Mike, shining his light on a small, gated area.

Teresa hurried and opened a rusted gate. She shined her flashlight down on a tangled mass of overgrown shrubbery and high weeds. When she lifted the light, she saw graves dating back to the 1800s and a small stone building without markings.

"Could be a storage area," Mike said, giving the door a hard bang. He kicked it, but it didn't budge.

Teresa walked around to the back and followed the stone wall. "Nothing here!" she shouted. "Unless...."

"I don't think they're here," Mike said, examining the ground. "There aren't any footprints or signs of anyone being dragged. It appears that no one has been in here for some time."

They left the burial site and continued along the pathway until it curved, leading around and back out of the cemetery.

"I'll go right, you go left," Mike said. "We're missing something."

Teresa shook her head but didn't move. A dense thicket of tangled shrubbery, high bushes, and a bank of towering trees curved in line with the path and looked strangely out of place.

"What's wrong?" Mike asked.

"Is this where the property ends?"

"I'm not sure." He aimed his light to the right. "There's the wall. We should be able to see the rest of it as it continues behind all this shrubbery."

"You're right!" Teresa said.

He tried to make his way into the underbrush but found that it was impassable. "We'll need a machete to get in there!" he yelled.

Teresa disappeared around the opposite side.

Mike called her name, but she didn't respond. He was just about to call again when he heard a loud yell.

"Over here! Over here!" she screamed.

Mike followed the sound of her voice. "What is this, another Civil War burial plot?" He stopped short, bumping into Teresa, whose light was aimed at the top of a mausoleum, revealing the names Addison-Rhodes.

Without a moment's hesitation, they called Jennifer's name and banged sharply on the ornately decorated door.

From inside, Jennifer's head rested against Jonathan. In the distance, she heard something.

"Jennifer," Jonathan said softly. "Something's hitting the door. I can't move."

"Oh, my head," she cried, struggling to get up. She turned on her flashlight and tried to scream but couldn't.

Mike continued banging the door with his flashlight.

Jennifer put the flashlight into her mouth and crawled along the floor until she reached the door. She slumped against it and began tapping the flashlight.

Teresa pressed her ear to the door. She lifted her hand to stop Mike from making any further noise.

"We're here," Jennifer whimpered. She gave a few more taps before passing out.

"We found them!" Teresa yelled.

CHAPTER 29

Early the next morning, from inside the emergency room at Emory Hospital, Jennifer sat in a wheelchair and looked across at Jonathan. He was talking with the nurse when the ER doctor came in.

"I have good news. You're both ready to go home," he said, smiling at Jennifer. "Your CT scans show what we already diagnosed when you were admitted. Jonathan, you have a fractured rib. We didn't see any bruising or bleeding in the brain for Jennifer, but she does have a mild concussion. The prognosis for complete recovery is extremely favorable for both of you, but rest is imperative."

"Great news," Jonathan said, nodding in agreement.

Release papers were signed, and within two hours they were in the car with Oscar at the wheel.

"We're going home," Mrs. B said from the front seat.

"Those are the sweetest three words I could ever hear," Jonathan answered.

"Ditto that," Jennifer echoed.

"Did you hear about Rhodes?" Oscar asked.

"Yes. Mike told us when we were in the ambulance," Jonathan replied.

Oscar looked in the rear view mirror. "When we left the house earlier, the media was lying in wait."

"I called the police to complain," Mrs. B said. "But there's nothing they can do."

"Must be a slow news day," Jonathan said. "As soon as the next story breaks, we'll be forgotten."

Mrs. B wasted no time laying down the law. "Rest is the only thing the two of you will be doing for the next few weeks. I'll take care of the press."

Oscar laughed. "Glad I'm not a news reporter."

All through the early morning hours, texts flooded Jennifer's cell. Everyone at the magazine, including Ann Baldwin, sent messages. Thankfully, no one called. But Jennifer had a difficult time trying to convince Alex and Billy by phone that she was going to be fine. Even speaking to Jonathan didn't ease their concerns.

"Dad and I got an early flight tomorrow…we're coming, and that's that!" Billy said. "I have a surprise for you, but don't tell Dad I told you."

"What? You haven't said anything yet. You know you can't keep secrets from me."

"I'll keep this one, or I'll have to deal with both Dad and Jonathan."

Late that afternoon, Jennifer gave her pen recorder to Mike and Teresa. Although parts of the recording were muffled, Rhodes's confession to murdering three women was distinctly heard.

"I printed out my notes listing the people and events leading up to meeting him. I hope it helps," Jennifer said, handing each a copy.

"Thanks to you, Jennifer," Mike said, "we found two women who have been missing for over three years. They were buried behind Rhodes's mausoleum. But neither of them is Katie Bentley."

"Sadly," Teresa interjected, "another body was discovered early this morning buried at the Civil War site. We think it might be Katie Bentley."

Two pairs of shocked eyes stared at her, and she realized that neither Jonathan nor Jennifer heard the continuous coverage, as well as in-depth analysis and repeated commentaries on cable and local stations.

"We haven't had the TV on...too distressing," Jonathan said, holding Jennifer's hand.

"Is this investigation over now that he's killed himself?" Jennifer asked.

"No. This is just the beginning," Mike explained. "There will be a new investigation, which will also bring another IRS audit, especially in the area where church funds were used to silence certain individuals."

"Do you know who these individuals are?" Jennifer asked.

"Yes, we do," Teresa replied. "The story is going to break in the news, and the names will be revealed once arrests have been made."

"One person, in particular, has been of interest to us for some time, but we were unable to prove his involvement," Mike added. "We believe he remained quiet about Katie Bentley's disappearance because he was the catalyst in the cover-up and would lose his career if he came forward. It's nasty all around, but thanks to you, he and the others will serve time."

"It's not going to be good for the church either," Teresa explained, shaking her head. "And, unfortunately, the congregation will have to deal with his deplorable acts. Fraud, as it turns out, is secondary compared to his sexual misconducts and murders."

"By the way," Mike said, "we found the bullet that hit the marker. It was on the floor in the mausoleum. It's at forensics now, but we're sure it's a match to the gun Rhodes used to kill himself."

The next morning, while Jonathan slept, Jennifer worked in the library on her book. The complicated pieces to a puzzle that began with the purchase of a memorial marker were finally set in place. She leaned back in her chair and gazed outside. The day was bright and cloudless.

She went out and walked to the patio where the table was already set for breakfast. Her cell pinged. It was a text from Ralph with a bunch of cute emojis. She immediately called him.

"I was hoping to talk to you today. What are you doing up so early?" he asked.

"I'm working on the book. How are things in New York?"

"Nothing new on this end. By the way, thanks for the updates. I was frantic until Mike called with the news that you were found. I hope you're taking it easy."

"I'm following the doctor's orders."

"Mike filled me in on everything. But I have a feeling you have better news to share."

"My dad and Billy are coming today. I'm in love...but I think you already know that. It's not official yet, but Jonathan asked me to marry him when we were locked in the mausoleum. Not the greatest place for a proposal. Anyway, I don't think he even remembers it."

Ralph laughed. "Knowing you, he'll be reminded of it soon enough. Let me know when it's official. Alice and I are very thankful that you're both okay."

"We're not done, yet, Mr. Mancuso. I intend to give the story rights to the magazine, along with a whopping bill for your services. And I'm certainly going to need your help as a consultant on certain aspects of the book. In the meantime, take care, and give Alice my best."

Under a breathtakingly beautiful sky, Jonathan strolled out to the patio, followed by Mrs. B, carrying a breakfast tray. Atop the tray was a single pink rose tied with a satin ribbon.

He bent over and kissed Jennifer. "Good morning," he whispered, and her heart melted.

Mrs. B cleared her throat. "Let me know if there's anything else you two need," she said, locking eyes with Jonathan. She walked away with a knowing grin.

Jonathan bent down on one knee, resting his arm on the table for support. With his other hand, he held the rose. "Got to do this quickly," he said. "Not sure how long I can hold this position. I love you, Jennifer Beasley…more than you'll ever know. You are my beginning, middle, and end. Everything I want is in you. You taught me about love and faith and how to believe again. Will you marry me and make me the happiest man in the world? And will you accept this ring that belonged to my mother?" He unfastened the ribbon and held up an exquisite diamond.

"Yes, I will marry you. You're the one I've been waiting for all my life. There has never been another man whom I've loved and adored as I do you."

He slipped the ring on her finger and slowly bent forward to kiss her.

She got up and helped him into a chair.

"I spoke to your dad last night and asked for your hand in marriage. He gave us his blessing."

"What if he'd said no?"

"Then we'd elope and leave the country."

"Oh, Dr. Powell, you're so romantic."

"As soon as your dad and Billy get here we'll plan the wedding. I think they'll want to be included."

"Included? They'll both want to take over."

Jonathan laughed. "Between them and Mrs. B, all we'll have to do is sit back and show up when the time comes. Where do you want to get married? Here or in New York?"

"Right here. I want a small wedding and reception in the garden. Just family and close friends."

"Your wish is my command. Mrs. B will be delighted."

Jennifer gazed at her ring finger and smiled. Within seconds, she texted Ralph a ring emoji and two words: *It's official!*

By mid-afternoon, Alex and Billy walked through the front door of the Powell home. Tears welled in Jennifer's eyes when she saw her dad and Jonathan embrace. Billy wouldn't let go of her and kept expressing how thankful he was that she was safe.

Oscar, trailing behind, stepped to the side. "Jennifer," he called. "There's someone else here to see you."

She looked over her shoulder and let out a squeal of surprise when she saw Morton. The inquisitive cat wiggled, wanting out of protective arms. He needed to explore, investigate, and mark his new territory. Instead of greeting Jennifer with happy purrs and snuggly nudges, he sauntered over to Jonathan. A quick swish of his tail against his new master's leg sent a message of approval.

Mrs. B headed to the kitchen with Morton close behind. "I have your food and litter box all set up for you," she said happily. "I hope it meets with your approval."

After dinner, Jonathan, Alex, and Billy sat by the pool. They talked about gardening, and Alex offered a few suggestions for where a vegetable garden would do well.

"As soon as I'm able," Jonathan said, "I'm going to take an active role in the gardening. I think Jennifer will like that. She's told me so much about your garden in New York and how much you and Billy enjoy it."

"It's relaxing and fun," Billy said.

"I think you and Jennifer are a perfect fit," Alex said. "This whole thing with Dr. Taylor began as a mystery that turned into an incredible love story."

Early Monday morning, Sam called without so much as a pleasant greeting. "Why am I always the last to know things?"

"Sam, you know that's not true," Jennifer said, holding back a laugh. "I'm sure that between the wire services and your Atlanta connections, you know more than I do. Anyway, I was just getting ready to call you. We're okay but a little worn out and hurting. It's been—"

"Is it true? Are you getting married?"

"Wow, news travels fast. Who told you?"

"Missy said she heard it on the news. But that's a lie. I was talking to Ralph this morning, and she overheard the conversation. I should fire her."

"On what grounds?"

"Snooping! She told everyone that you're marrying a man you've only known for a short time. It sent ripples of gossipy crap through the office. I won't have it!"

"How's Jake?" Jennifer asked, changing the subject.

"He's not okay! Have you heard from him? He's distraught."

"He sent a text saying he's relieved that I wasn't harmed, but nothing more was offered."

"See! I told you so. When are you coming home?"

"Sam, I'm staying right here in Georgia."

His voice raised ten octaves. "I'll give you a raise! Vacation time! Whatever you want...you name it!"

"Tell you what," she began, hoping to appease him. "You can have the exclusive story about Rhodes."

"Great! Come back to New York, write the feature, and we'll—"

"Sam! I'm not going to write it. You'll have to find someone else to do it."

"Please don't tell me that your writing career is over because you found Mr. Right."

"No. Actually, it's just beginning. The Marker should be finished before the holidays."

"A wedding, a book, and...what's next? A big family, a house with a picket fence, a slew of dogs and more cats?"

"Sam, calm down. You're going to be fine without me. Please

give my best to Ann."

"My mother? She wants nothing to do with you. She called you a traitor."

Jennifer laughed. "She did no such thing. I'll call her—"

"Don't bother," Sam said quickly. "She's out of town, won't be back for years."

"I hope you'll bring her to the wedding. I'll let you know the date. And by the way, Sam, I want to thank you for sending me to Florida. Had it not been for you, I wouldn't have found the marker. Take care, sweetie. Everything's going to be fine."

The night before Alex and Billy were to return to New York, Jonathan invited Judge Aguda for dinner to meet the family and discuss the procedure needed to get a court order to exhume Bradley's remains.

Billy was delighted to be involved, knowing that Elaine would want all the details when he returned home. He even took notes.

Judge Aguda took his cell and forwarded an email with two attachments to Jonathan. "Just before I left my house, I got word from my secretary with information regarding disinterment from the cemeteries in Brandon and Natchez. One is a Request for Disinterment form from the Veteran's Administration for Dr. Taylor. The other is for Bradley's mother. You can fill them out at your leisure," he explained. "Both exhumations are not involved procedures, but rather ones that need to follow protocol. The family of the deceased may request that their remains be moved to another burial site. But Dr. Taylor's case is unique…and herein is the problem. We're requesting the disinterment of an Unknown Soldier based solely on no proof that this person is your relative. So, no doubt I will have to issue a court order based on facts and findings documented by Jennifer. Right now, everything you have is circumstantial evidence. On a more positive note, when will the wedding take place?"

"July 24th, in the evening, right here in the garden," Jennifer said happily.

"I like that. I wish my Sarah were here to share in this joyous time."

"She's here in spirit," Jonathan said.

And with that, Judge Aguda's face brightened.

And so, in the quiet of a lovely evening under the stars, a string quartet played Mendelssohn's Wedding March as Alex Beasley walked his daughter along a lighted path to a gazebo where Judge Aguda waited with Jonathan to perform the ceremony.

Jennifer looked radiant in a pale lavender lace and chiffon dress. They exchanged vows in the company of the most important people in their lives. Ralph and Alice were there, as well as Sam and Ann Baldwin.

At the reception in the garden, guests dined under arbors entwined with twinkling lights and trimmed with flowers in the colors of fuchsia, plum, and lavender.

Judge Aguda offered a toast to the bride and groom. "Jonathan and Jennifer, you found each other under mysterious and, what some might call, odd circumstances. When your paths crossed, you both discovered that your destiny was set long before you were born. You have everything in life because you have each other. May the joy and love you feel today, last a lifetime. I believe it will. We're so thankful to have you both in our lives."

Later in the evening, Judge Aguda shared the news that approval had been given to exhume Olivia Taylor's remains for interment in the family mausoleum in Atlanta. "Together with my court order and the recommendation from Alfred Copeland, the VA has also approved DNA testing on the Unknown Soldier," he said. "The analysis of Dr. Taylor's remains, along with the hair in the locket, will be performed in Natchez. Once confirmed, Bradley and Olivia's remains will be moved here." He took Jennifer's hands in his and asked, "Any doubts?"

"From the first day of this journey to this very moment, I'm convinced that Bradley and Jonathan are a match."

One month later, confirmation arrived that Jonathan's DNA was a match to the Unknown Soldier, now documented as Dr. Bradley Taylor. The US buckle in his hand was given to the Mississippi Historical Society.

And so, on a stormy September day, two mahogany caskets, draped in matching sprays of lilies, roses, and carnations, were carried into Oakland Cemetery. The clouds may have been dark and gloomy, but the atmosphere around the mausoleum was anything but that.

Family and close friends listened as Jonathan's pastor paid tribute to those who passed. "The Taylor family came from an era where difficult times revealed both good and evil in humanity. I've had the distinct privilege to read some of the documentation of their lives written by Jennifer Powell. This was a caring family to all those whom they loved and protected. Future generations will benefit from what we've learned through the events leading to this very day."

Serenity embraced all those present.

Joy and anticipation for the future prompted Jennifer to tell Jonathan the news she'd learned this morning. Just as she was about to tell him, Judge Aguda, Alex, and Ralph joined them. *It will have to wait until we're alone,* she thought.

Billy and Carolyn sat on the stone bench, talking to Susie Metcalf.

Elaine was telling Mike and Teresa that there was an aura of mystery surrounding them. Mike was eager to hear more, but Teresa shook her head in disbelief and walked away.

Jennifer's attention was drawn to a man standing alone at the end of the pathway. The unfamiliar face smiled when their eyes met.

She walked toward him. "I'm sorry, do I know you?" she asked.

"In a way, you do. I know you've accepted a difficult task, and your commitment to it changed many lives," he answered softly.

"I only regret that those who have passed are unable to see what has happened here."

"Oh, Mrs. Powell, they already know. Heaven has received the message of this day, and there is great rejoicing. And they also know that you have been doubly blessed. Go in peace; all is well."

A feeling of excitement swept over her. She turned and called to Jonathan. By the time he came over, the man was gone.

"Did you see the gentleman I was speaking to?" she asked excitedly.

"I didn't see anyone. Who was he?"

"Someone who knows us. Someone who knows that…." She paused and took a deep breath. She closed her eyes and leaned into her husband.

"You look pale and tired," he said, putting his arms around her. "I think we'll go home now. It's been an exhausting day for all of us. But all is well."

"That's exactly what he said!"

"Well, there it is. Confirmation."

"There's one more thing, Jonathan. Well, two to be precise. You see, I just found out something this morning, but that man already knew it."

Jonathan narrowed his eyes. "I'm confused."

"We're expecting!"

He hugged her tightly and shouted, "Hurrah! I don't think my life could get any better."

"Yes, it can. If being doubly blessed means what I think it does, then we're going to have twins."

And at that moment, the clouds parted, revealing a boundless universe where a mighty congregation of angels surrounded the perimeter of earth and lined the corridors of heaven.

www.ingramcontent.com/pod-product-compliance
Lightning Source LLC
Chambersburg PA
CBHW020226180626
46810CB00006B/2057